THE BONES AT POINT NO POINT

A THOMAS AUSTIN CRIME THRILLER, BOOK 1

D.D. BLACK

DARKNESS AND LIGHT PUBLISHING

A Note on Setting

Hansville is a real town, Point No Point a real beach with a famous lighthouse. And while many locations in this book are true to life, some details of the setting have been changed.

Only one character in these pages exists in the real world: Thomas Austin's corgi, *Run*. Her personality mirrors that of my own corgi, Pearl. Any other resemblances between characters in this book and actual people is purely coincidental. In other words, I made them all up.

Thanks for reading,

D.D. Black

PART 1

THE BONES AND THE BEACH

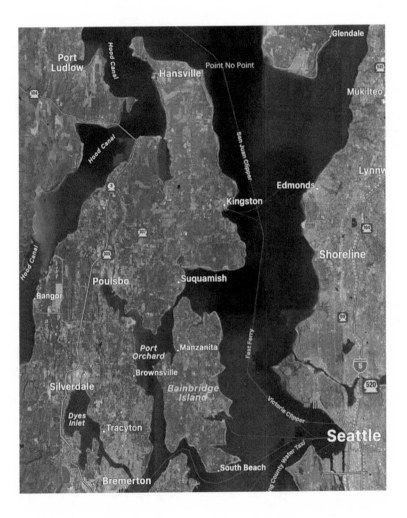

CHAPTER ONE

Norwegian Point Beach, Hansville, WA

SARAH KNEW she shouldn't be here. She'd told Benny she couldn't come, *wouldn't* come. But by his third text, she'd agreed. And now *he* was the one running late.

She'd been sitting on the massive driftwood log for ten minutes, staring out at the Puget Sound, as a light drizzle began. It was the kind of rain she'd grown up with, the sort she could be out in all day long and never get wet through her thin buffalo plaid fleece. She'd broken up with Benny three or four times now and had assured herself—not to mention her parents—that they would *not* be getting back together. But Benny had the best weed in Kitsap County—his cousin worked at one of the shops—and after the stress of finals and college applications, she needed to laugh and to green out.

Finally. She smiled when she saw him coming down the beach. He wore a black hoodie and blue jeans, and walked with more swagger than he'd earned. They were never getting back together, she assured herself, but she *did* like his swagger. It was exaggerated, as though he was doing an impression of someone swaggering. Ironic, which somehow made it endearing. Maybe she could take him back, just for the Christmas break, which started in a couple weeks.

He caught her eye and flashed a big smile. She smiled back.

She ran her hands over her damp jeans and let out a long breath. "Hey," she said as he plopped down on the log next to her, stretching his long legs.

"Hey." His voice was deep and sleepy, like he'd just rolled out of bed, which he probably had.

What the hell was she doing? She'd told herself there was no way they were getting back together and yet here she was, sitting on the log where they'd first kissed, flashing a newly-tightened-braces smile at him. She should leave.

Then again, the semester was almost over, and she'd already finished her essays. She deserved a break. Sarah jumped down from the log. "You wanna walk?"

"We can blaze one right here." He glanced up and down the deserted beach.

Everything was shades of gray: the blue-gray water lapping against green-gray beach stones and brown-gray driftwood. Even the sand looked dull and lifeless under the dark gray sky.

"Who the hell comes to the beach on a rainy day the week after Thanksgiving?" He chuckled. "Besides a former couple who are still madly in love and want to smoke a little."

Sarah slapped his arm, then looked toward the little café and general store, its entryway decorated with faint blue and white Christmas lights. It was the only business in town besides the post office, and there were two cars in the parking lot, and one was Benny's. In the other direction, there were the abandoned shacks of Norwegian Point.

December in Hansville was a dreary affair, most of the time. She doubted anyone would show up on the beach, but still. "Let's go to the bluff," she insisted.

Benny shrugged and followed her down from the log.

They took their usual route, following a mile-long stretch of beach that led past a row of waterfront homes and into the Point

No Point Park. There were a few cars in the parking lot and a pair of kayakers in wetsuits trudged toward the water.

In silence they walked just along the water's edge and rounded the tip of the peninsula past the lighthouse. The water swayed gently in front of them. On a clear day, she would have been able to see Edmonds and Seattle across the water and all the way to Mount Rainier, hundreds of miles to the southeast.

Sarah nodded toward the trail that led away from the beach, through the marshlands, and up to the bluff.

Benny followed, hands in his pockets. "You think we'll stay friends when you go away to college?"

"Sure we will," Sarah said, but she didn't know if it was true. She didn't even know where she'd go to college, and they both knew Benny wouldn't be going at all.

He caught her eye. "You're humming that song again."

"No, I'm not," she protested.

"I've literally been listening to it for like two minutes."

Had she been? It popped back into her head.

Da-da-dee-da-da-*deeeeee*-da, Da-da-dee-da-*da*-deeeeee.

It was an old indie rock song about a girl who was *never* getting back together with her boyfriend. The first time they'd broken up she'd played it on repeat, and they'd laughed about it when they'd gotten back together a few weeks later. Now that they'd broken up three or four times—she'd lost track—it was more than a running joke.

Benny dropped to his knees in the sand, holding up a stick as a microphone as he belted the chorus.

"The last time I saw your *briiiight* eyes...

The last time we said *gooooood* bye."

He'd been in a mediocre band for a little over a year and had a pretty decent voice for a guy who put in next to no effort.

"Enough," Sarah said, laughing and pulling him up by his elbow.

They continued up the trail, leaving behind the famous lighthouse and the plaque commemorating the treaty signed by the local tribes and the state government in 1855.

When they reached the top of the stairs, they sat on a bench that offered a narrow view of the beach through a cutout in the blackberry bushes. Benny pulled a joint out of a little glass vial and held it out, lighter poised in the other hand. "Ladies first."

She was about to take it when she saw a figure down on the beach, walking close to the water. "Hold on." She pointed.

"Dude, she can't see us from there. Not to mention, weed is *legal* now."

"Not for seventeen-year-olds. And if I can see her, then she can see us. And don't call me dude. I mean, why do boys your age call everyone dude?"

Benny smirked. "Fine, *bro.*"

Sarah squinted. The woman was slight, with sandy brown hair and a quick, purposeful walk, but she couldn't make out much about her face. "You recognize her?"

Benny put the joint and lighter on his lap and held his hands in front of his eyes like they were binoculars. "Nope." He went to light the joint and Sarah swatted his hands down.

"No. She'll smell it. Just wait 'til she goes by."

They watched in silence as the woman walked along the beach, jutting up from the Sound toward a patch of driftwood thirty feet from the waterline. "What's she carrying?" Sarah asked.

"Picnic lunch?"

Benny laughed, but Sarah ignored him. He was always making jokes. Or trying to.

Moving with purpose, the woman stopped about halfway between the lighthouse and the bottom of the trail that led up the bluff. After a quick glance around, she set something on a log. From the bluff, it looked like a green bag.

Next, the woman pulled out her phone and appeared to take a few pictures of the bag. Then she turned around and hurried back to the parking lot near the lighthouse, leaving the bag behind.

"What the hell?" Sarah asked.

Benny seemed unconcerned. "Maybe she's doin' one of those online treasure hunts or somethin'? Seen 'em on Insta."

Sarah looked at him skeptically. "In Hansville, population, like, two thousand? In December?"

Benny lit the joint and took a long drag, the sweet smell of high-end marijuana mingling with the moist, salty air. Sarah pulled up the collar on her jacket. Benny offered her the joint and, when she declined, he took another puff and put it out on the bench, then stowed it back in the vial.

"Only one thing to do." He leapt up and bolted down the stairs toward the beach, flapping his arms like the wings of a bird in flight and belting the breakup song.

"The last time I saw your *briiiight* eyes

The last time we said *gooooood* bye."

Sarah followed, smiling in spite of herself. He was funny when he was high. She was definitely not getting back together with him, but maybe they could have a little Christmas Break fling.

Benny skidded to a stop in the sand. Dropping to his knees in front of the bag, he leaned back, wiggling his fingers in a trance-like, prayerful gesture, an impression of the famous Jimi Hendrix moment when he'd lit his guitar on fire and implored the flames to rise. Benny knew this one always got a laugh out of Sarah.

The sack was roughly the size of a plastic grocery bag but made of green felt in the style of a holiday gift bag. It was decorated with cheesy cutouts of Thanksgiving turkeys and cranberries.

Benny reached for it.

"Don't touch it!"

He offered a dumb smile. "She clearly meant for us to have whatever is in here."

Sarah crouched next to him. "What if it's a bomb or something?"

"Ahh yes, because terrorists always want to blow up logs on empty beaches on mostly empty peninsulas at the edge of the known world." He reached for it again. "How could we *not* look inside?"

She glanced up and down the beach. Not a person in sight. "Why would she just leave it here?"

"The world is a strange place, Sarah." He looked up at the sky. "Why does anyone do anything?"

"You're *sooooooo* high."

Benny laughed and rolled into a patch of sand, spreading his arms and legs wide and flailing like he was trying to make a snow angel.

Sarah took one more look around her, then reached for the bag.

Bang!

A thunderous pop cut the silence.

Sarah's shoulders tightened.

Benny sat up, looking in the direction of the parking lot.

"Was that a gunshot?" Sarah asked.

Benny laughed. "Pro'lly a car backfiring."

She heard the quiet whooshing of a car passing on the road behind them.

"You were so freaked out." Benny spoke in a high-pitched mimic. "*Was that a gunshot?*"

"Shut up, asshole."

He continued rolling in the sand, laughing. "This is some good shit."

Gently, Sarah inched the red drawstring between her fingers. The contents of the bag rattled softly as she tugged it open. At first, she saw only shadow. Then, angling her body so the light filtering through the cloud cover seeped into the bag, she gasped.

"What?" Benny was looking over her shoulder now. "Is it a prize? Christmas come early? Cash? Oh, please tell me it's cash."

He whipped out his phone. "Smile." Before she could object, before she could turn, he snapped a picture.

"You're a jerk, Benny." Sarah looked down, shaking the bag slightly. Maybe she hadn't seen what she thought she'd seen. Maybe they were plastic or something. Maybe they were... She peered inside, opening the bag a little wider.

Bones. A hundred, maybe two hundred. Scattered at random as though fighting for space in the bag.

Tiny. Bones.

She rolled down the edges of the cloth, letting more light into the bag, and then she saw it.

A human skull, the tiniest she'd ever seen.

Jumping back, Sarah dropped the bag and screamed, causing the birds to rise from the marshland and take flight for safer ground.

CHAPTER TWO

Hansville Café, General Store, and Bait Shop

Three Weeks Later

HANSVILLE WAS the kind of quiet beach town where Thomas Austin didn't even bother locking his door. After twenty years in New York City, it was a welcome change.

He was on his third attempt at making the perfect hamburger when his cellphone rang again. He didn't recognize the number, so he silenced it and turned back to the grill. He flipped the patty, added a slice of pepper jack, and covered it with a lid. The crisp bacon and charred green chiles lay on a plate next to the grill. The bun was in the toaster, almost ready to be spread with the peppered tomato jam he'd spent the weekend perfecting.

"Boss, why don't you answer your phone?" Andy, his head cook, was doing dishes on the other side of the kitchen, which was, in truth, only about five feet from him. The commercial kitchen in the back of his store was just big enough to service the twelve-seat café, which was empty despite the fact that it was seven in the morning, theoretically the time for the breakfast rush. Slow mornings, he told himself, were perfect for testing new recipes.

Austin shrugged. "If it's important they'll call back."

"Uhh, that's the third time your phone's rang in the last five minutes."

"If it's important they'll leave a message."

Andy laughed.

"Plus," Austin said, pulling the bun out of the toaster, "the damn calls drop half the time, other times they go straight to voicemail."

"My girlfriend calls Hansville an Instagram desert, a one-bar backwater."

Austin looked at him blankly.

"One bar, as in, one bar of reception on the cellphone. And Instagram—"

"I've heard of it. I think." At 43, Austin didn't *feel* old, but being around a cook in his mid-twenties made him realize that the world had passed him by in more ways than one.

The store phone rang and Andy hurried to the wall to grab it. "Hansville General Store, Café, and Bait Shop. How can I help you?"

Austin slid a spatula under the burger and placed it on the bun.

He was about to add the toppings when Andy extended the red cordless phone toward him. "Boss, you might want to take this."

"Who is it?"

"Riley, um, something. Or Reynold? Said he was a Detective with Kitsap County. That was him on the cell. Sounds important."

Austin traded him the plate for the phone. "You finish this, see how it comes out." He leaned on the sink and held the phone to his ear. "Thomas Austin."

"Mr. Austin, this is Ridley Calvin, homicide detective, Kitsap County Sheriff's Department. You're a hard man to reach."

Austin paused. "Thank you."

"That wasn't a... um, you're welcome."

"Bad joke, Detective Calvin. And please, I go by Austin, not 'Mr.' What's this regarding?" Since leaving the NYPD a year earlier, Austin had gotten a few calls about old cases, but always from former colleagues. Never from a local detective. "One of my old cases, I'm guessing?"

"You guessed right," Ridley said. "But before I say more, just to confirm, this is Thomas Aaron Austin, retired detective. NYPD from 2002 to 2022?"

"That's correct."

Across the cramped kitchen, Andy held up the finished burger proudly and took a huge, dramatic bite. Austin smiled. On their honeymoon, at a little hotel bar in Texas, Austin and his wife had shared the perfect hamburger, and he'd been working for a week to recreate it to add it to his menu.

Detective Calvin continued. "You were the lead investigator on the Lorraine D'Antonia case, aka The Holiday Baby Butcher, correct?"

Austin's smile dropped. "I was lead detective on the abduction and murder she committed in New York, yes. The Seattle murders and investigation I had nothing to do with."

"Understood. Before I get into it, may I ask, why New York City to Kitsap County, and why Hansville of all places?"

Austin stared out the little window to the parking lot that ran right up to the beach. The day was sunny and crisp, the kind of day he craved in a winter mostly populated by gray drizzle. "You know about my wife, I assume?"

Austin's corgi, Run, squeezed herself under the swinging wooden doors that led from the store area into the tiny kitchen. She stared at the grill and sniffed. When no one offered up a treat, she lay in the patch of sun that streamed through the window onto the linoleum floor, taking up about a third of the available floor space.

"Yes," Ridley said. "That story made the news even out here. And I'm sorry."

"Thank you. She was from one town over. Kingston. We had talked about retiring out here. And I lived two years in Bremerton as a kid."

"Navy brat, I assume?"

"Exactly. Never thought I'd retire so soon, but here I am."

"And you bought the little store?"

"And bait shop, and café, yes. Can you tell me what this is about?"

An iron knot had tied itself in Austin's stomach over the last minute. The mention of Lorraine D'Antonia was enough to do that.

Ridley let out a long slow breath, the kind of breath Austin knew well. He'd heard a thousand like it and had let out a thousand of his own over the years. It was a breath that said, *You're gonna hate hearing this as much as I'm gonna hate telling it.*

"Three weeks ago," Ridley said, "a couple teenagers found a bag on a beach just up the road from you. Point No Point. A decorative Thanksgiving gift bag. Felt."

Austin listened to Ridley's breathing, then listened to his own. "I don't want anything to do with this."

"I know but—"

"Really, I moved out here to get away from this kind of thing."

"Austin, please. I'm sending you a photo right now. Check your cell."

"Our service sucks out here and—"

Andy waved to get his attention. "Wi-Fi, boss. Photos come in over Wi-Fi."

Austin's cellphone dinged with a new text.

"Did you get it?" Ridley asked. "No obligation, just look at it. Tell me you're not intrigued and I'll hang up right now."

Austin swiped open the photo. As Ridley had said, it was a decorative gift bag, Thanksgiving themed, sitting on a beige table. An evidence table. Austin tasted a saline bitterness in his mouth. Like salted grapefruit rind. Frustration.

"Now look at this one," Ridley said.

Another photo appeared, a shot of the inside of the bag taken from a couple feet above it. Austin tasted moldy bread. Disgust. Inside the bag were dozens of tiny white bones. He knew what was coming next.

"The bones belonged to a baby," Ridley said. "Four weeks old. She was kidnapped from Bremerton a few days before Thanksgiving. A little less than a month ago now." He paused, and when he spoke again, his voice cracked. "Four. Weeks. Old. Her name was Allie."

Austin stared at the picture, the iron knot in his belly tightening. He said the only word he could think of, the only word that would form on his lips. "Copycat."

"That's what we're assuming, but still, I'd love to get your perspective on this."

"Hold on a sec," Austin said.

Across the kitchen, Andy had stopped eating the burger. He shrugged as if to ask, *What's going on?*

Austin covered the receiver with his hand. "Can you handle the rest of the day?"

"We've had seven customers in the last week, boss. A tumbleweed just blew through the kitchen and a lonesome coyote is currently howling in the dining room. Yeah, I think I got it."

"Where's your office?" Austin asked, uncovering the receiver.

"Silverdale."

Austin sighed. "Give me forty minutes."

He hung up. "How was the burger?"

"Good, but..."

"Not perfect?" He picked it up, considered taking a bite, then set it down. The taste of moldy bread still coated his tongue.

Andy eyed him thoughtfully. "Is your thing acting up?"

Austin nodded. He'd tried to explain his lexical-gustatory synesthesia to Andy a few times, but he knew how odd he sounded when he tried. Words and emotions sometimes brought tastes and occasionally, strong emotions kept him from tasting food altogether. "If I taste it now, well, I'm too pissed off to taste it right."

"What's going on?"

Ignoring the question, Austin took off his apron. "I'll be gone for a while. Will you feed Run? Apartment is unlocked." The building housed the tiny café, the store, and a small apartment where Austin lived with Run.

"Of course, but why did the detective call? What did he want?"

Austin tossed the apron into the bin of dirty rags in the corner. "He wanted me to take a leisurely stroll down nightmare lane."

CHAPTER THREE

THE DRIVE TOOK Austin past the Port Gamble S'Klallam casino, through Poulsbo—a city known for its Viking-themed parade, stunning views of the Olympics, and legendary donut shop—and along a pretty stretch of highway into Silverdale. He'd lived in the area for a little over a year and still couldn't get used to all the green. It was a few days until Christmas and the trees were a deep shade of green and stretched as far as he could see on both sides of the highway. In the distance, snow-capped mountains peered out from behind thin clouds.

When he'd left the NYPD, he'd moved west for a lot of reasons, not the least of which was to get away from cases like the one that led to the arrest of Lorraine D'Antonia. Every detective who'd been on the job for a decade or two had *The One*. A case that made their career, defined their career, or, in some cases, destroyed their career. Austin's *One* was the serial murder case of Lorraine D'Antonia or, as the New York City tabloids had branded her, "The Holiday Baby Butcher."

The case hadn't made his career—he was already one of the top detectives in the NYPD when it landed on his desk. It hadn't destroyed his career, either. His career hadn't been destroyed until a Tuesday in September, when two gunmen opened fire on Austin and his wife as they strolled out of an Upper East Side steakhouse on their tenth wedding anniversary. He'd caught four bullets and lived. Fiona, an assistant DA for Manhattan County, had been struck once in the head and died at the scene. He still wasn't sure—no one was because the case remained unsolved—but Austin assumed all the bullets had been meant for her.

No, the Lorraine D'Antonia case hadn't been the one to make or break his career, but it was the one that haunted him more than any other. D'Antonia had grown up in Seattle in the seventies and eighties and worked as a travel nurse for twenty years before returning home. Her first victim was Johnathan Gruber, a three-week old whom she'd stolen in the dead of night three days before the Fourth of July, 2014. On July 5th, his bones were found in a decorative bag—red, white, and blue, complete with stars and stripes—next to Green Lake in Seattle. She'd committed four more murders over the next two years: Thanksgiving of 2014, Christmas of 2014, Easter of 2015, and Thanksgiving of 2015. After that she'd gone dark.

She'd popped up again three years later in New York, Austin's territory. Her victim was tiny Sonya Lopez, a premature baby who'd only been home from the hospital for six days when D'Antonia stole her. The little girl's bones were found the day after Christmas, stuffed into a felt Christmas gift bag decorated with a jolly Santa Claus. That was her first murder in New York.

It was also her last.

Coordinating with the Seattle Police and the FBI, Austin had led the team that eventually apprehended D'Antonia. A negotiation above Austin's pay grade had led to D'Antonia being sent back to Seattle to stand trial and, for the last twenty-six months, she'd been exactly where she belonged: rotting behind bars in the maximum-security wing of the Washington Corrections Center for Women.

Austin parked his truck in front of the Kitsap Sheriff's Office, a two-story building that looked a lot like a regular house, complete with a Christmas tree sparkling with silver tinsel and lights visible through the glass door. The only evidence it was a law enforcement office was the huge Sheriff's star stenciled on a wide window facing the parking lot.

As he approached the door, a car pulled in behind him. A man hopped out and strode toward him wearing black jeans, a blue blazer, and a smile that showed absolutely zero warmth.

"You Thomas Austin?" He called, hurrying up to him and extending a hand. He was tall, around Austin's height, but stouter, with a round face with red, fleshy cheeks that made Austin think he was a heavy drinker.

Austin held out a hand to shake. "That's me."

"Sheriff Grayson Daniels. Detective Calvin told me you might be dropping by."

"Ahh. Good to meet you. I told him I'd talk through the old case. Tell him what I know."

The Sheriff's smile had faded, his lips forming a tight line. "You're the one who bought the Hansville Café, right?"

"And general store and bait shop, yeah."

"Right out from under me. Flew in from New York and just grabbed it right up, didn't you, Mr. Moneybags?"

Austin cocked his head to the side. Was this guy serious? He'd driven half an hour in the middle of the day to talk about a case he'd never wanted to think about again. And now this? "I'm sorry, were you trying to buy it, too?"

"Damn right I was."

Austin stepped back. This guy's breath smelled both of whiskey and the mint mouthwash he'd used to try to cover up the whiskey. "My real estate lady never said anything about... I mean, I just put in an offer, they accepted, and I moved."

"Well, no hard feelings. My wife and I had saved a long time, hoping to buy that café for her and, well, I guess we couldn't all compete with New York money."

As a Navy brat, Austin had grown up all over, but his twenty years in New York had taught him how valuable a frosty glare could be. He offered one of his coldest to Sheriff Daniels. "Can I help you?" He'd purchased the building with money from Fiona's death benefit and the pension he got for early retirement after taking four bullets. Not that he was going to tell this bastard any of that.

Sheriff Daniels cleared his throat. "Well, water under the bridge now." He pushed open the door and led Austin into the building. They stopped in the foyer. "Now listen, Austin, I told Detective Calvin we don't need any outside help on this, especially since this looks like a copycat."

"It *is* a copycat. Unless Lorraine D'Antonia escaped and it didn't make the news."

Sheriff Daniels offered a polite chuckle. "She's very much behind bars. In fact, Ridley interviewed her last week." He waved a hand at nothing. "I'm sure he'll tell you about it."

"I imagine so."

Sheriff Daniels pointed down a hallway. "Second door on the right." He turned to go, then stopped himself. "One more thing, *former* Detective Austin. I've heard you used to play it fast and loose from time to time. We do things a little slower out here. By the book. You sure you got the right woman?"

Was this guy for real? Austin spoke through gritted teeth. "Lorraine D'Antonia was convicted of four murders. In *your* courts. Yeah, I'm pretty sure we got her."

"Well, like I told Ridley, fine by me if you want to help out—"

"I *don't* want to help out."

"Alright, alright. Well, thanks for coming out to chat with Ridley. He's the best detective we have, so if he's stumped..." He leveled the most serious look he could muster on Austin. "Just make sure you don't go breaking any eggs that belong in the crate."

It wasn't an expression Austin had heard before, but he got the point. Sheriff Daniels was only five or six months out from the beginning of his next election campaign. He didn't want any bad press, especially in a high-profile case. Of course, in Austin's mind, it was worth cracking eggs—and skulls—to get people like Lorraine D'Antonia off the street.

As he knocked on the door to Ridley's office, all he could think about was how he'd left his job, traveled three thousand miles across the country, and he was still eating shit from a commanding officer.

CHAPTER FOUR

DETECTIVE RIDLEY CALVIN was too big for his office. Austin was above average height, but Ridley had at least four inches on him, with broad shoulders and a neck as thick as one of Austin's thighs. When Austin entered, Ridley was scrunched behind a desk that looked like doll furniture as he stood and extended a meaty hand. His grip was like a vise.

"I take it you work out," Austin said, taking the seat that was offered.

"Relieves the stress. Keeps me looking younger than I feel."

"Good to meet you, Detective."

"Call me Rid," he said, wedging his legs back under the desk.

"Actually, call him Black Sherlock." It was a woman's voice from the hall.

Austin turned to see a young woman, her freckled complexion as pale white as Ridley's was a rich, onyx black. She stood in the doorway, grinning.

"Austin, this is Lucy O'Rourke, deputy detective, aka Lucy O'Licorice, aka Lucy O'Law-and-Order, aka Lucy O'Lager, aka Lucy O'Lexus, aka—"

"Hey, I don't drive a Lexus."

"And I don't go by Black Sherlock."

Lucy strolled into the office, leaned on Ridley's desk, and addressed Austin as though they were old friends. "One time he texted me—he meant to text his wife but her name is Luanne so I guess she's right next to me in his contacts or whatever—and he texted *me* instead. Nothing *too* inappropriate, thankfully, but he signed the text, *Black Sherlock*." She paused. "In this office, he will *never* be known by another name. Not *only* did he refer to himself by a nickname to his wife, but who signs their texts?"

Lucy looked to be about ten years younger than Austin, probably early thirties, while Ridley's beard—neatly trimmed but graying—made him look about ten years older.

Lucy extended a hand. "I'll answer to any of those other names, or any you make up. As long as they refer to things I like. I'm especially fond of Lucy O'Lemonade and Lucy O'Latte. Pretty much anything I can drink. And don't let this man tell you he's not Black Sherlock. He *earned* that gray in his beard." Her phone buzzed and she glanced at the caller-ID, then headed out, pausing in the doorway. "Welcome to Kitsap, NYPD Austin."

Ridley waved her out and she closed the door behind her. "She's a ball of energy," he said. "Remember being thirty?"

Austin smiled. "Don't feel too bad. I only recently stopped signing my texts. The cook at my café is five years younger than Lucy and he speaks an entirely different language. He installed Wi-Fi at my place and the way he talked about how it worked, he may as well have been reciting ancient spells or something."

Ridley laughed. "The generational divide seems to be widening at lightning speed."

"Fine by me. I was always about ten years behind my age group when it came to computers and phones and all that. I'm perfectly content fossilizing out in Hansville all on my own."

Ridley eyed him skeptically. "You were one of the youngest detectives in the NYPD, and, from what I hear, one of the best. You're what, forty?"

"Forty-three."

"Hard to believe you'll be happy selling salmon bait for the rest of your life."

Austin's jaw clenched. "I will be." His tone was a little more forceful than he'd intended, like he was trying hard to convince Ridley. Or maybe he was trying to convince himself.

The silence that followed was awkward, Ridley fiddled with a stack of papers on his desk. Finally, he let out a long breath. "So."

"So," Austin agreed.

"No good way to make this transition, so I'll just go for it: The Holiday Baby Butcher."

Austin grimaced. "Listen, I lived with the New York tabloids making money off her nickname and, well...let's just call her by her name, okay?"

"Gotcha," Ridley said. "Makes sense. Can you tell me what you know of her?"

Austin sighed. "Where should I start? How much of the files have you read?"

"All I could get so far, but still waiting on some pieces from your neck of the woods, and the FBI is—well—slow to share their work."

Austin chuckled. "You don't say?"

Ridley smiled, but quickly moved on. He slid a picture across the desk. It was a beautiful baby, cradled in the deeply-tanned arms of someone, likely the mother since Austin could make out the sleeve of a hospital gown. "Allie Shreever. That's when she was one day old. The next day, she was home with her parents in Bremerton. Nineteen days later, sometime between one and five in the morning, she was taken out of her crib. No footprints, no fingerprints, no forensic evidence, no security footage, no witnesses. Roughly three days later, she was murdered. Couple days after that, the bag of bones I texted you was found on the beach. Coincidentally, only a mile from your place."

Austin exhaled slowly, trying to keep his cool as he slid the photo back across the table. His jaw had tightened during

Ridley's summary, his back teeth grinding. It sounded exactly like every murder Lorraine D'Antonia had ever committed.

"So," Ridley continued, "I want to get your take on what we have, but first, what's your read on her? D'Antonia, I mean."

"Why? She's in prison for life. You've clearly got a copycat here so—"

"I get it," Ridley said, "and no one is questioning whether you got the right woman. I've been through this with the folks in Seattle. Everyone knows you got the right woman. That's why they prosecuted. Why she confessed. My thinking is, assuming we have a copycat, he or she is a *damn* good one. Maybe you can give me something that's not in the files, something in the way D'Antonia thinks or does things that a copycat might use." Ridley stood and walked a slow lap around his desk, looking like a giant lion trapped in a small cage. "I've been on this case for three weeks and, other than a couple stoners who saw a woman drop the bones on the beach, I've got nothing. I'm looking for any help I can get."

Austin liked this guy. On TV, detectives often came off as brilliant loners single-handedly bringing down evil. In practice, catching killers was much more of a team sport, even for the most brilliant detectives out there.

"Short version?" Austin asked.

Ridley nodded.

"Lorraine D'Antonia was a registered nurse. Worked labor and delivery. But she didn't target babies born in the hospitals where she worked except for the New York kidnapping of Sonya Lopez. She targeted two-parent heterosexual couples, couples with happy, loving marriages, stable family lives. *Not* the most vulnerable, which is interesting because it spoke to motive. She was viciously jealous of these infants—as deranged as that sounds. She *did* confess to loitering in hospitals, following parents home, that kind of thing. Each time it was a kidnapping in the dead of night, no fingerprints or DNA, no direct surveillance. And you know what she did after she took the children."

Ridley tugged gently on his beard, deep in thought. "The psych profile the FBI put together, that match your read on her?"

Austin nodded. "She told a story of being adopted and missing her birth mother, but D'Antonia actually had it pretty good. FBI says sociopathy and psychopathy. Add a couple other brands of crazy, and you have Lorraine D'Antonia." Austin winced internally, remembering some of the details of the case. "She always took the babies a few days before the holidays, dressed them up in cute little outfits, and played mommy for a few days. Treated them incredibly well, like little princes and princesses. Presents related to the holidays—easter baskets and whatnot—fed them formula, took photos with them, then..."

Austin trailed off, but Ridley finished his thought. "Then drugged them and boiled the bodies until the flesh sloughed off the bones. Stashed the bones in holiday bags and dropped them places where they'd be found. Written about. Cause a panic in parents everywhere."

"Exactly. Some people thought the process she went through —the kidnapping, pampering, then murdering—fulfilled some deep, nagging pain in her. For whatever that's worth. Me? I don't claim to know why, but I know she's one of the most evil people to ever live."

Ridley scooched his chair back and crossed one leg over the other. "I've read the case files. Anything major that didn't make it to the trial?"

"The poems. Never came out at trial or in the press—she carved holiday poems into the bones of her victims. Used a Dremel tool."

Ridley nodded. "The poems. In a case as sickening as any I've ever seen, that detail takes it to a new level."

They both shook their heads, sitting in silence as that fact filled the room. Faced with a case this disgusting, this disturbing, there was often nothing to say.

Finally, Ridley said, "We've got a little budget for expert consultants. Any chance you'd—"

Austin held up both hands as if to say, *Whoa, hold up.*

"Hear me out," Ridley said. "Lucy is gonna be working a few leads on this, and I'm hoping you'll agree to work alongside her, just for a week or two in a very limited consulting role. You know the case and the files better than anyone. And Lucy is more street smart than book smart. I can hardly get her to read the files. I—"

"I don't want any part of this."

"None of us *want* any part of this. I'd rather be home helping my son study for the SATs, or teaching my daughter how to drive. I'd rather be eating a shit sandwich sprinkled with tacks, for God's sake. But here I am." Ridley implored Austin with a look. "Tell you what. Last week I went to the prison, did a twenty-minute interview with The Holiday Baby Bu-, with D'Antonia. Watch it, and if you can walk out of here afterwards, I'll let you go and you won't hear from me again."

Austin said nothing.

"Watch the video," Ridley said. "She mentions you by name."

Austin was hit with a ping of curiosity accompanied by the flavor of tart cherries, the taste he always got at the beginning of a case. Then he got another ping, a thought about something Ridley had said. "Wait, when I mentioned the poems, you said, 'That detail *takes* it to a new level.' Present tense."

He leveled his eyes on Ridley, who uncrossed his legs and offered another one of those sighs that Austin knew well. "We'll get to that."

CHAPTER FIVE

RIDLEY WHEELED in a TV and dimmed the lights in his office. He couldn't get the interview to stream from his phone onto the TV, so he grabbed a young deputy named Jimmy from the other room. Jimmy was just as muscular as Ridley, though half a head shorter, and he quickly got the TV working.

The video began with a quick zoom from a wide shot of the room to a tighter shot that started at Lorraine D'Antonia's shackled feet and ended at the top of her head of thin, wispy hair. Her face was sallow, approaching the color of the white prison garb she wore, and she'd aged more than Austin had expected. Her hair had been thick and voluminous when he'd arrested her. Maybe she'd lost it from stress, or maybe it had just fallen into its natural state when deprived of the hair products she was known to love. Her nails were no longer the thick, well-manicured artificial ones she'd worn on the outside. They were neatly manicured to rounded points and painted a light gray, the same color as the prison walls. Nail polish wasn't allowed in prison, but D'Antonia had found a way. Paint and floor sealer, Austin thought.

In any case, she looked like she'd aged ten years in the three she'd been locked up. He'd hoped never to see her face again.

Never to hear her low, monotonous voice, and the strange way she spoke—not like some caricature of evil—though she was as evil as they came—but also not like a regular person. Hers was a pathology he had never experienced before or since.

Austin heard Ridley's voice off camera. "Please state your name."

"Lorraine D'Antonia." Though she'd been adopted by an Italian-American family, she'd lived all over the country—like Austin himself—leaving her with no discernible accent.

"Thank you, Ms. D'Antonia. I am Detective Ridley Calvin of the Kitsap County Sheriff's Department. I appreciate you meeting with me today. I am here because a kidnapping and murder occurred recently, and I'd like to ask you a few questions."

"You are so tall!"

Ridley said, "I am."

"I am only five foot two," D'Antonia said. Her voice still had a deeply disturbing timbre. Low and steady, like a loud whisper. "I've been reading a lot lately. Harry Potter. You are as big as Hagrid."

From off camera, Ridley said, "I took my kids to the Harry Potter exhibit in Seattle once and they had Hagrid's chair from the movie set for people to sit in. So, I took pictures of my kids in it and they looked tiny. Then *I* sat in it and my kids laughed because it looked just the right size."

D'Antonia's laugh was even more disturbing than her voice. Dry and forced, like she had a can of laughter stuck in her throat and released bursts from it one by one.

Ridley's approach to the interview confirmed Austin's hunch that he was damn good at his job. Austin knew how revolting it was to make small talk with the world's most vicious killers. He also knew that it was part of the job, a part that could solve crimes and save lives when one was good at it. And Ridley was. He'd read D'Antonia right from the moment he walked in the room. Sometimes it was a good idea to go into an interview with guns blazing, aggressive and confrontational. But not with someone like D'Antonia. She genuinely believed she'd done nothing wrong. She wanted to be heard, needed to be appreciated. In short, she definitely required a "catch more flies with honey" kind of interview.

When her laughter faded, D'Antonia said, "What would you like to ask me, Mr. Calvin?"

"Please, Mr. Calvin is my father. Call me Rid." He cleared his throat. "Now, I want to say, we know you had nothing to do with what I'm here to talk about, and I'm not here to relitigate the past, what happened in Seattle or New York."

"I loved those children. And they loved me."

Austin tensed. He tasted moldy bread again. She'd overdosed those babies with strychnine, then boiled them in massive canning pots. Even Ridley playing the good cop couldn't muster a conversational response to this.

Ignoring her statement, he asked, "Do you know anyone who might have admired you, might have wanted to celebrate holidays with babies the way you did?"

Austin's stomach turned and he glanced at Ridley, whose feet were up on his desk. "You're a more patient man than I," Austin said.

"Took everything I had to stay level-headed," Ridley replied.

On the screen, D'Antonia said, "*Celebrate*, yes. You get it. Those babies loved the holidays just like I do." She was silent for a long time, staring straight ahead, motionless. Finally, she shifted in her chair slowly. It creaked beneath her. "No. I can't think of anyone."

"Did you ever have any help when you took the children? A boyfriend maybe, a girlfriend?"

She shook her head slowly. "I like boys."

"And what about after you were arrested? Did anyone contact you to find out about the case, anyone who seemed especially interested?"

"My lawyers."

"Other than them."

She shook her head again. Then, a flash in her eyes, some sort of recognition. "Is someone out in the world celebrating with new babies the way I did?"

"Yes, that's what I'm here about."

"But who?"

"Well..." he cleared his throat, and Austin could hear the frustration in his tone. "Like I said, that's why I'm here, Ms. D'Antonia. I'll ask you directly. Can you think of anyone you might have talked to about the specific nature of what you did, the details, someone who might know the things you did, who would want to do them similarly?"

Looking down at her nails, she folded and refolded her hands in her lap, the handcuffs clanging dully. "What was the name of the handsome one?"

"I'm sorry?"

"The one who arrested me in New York?"

Austin heard papers shuffling in the video. Ridley said, "Arresting officer was Thomas Austin."

"Mmm, yes, Austin. He asked *a lot* of questions."

"That was his job, Ms. D'Antonia."

She shrugged. "He was not as big as you."

"Few are."

"You are bigger than most."

"I am."

"He was not. But he is more handsome."

D'Antonia had an odd conversational style. Sometimes she could carry on a seemingly normal conversation, other times she dropped into a strange, literal directness. And at other times she could describe her own acts, the most heinous crimes he'd ever seen, as though reading the assembly instructions for a piece of furniture. It was almost as though she was heavily drugged. Downers, maybe. But they'd found no evidence of drug use anywhere in her past.

D'Antonia said, "My lawyer told me that I will not be able to have a new trial. That the judge was unwilling to throw out my confession. Is that something you can help me with? I do not belong here."

"I'm not going to lie, I don't know if I can help you. But I will tell you this: if you can give me information that helps me figure out who is taking children like you used to, I will put in a good word with the judge."

She considered this. "I don't know if it can help anymore. My appeal was denied."

Ridley paused the playback and turned to Austin. "Couple months back, her bastard lawyer was trying for a new trial based on some bullshit. False confession. Judge threw it out, reconfirmed her sentence. She will never see the light of day."

Austin had been in the room when she confessed to the kidnapping and murder of Sonya Lopez. There was nothing false about it and he was glad a judge had agreed.

When Ridley started the video again, he summarized the meeting while fast-forwarding through a long section. "She talked around stuff for a while, asked me about other books— she loves fantasy, mostly for younger audiences. Kinda sickened me, a lot of the same stuff my kids read. Sometimes she comes off as an adult, sometimes she feels like a little girl still. Sometimes it seems she's on the spectrum, other times not at all. There's a part at the end I want to show you."

When he re-started the video, he was halfway through a question. "...else can you tell me about that?"

"I never told anyone else about the poems. Except for Detective Austin. He told me he didn't like my poems, but I didn't believe him. After all, the handsome detective moved across the country, just like me. New York to Washington State, though I think his new home is likely nicer than mine." She giggled at her joke, a sickening, girlish giggle that clashed with her pale face and wisps of gray hair.

Ridley turned off the video and flicked on the lights. "I spent a lot of time asking her about the poems. She gave me nothing."

"Why spend so much time on that?"

Ridley slid his phone across the desk. "There's something I didn't tell you yet." The screen showed a photograph, the same one Ridley had sent him earlier in the day, looking into the bag of bones from above. "Swipe right."

Austin did. In the next photo, a couple dozen bones were spread out on a shiny metal table. The next showed a closeup of a single bone.

Austin tried to swallow the taste of dread, a dry burnt-toast bitterness. He zoomed in on the bone. In tiny scratches, but clear enough to read, he saw two words: "Thanksgiving is."

A month or so before Fiona had been killed, she and Austin had spent an evening—and a couple bottles of good Burgundy—debating whether truly evil criminals like D'Antonia were born that way, or created by circumstance. The classic nature vs. nurture argument. Austin tended to fall on the side of nurture: upbringing, trauma, abuse, and desperation leading to most crimes. But Fiona had used his own case against him, specifically D'Antonia's decent upbringing and the poems she'd carved into the tiny bones of her victims. What could happen to a person that would make them do something like this?

He swiped left again, zoomed in on another bone: "A time to praise."

Swiping and zooming as fast as he could, he read the entire poem, etched into a dozen tiny rib bones. Just as Lorraine D'Antonia had done, the killer had written twelve lines using the baby's twelve rib bones, the first line written on the top rib and the rest descending from there.

Thanksgiving is
A time to praise
To love each other
And cherish each day
To gather around
A feast fit for a king
To laugh and toast

To love and sing
So come ye all
To our table this fall
And savor each moment
And love one and all

He handed Ridley the phone. Assuming Austin hadn't missed something, the poems had never hit the press and had been left out of the trial.

Ridley could tell what he was thinking. "Like I said, NYPD Austin, it's gotta be a copycat, but it may be the best we've ever seen."

CHAPTER SIX

AUSTIN TOOK A SLOW SIP, sucking air into his mouth to cool the scalding hot coffee. Something was wrong with the temperature control on the pot. It kept the coffee just below boiling and gave it a bitter, burnt taste. He considered going to the store to grab an iced coffee from the cold case, but he'd slept badly and needed the caffeine immediately. He added a spritz of cold water from the faucet.

Run scrambled in through the dog door and nudged her nose against his shin repeatedly to get his attention. He crouched down to pet her, but she quickly leapt back and grabbed a ball from the floor, then dropped it dramatically at his feet. She was the smartest, most active dog he'd ever met, and she wasn't much for cuddling. But in the year he'd had her, she'd never once gotten tired of chasing anything he threw. He opened the sliding glass door and tossed the ball into the small, fenced-in yard.

When she raced out to find it, he looked up to the plaque hanging above the coffeemaker. It looked like the kind of thing you'd get from your boss to commemorate five years on the job. It was faux-wood, the lacquer faded, and stamped with a metal plate where three lines of words had been etched:

Every single second,

Of every single day,
Every victim deserves my best.

On her first day in the DA's office, Fiona had ordered it from an online store that did custom trophies and plaques. She'd placed it on her desk next to a single plant and a picture from their wedding. For six years, she'd lived that motto. And for longer than that, it had been what they both believed.

Now it was just a plaque, a memory. Austin had never stopped believing it. But when he went back to his job after getting out of the hospital, he'd no longer been able to live it. Whatever it was that had allowed him to care enough to do his job well had died along with Fiona.

After reading the poems on the bones of little Allie Shreever, Austin had told Detective Calvin that he'd be willing to answer any questions they had by phone, but he was not interested in anything official. He'd had enough of police work and had moved three thousand miles to get away from it. He was content selling bait, beer, and burgers to locals in the winter and the swarms of visitors and returning snowbirds in the summer.

Run busted through the dog door and dropped the ball with a flourish before doing a full 360 spin in excitement. Austin added a little more tap water to his coffee, swigged it, and put the cup in the sink. He held up his empty hands and turned them back and forth like a magician proving the object had disappeared. "Sorry, Run, all done."

Run gave him her best wide-eyed-cuteness stare, then retreated to the living room to gnaw on a bone.

Austin tossed on a jacket and eased out the back door, crossing the one road through town and slipping in through the unlocked back door of the West Sound Community Church. The door led into a small storage room, which opened into a kitchenette. Austin walked through the darkness, holding his breath, and made his way into the nave, an area about six-hundred square feet, with ten rows of seating. He sat on a wooden pew in the back row and closed his eyes, though all the lights in the place were off. Finally releasing his breath, he inhaled deeply.

And, just like that, Fiona was back.

His parents had brought him to church every now and then as a kid, but he'd lost touch with it in college and had never gone as an adult. He'd told Fiona once that after seeing the kinds of things he saw on the job, going to church just didn't make sense any more. She'd replied that after seeing the kind of things *she'd* seen on the job, going to church was one of the *only* things that made sense. They'd agreed to disagree, but he'd come with her on Christmas Eve every year. He didn't come now because she'd want him to. He came because of the smell.

He opened his eyes when he heard the gentle swoosh of a broom on a wooden floor. Looking up, he saw Pastor Johnson coming toward him, sweeping as he inched up the aisle. "Thought I heard you come in," the Pastor said. "What is this, three days in a row now?" He was an older man, likely seventies from the wrinkles on his face, but as spry and active as Austin himself. In addition to running a food bank and countless community meetings, he was an amateur photographer, known in the community for his stunning pictures of sunrises over the Cascades and sunsets over the Olympics.

"Four," Austin said. "I hope it's no bother."

"Not at all. We'd love to see you at regular service, but, well, I understand."

"Thank you."

"You stay as long as you need."

"Thank you."

The Pastor began sweeping again, but stopped, leaning on the broom. "How does it work, with your wife?"

Austin said, "You know how you can smell something, like your grandma's old sweater, and be transported back to a memory? Sitting on her lap as a child, or standing next to her on the porch. Smells carry memories. Most people experience that."

"For me it's instant coffee. We drink the fancy stuff now, but

I was raised by my grandpa and he drank Folger's all day every day. Maybe ten cups. One whiff and I'm back in his kitchen."

"Right, most people have something like that."

"But for you it's different?"

"First time I walked in here, my wife was back with me. My senses kind of cross over each other. Usually with tastes and words and feelings. When I'm here, something in the air— maybe the age of the wood mixed with the paint, mixed with... I don't know. Usually I can pinpoint it. Here I can't."

"What do you feel?"

"What do I feel?" Austin wasn't one to talk much about his feelings. Anyone else who'd asked, he would have given a look, that New Yorker look that implied, *this conversation is over*. But Pastor Johnson left the place unlocked for him, let him sneak in and sit as long as he wanted, and had never been anything but kind. "You do photography, right?"

Pastor Johnson nodded.

"Imagine you're out at dawn, all by yourself, just you and the camera. Maybe it rained the day before, but now it's clear so everything is fresh and clean. You stroll along the beach, a few birds chirping, a bright white sailboat gliding by. Then the first glow of sunrise creeps over the mountains to the east, bathing you in golden light. How do you feel?"

Pastor Johnson smiled sadly, but said nothing.

"That's how I feel when I'm here. That's how it used to feel with Fiona."

The pastor held his eye for a moment, then nodded and went back to sweeping.

~

Andy handled the café's breakfast crowd—if it could be called 'a crowd'—on his own. Today, Mr. and Mrs. McGuilicutty were the only two patrons, both hunched over the exact same breakfast they ordered every day: two scrambled eggs, two pieces of toast burned black, a single strip of bacon each, and coffee so sweet Andy had to refill the sugar dispenser at their regular table twice as often as the others.

"Morning, New York." That's what Mr. McGuilicutty always called him, despite the fact that he'd lived in San Diego, Virginia, Connecticut, and pretty much every other state with a Navy base.

"Morning," Austin replied, slapping him on the back. "Andy taking good care of you?"

Mrs. McGuilicutty crunched her blackened toast. "They say burnt toast'll give you cancer. Look at me. I'm ninety-one!"

"She is," Mr. McGuilicutty said. "Ain't that right. And I'm ninety-four." He waved a piece of burnt toast in the air. "I could beat you in a footrace right now, I could!"

"Oh, no!" Mrs. McGuilicutty's eyes were on the TV above the bar.

"Oh yes, I could beat him," Mr. McGuilicutty insisted. "My legs are strong as—"

"No, look at the TV." Mrs. McGuilicutty waved her toast toward the screen.

Austin let his gaze drift up. The TV was usually tuned to sports—Mariners, Seahawks, UW, and Mystics games. Today it was the local news, which Austin tried to avoid the way he tried to avoid everything that wasn't his dog or his business.

The knot in his stomach returned in a flash as he read the scroll along the bottom of the screen: *Newborn kidnapped from home in upscale Bainbridge Island neighborhood.*

CHAPTER SEVEN

"TURN UP THE SOUND!" Austin said, walking toward the bar, where the TV was mounted on the wall.

Andy unmuted the TV and the voice of a solemn-sounding male news anchor filled the tiny café. "Tragic news out of Bainbridge Island, Washington today, where an infant boy was apparently kidnapped overnight. Details are few and far between at this time, but our reporter Sandra Chang has been at the scene all morning, trying to learn more. Sandra, what can you tell us?"

The shot changed to a wide-angle of a residential street, where a reporter stood in front of a backdrop of large homes with lovely gardens and pristine, manicured yards. As the shot zoomed in on the reporter, one house in particular stood out. Surrounded by yellow police tape, it was an impressive modern home—right angles of steel and glass and fine wood—with a silver BMW parked on a gorgeous stone driveway. "Thanks, Chet, and yes, I'm live on the western edge of Bainbridge Island, where police say a boy of only three weeks was taken from his crib either late last night or early this morning. The family is not speaking at this time, and names are being withheld for privacy, but sources say the family is distraught. So far, police say, no suspects have emerged, but in the minds of many, the similarities to a recent kidnapping in Bremerton are unavoidable. The victim in that case was recently found deceased after a desperate search for the missing child came up empty."

The shot changed to footage from earlier in the day—based on the darker sky it looked like dawn. The reporter hurried after a uniformed officer, shouting questions. "Officer, can you comment on the similarities between this case and the kidnapping and murder of Allie Shreever? Officer, is there a serial kidnapper on the loose in Kitsap County?"

The officer, who'd been hurrying into the house, stopped and turned. It was Jimmy, the younger deputy detective who'd helped with the video the day before. He had a frustrated look on his face, a look Austin knew well. Most detectives were desperate to find information and clues, especially in the early hours of a case. The last thing they wanted to do was answer questions, especially when the answer would require wild speculation. Jimmy opened his mouth to speak, bit his lower lip, then continued past the police tape and into the house.

"Damn pirates. So sad," Mrs. McGuilicutty said. "Used to be such a safe area."

Austin looked confused. "Pirates?"

"Yeah *New York*, she calls them pirates." Mr. McGuilicutty shook his head and sucked air through his teeth.

Mrs. McGuilicutty grew animated. "Robbers come in on their boats, stop on the beaches, and take what they please before escaping on the water. Stole my jewelry."

Mr. McGuilicutty waved a hand dismissively. "It happened *one* time. In 1974. Now everything is *pirates this and pirates that*."

"Turn it off," Austin said. "Or turn to something else."

Andy flicked over to the sports news.

Austin retrieved the coffee pot from behind the bar, refilled the cups for his only two patrons, then walked out to the small beach area in front of his café. A lone fisherman stood in the Sound, water up to his waist, dressed in rubber coveralls and a thick hooded sweatshirt. A cigarette dangled from the corner of his mouth, leaving his hands free as he cast his line far out in the water, then slowly reeled it back in. Austin had learned during his first winter in Hansville that, while the summer was by far the busiest, a handful of locals fished year round, even though the best salmon didn't run in the winter. If the guy was lucky, he might nab a chum or dog salmon, but the King and Chinook wouldn't be back for months.

Far out in the water, halfway between Hansville and Edmonds, a tugboat pulled a giant flat of scrap metal, probably on its way to China. From May to September, dozens of cruise ships passed by his little stretch of beach regularly, heading to and from Alaska. Half of him wished he could hop on one right now. The report had sparked his curiosity, that sharp ping of tart cherries to which he'd once been addicted. It was the thrill of the unknown—the mystery—mingled with the righteous indignation he felt toward the perpetrators of crimes against children.

For years, that feeling had gotten him out of bed in the morning and kept him at the office late into the night. It's why he and Fiona worked like hell and never had children. He still felt it, but now there was a desire to flee alongside it.

As Detective Calvin had said, this was a copycat, but a damn good one. The details of the Allie Shreever kidnapping and murder were right out of Lorraine D'Antonia's playbook. Based on the news report, the new case appeared to follow the same pattern. Austin had worked copycat murder cases before. The perpetrators always turned out to be obsessed with the original killers, gathering everything they could from the news, trial records, even leaked police reports. But the poems etched into the bones had never come out—not in the news and not at trial. If D'Antonia hadn't been behind bars, Austin would have bet his life she was involved. Now, it had to be someone close to the case, or someone who'd gotten hold of photographs or files that had never seen the light of day. Either way, if the copycat was determined to follow D'Antonia's MO. It meant the baby had about three days to live.

A light drizzle began to fall. Austin shoved his hands in his pockets and watched the rain pitter-patter the water, colliding with the small ripples moving toward the shore from the wake of the ship.

Austin yanked his cellphone from his pocket and found a spot where his reception went from one bar to two, just enough to make a call.

Detective Calvin picked up after two rings. "Hello?"

"Rid, it's Thomas Austin."

"You heard?"

"I heard."

"And? I'm pretty damn busy right now."

"It's December 22nd. By Christmas morning, the bones of that child will be in a decorative Christmas bag unless we find... him? Her?"

"Him. Joshua Green." Austin heard voices in the background, cars passing. Ridley was likely at the scene of the kidnapping. "You said 'we'?"

"I won't take payment. I don't want anything to be official. Even if this *is* a copycat—and it is—I'll likely be able to help. Put me in where you need me and I'll do everything I can to catch the monster behind this."

"I'm heading back to the office. How soon can you get there?"

CHAPTER EIGHT

AFTER A QUICK STOP TO feed Run, throw her the ball once or twice, and apologize for not taking her to the beach yet, Austin drove out to the Sheriff's office.

As he got out of his truck, he spotted a woman on the other end of the parking lot, sitting on the hood of a beat-up old station wagon. She looked as though she'd been lurking, waiting for someone to arrive, because the second he shut the car door she began walking toward him purposefully, eyes locked on his face.

She was around his age, with dirty blond hair and a vaguely Northern European look that was common around here. Fiona had grown up in the area and had a similar look. Like many of the county's residents, Fiona's family had come from Europe in the early 1900s—her mom's side from Ireland, her dad's side from Sweden. On a trip to visit her parents just after they were married, Fiona had joked that half the women in Kitsap— including herself—looked like nineteenth-century Norwegian farmworkers wearing Nirvana t-shirts. The woman approaching wasn't wearing a t-shirt—blue jeans and the black puffer jacket that seemed to be the uniform of both women and men in the area—but she had the Norwegian farmworker thing down.

Austin stopped on the curb in front of the door. "Can I help you?"

The woman pulled a pair of sunglasses out of her purse and put them on, blocking out the glare as the sun cut through the clouds for the first time all day. She held a cellphone between them the way reporters used to hold recorders. He knew where this was going.

"I'm Anna Downey, reporter. Any chance I could speak with you about the kidnapping that occurred last night?"

When he was a detective, reporters had generally made Austin's job harder, though he'd been happy to use them, or let *them* use *him*, when it suited his purpose. But after his wife was killed, a special kind of animosity toward reporters had hardened within him. He offered the most polite smile he could manage. "I don't work here. You'll want to speak with someone else."

She pulled off her sunglasses, studying his face, then put them back on. "Are you Thomas Austin, by any chance?"

He stepped back. "How'd you know that?"

"Google."

He stared at her. "I'm sorry, what paper are you with?"

"I'm not with a paper."

"You said you were a reporter."

"Ever heard of the internet?"

He scowled, looking her up and down. She'd unzipped her puffer jacket, revealing a red button-down shirt that would have looked professional in some settings, but looked incongruous with her jeans and tennis shoes. "Yeah, I've heard of the internet, but usually reporters identify not only their job, but where they work."

"I do a weekly column for the *Kitsap Union*. Online only. It's a roundup of all the crimes from the week, reports on ongoing investigations, trials, that sort of thing. Basically, I'm the Carrie Bradshaw of Kitsap County crime reporters."

Austin stared at her blankly, the way he always did when people made references he knew he should get, but didn't.

She stared back. "She's, uh, from a show. *Sex and the City?* You don't get out much, huh?"

"No."

"I also do a blog, a podcast, and some freelance stuff. A girl's gotta eat, right?"

Austin turned to leave, then remembered something. "Wait, how did you know my name?"

She moved into the shadow of the building and took off her sunglasses, presumably for the last time as she stashed them in the pocket of her button down. "I know about the bones in the bag, the ones found on the beach." She said it casually, as though it was no big deal. "Don't worry, I'm not gonna write it. Yet. But I know about them, and of course that got me looking into the Baby Butcher, which led me to you, which made me realize you live here now. You bought the Hansville Café, right? Quick call to one of my sources and I learned you might be a consultant on this case."

"I'm not."

"Then why are you here?"

"Who's your source?"

She laughed. "Twenty years in the NYPD and you still don't know how the press works?"

He stepped closer, his eyes hard. "You said you looked into me, right?"

She nodded.

"Did you read what the tabloids wrote after I was shot, after my wife was killed?"

She nodded. "I was sorry to read about it. Really. Sounds like you went through hell. But please don't tell me you're one of those cops who blames the reporters."

"I'm not a cop." Austin took a deep breath, trying to cool himself down. "And I don't blame reporters for unloading a nine-millimeter into my shoulder, my ribs, my forearm and my thigh." He swallowed hard. "And I don't blame reporters for the bullet that killed my wife. You know what I blame them for? For headline after headline that questioned why I took four bullets and lived while she took one and died. For headline after headline that questioned whether she was killed because of a case *I* was working on. I blame them for the story that wondered in print whether I'd had her killed because she was having an affair, which she wasn't—taking four bullets strategically placed to leave me alive—as cover up. I blame them for..." He trailed off, letting out a long, slow breath. "I blame the bastards who fired the guns. You folks in the press made it a little worse. A sprinkling of bitterness on an unending nightmare."

Anna Downey looked at the ground. "I'm sorry. And that's poetic, but I still have to do my job. I don't work for the New York tabloids and I don't write BS." She looked up. "Assuming you're here to help on this case..." she slid a business card into the pocket of his jeans... "don't hesitate to call. Day or night. I grew up here. Know the area, know everyone here." She chuckled. "Half the cops in the county are my uncle."

"Thanks, but you won't be hearing from me. Trust me on that."

He turned and pushed open the door.

"Austin," she called after him. "I'm sorry about what went down with your wife. I really am. And I think I understand why you do what you do, or why you did what you did before you quit. I live here. I care about this place. My reporting has tipped detectives inside that building onto two murder suspects and brought home a kid who'd been kidnapped by his biological father. *I give a shit.* And I don't do things the way the New York tabloids do. But I have to ask you: was a little bad press enough to get you to quit, to walk away from a job that, by all accounts, you were damn good at?"

He thought for a moment, considered shutting the door in her face and walking away. But something made him want to answer. She had an earnestness about her that he'd never seen from a reporter in New York, most of whom were from someplace else, or working like hell to get someplace else. "For a long time my wife and I thought we could save the world. Or at least, save a city. Or at least save enough people in a city that it would feel like we'd done something. I quit because I decided the world can't be saved. Or maybe it's not worth saving."

Her look was neutral, her bright blue eyes scanning his face like she was searching for the truth in what he said. "And yet," she said, shoving her cellphone in the back pocket of her jeans, "here you are."

She walked back to her car as he eased through the door.

CHAPTER NINE

THE CONFERENCE ROOM at the end of the hall looked like a crummy breakout room at a 2-star conference center. A folding table and six chairs atop a thinning, patternless carpet. A coffee maker perched on a black mini-fridge next to a sink in the corner. A whiteboard clinging crookedly to a wall that had more pin pricks than a voodoo doll. That was it. Austin didn't know if the room smelled like stale instant ramen, or if the taste in his mouth made him think so.

Detective Ridley Calvin stood in front of the whiteboard, already covered with notes about the case. Next to him, Lucy O'Rourke was taping a Kitsap County map to a wall as Jimmy sat on a plastic chair, staring at his phone.

On the wall to his left, there was a large sketch of a generic-looking woman in her fifties or sixties with dirty blonde hair. Austin assumed that was the woman who'd been spotted leaving the bones on the beach. It was one of the worst sketches he'd ever seen, likely a combination of a bad artist and unreliable witnesses. Next to the sketch were two photos of tiny babies, one labeled "Joshua Green" and the other "Allie Shreever, deceased."

On the top left of the whiteboard, Ridley had written "Allie

Shreever—Bremerton." On the right side, he was adding a new name: "Joshua Green—Bainbridge Island." Below the name of the first victim were a couple dates—likely the abduction date, the suspected date of death, and the date the bones had been found, along with a half dozen names he didn't recognize. Family members, witnesses, and suspects, most likely. Under the second name was a big white space.

He knew that blank space well. It meant that they had nothing.

Austin cleared his throat. Jimmy looked up briefly, then back down at his phone. Ridley and Lucy turned.

"Take a seat," Ridley said. "And thanks for coming."

Ridley added the names of the parents of the latest victim to the white board—Deidre Gailhammer and Damian Green—then leaned against the wall. "Jimmy, off the phone, let's go, what do you have?"

Lucy sat next to Jimmy, kicking his boot as she sat. "Off the phone, dumbass."

He set the phone on his lap. "You should talk, Lucy O'Please-Like-My-Instagram-Post. You're on your phone way more than me. And anyway, I wasn't scrolling. We got the first surveillance footage from Hansville."

"That's good news," Ridley said, "but hold on. Let me say first, to make it official: this is Thomas Austin, retired NYPD detective. He's gonna help us out on this. Lucy, he'll be accompanying you. Knows the D'Antonia case inside and out. His insight will no doubt be valuable. Copycats are often obsessed with the original, try to mimic every detail. Thomas, you'll have to sign some stuff on the way out the door. I don't know what, just, well, sign it. Something about liability and not putting yourself in harm's way."

Austin nodded. "Got it. And please, call me Austin."

"Right. Will do." He waved a hand toward Jimmy. "This is Jimmy Jule, aka 'Not-JJ.' Only man I know who can bench press four times his IQ."

Austin laughed. "That supposed to be a compliment?"

Jimmy said, "I take it as one. And yeah, don't call me JJ." He looked to be in his late-twenties, with skin tanned so evenly it had to be artificial, especially in December. His short brown hair had been gelled into place and he had a tattoo of an eagle on his muscular forearm.

"Why not?" Austin asked.

"He doesn't like to talk about it," Lucy said. "Under all those muscles he's a sensitive flower of a man."

Jimmy's face reddened. "Look, I had a cat named JJ. It didn't end well."

Lucy tossed a crumpled piece of paper at his head. "Tell him what the 'JJ' stood for."

"Justice Jellybean." He tossed the paper back at her, but she dodged, allowing it to sail past her head. "What do you want? I was five and those were the two things I loved. Anyway, thanks for pitching in, Austin. Why do you go by your last name?"

"As a kid I was really into reruns of *The Six Million Dollar Man*. Told my parents I wanted to go by 'Austin.' They kept calling me 'Tommy,' but in college my roommate was into wrestling and thought Stone Cold Steve Austin was the coolest dude ever. So he started calling me Austin, and from there we just ran with it."

"You *do* look kind of like Lee Majors," Ridley said.

Lucy and Jimmy were staring blankly. Austin said, "You have no idea who we're talking about, do you?"

Jimmy shook his head. "Friend of yours?"

Lucy threw another ball of paper at his head.

Ridley began pacing. "I just got back from the home of the victims on Bainbridge. The mom, Deirdre, was frantic. Could barely get anything out of her. Her mother arrived from the other side of the island and is trying to calm her down. The husband was out of town and will be back soon."

"Out of town?" Lucy asked. "We sure about that?"

"I'll be interviewing him myself," Ridley said. "Already looking into his alibi."

Ridley knew as well as Austin that most kidnappings were committed by someone who knew the victim. Fathers taking kids in the midst of a custody battle, that sort of thing. This didn't appear to be one of those times, but they had to look into everything.

"As of this moment," Ridley said, "we are treating the Green kidnapping as directly connected to the kidnapping and murder of Allie Shreever. Other than the similarity in the abductions, we don't have any direct evidence they are connected, but my gut says they are."

"Mine, too," Jimmy added.

"Your gut probably just wants another protein shake," Lucy said.

Jimmy flexed a perfectly-tanned bicep. "Gotta feed the guns, Lucy O'Lemon Drop Shots."

"So," Austin said, "I assume we work both avenues: the fresh case, Joshua Green, and the older one, Allie Shreever."

Ridley nodded. "Directly following this meeting, the three of us will head out to Bainbridge to interview the Greens." He pointed at Jimmy. "You stay here and go through that surveillance footage like you're getting paid a million bucks per lead."

"*Am* I getting a million bucks per lead?" Jimmy asked.

Ridley ignored him.

Austin flashed back to the news report. "The Green house looked fancy, modern. Security cameras?"

"Nope," Jimmy said. "They're, I don't know how to say it, kinda hippy-ish was the vibe I got. Dad runs some big organic juice thing in Seattle. I asked the mom about it and she said something about 'the surveillance state.' House smelled funny— incense and kombucha."

"We'll double check on surveillance footage," Ridley added,

"but Jimmy is right, as far as we know. I'm sure we'll get footage from another house on the block, or from a traffic light nearby, but that could take a few days, and we may not have that long." He paced for a moment, then continued. "Lucy, take Austin back to the beginning of the Shreever case. Fill him in on what we have." He glanced at Austin, apologetically. "It isn't much. Parents, suspects we've looked at. And the witnesses. Go talk to Benny and Sarah again. Maybe Austin can get something new out of them."

Lucy nodded. "Already called them. After we talk to the Green and Gailhammer family, Benny and Sarah are our first stop."

Ridley turned to Jimmy, who was back on his phone. "Bicep man, what do you have on surveillance?"

Jimmy walked over to the whiteboard. "I'll get to that, but first, I've got every digital file that's available on the D'Antonia case. I'll be going over them later, but in the meantime I have an AI running through them looking for anomalies."

"Wait," Austin said, "What?" Yesterday, Ridley had introduced Jimmy as a deputy and also their resident "tech guy." Austin assumed that meant he could restart the Wi-Fi or get the TV to work. Looks could be deceiving, but Austin thought he looked like a bit of a meathead. Austin's mentor had told him once that there were two kinds of cops, thinkers and door-bashers. That was, of course, an oversimplification, but Jimmy looked like a door-basher if anyone did.

Jimmy said, "It rarely gets us anything, but it's low-hanging fruit. Any files that are readable digitally, I run a series of algorithms on them to look for patterns. Words mentioned again and again, names mentioned once and never followed up on." Apparently he could see the skepticism on Austin's face. "I know, I know. This isn't *Minority Report*. We're not actually basing anything on this. It's one more arrow in our quiver. Occasionally it spits out something we missed. It's really Samantha's thing. Intern. You'll meet her later, I'm sure."

Austin nodded. "What were you saying about the surveillance videos? That's more my thing."

"The bones of Allie Shreever were found three weeks ago now. There's no footage from the beach, of course, but we've knocked on every door, watched hours of useless footage from people's home security cameras, hoping to get a suspect, an unusual car passing, something."

Austin's door had been one of the ones knocked on. When the bones had been found, an officer had come into his café and questioned him, Andy, and a few patrons, who were happy to share details about everything they'd ever seen, though none of it had seemed useful. The officers had, of course, not mentioned that the bones were found in a holiday gift bag.

"Finally got a hit," Jimmy said. "Driveway cam pointing toward a mailbox on Hansville Highway. Owners were out of town the last couple weeks, but they have some footage from that morning. It's not great, but it has cars coming and going toward that beach on the morning in question."

"Hot damn!" Lucy said. "Lucy O'Likes-That."

Jimmy stood and performed a gesture halfway between a bow and sneezing into the crook of his elbow.

Austin was pretty sure the kids called it 'dabbing.' He glanced at Ridley and waved a hand toward Lucy and Jimmy. "This normal?"

Ridley shook his head. "Sadly, yes." Then, to Jimmy, he asked, "How soon can you have more?"

"I'll watch the footage as soon as we're done."

Ridley nodded and took a long swig out of a giant silver coffee cup. "One more thing. I'm fighting to keep Sheriff Daniels off our ass, but we have to deliver, and fast. We're treating this case as though we have three days—two and a half now—before Joshua Green shows up in a bag. We *cannot* allow that to happen. Sheriff already got a call from the FBI. He told me that, for now, they are kindly offering assistance. Profiling. More advanced forensics than we can manage. He stressed the *for now* part of that. He told them about the bones, the similarities to the D'Antonia case. They're not taking over yet, but they can and will if the mood hits them. And if it leaks in the press that Allie Shreever's bones were found in the bag..." he grimaced, as though the thought alone pained him... "if that leaks, national media will descend and the FBI will have no choice but to follow. That happens and I'll be grabbing lattes for buzzcut FBI assholes half my age. Lucy and Jimmy, you don't even want to think about where that will leave you in the pecking order. It may involve shining wingtips."

Austin raised a finger. "Might have a problem there. Ran into a reporter, or blogger, or, well, I don't know what she was but—"

Ridley smiled. "Anna?"

"Yeah, that's her."

"Pain in the ass, but she's a friend. Not a friend, but, well, I hate her a lot less than I hate most reporters."

"Fine," Austin said, "but she has the bones. The Thanksgiving bag. Said she wasn't gonna run it yet."

Austin could make out the lines on Ridley's temples as they flared. "She what?" He looked from Jimmy to Lucy. He could go from relaxed to enraged in a heartbeat, and he just had.

Jimmy stood up. "That's probably on me. I'm sorry. I was on my cellphone and she heard me mention the witnesses—Benny and Sarah. She knows *everyone*. Likely tracked them down and got it from them."

"Jimmy O'Jackass," Lucy said, swinging a fist at his shoulder but missing as he leapt back. "Stay the hell off your phone."

"I know." He looked at the floor. "She was lurking in the parking lot."

Ridley walked a slow lap around the folding table. "Why wouldn't she have run it yet?"

"Called me for comment," Jimmy said. "I convinced her to hold it for a day or two in exchange for an exclusive interview with whoever catches the bastard behind this."

Ridley frowned. "We solve crimes as a team, Jimmy. And we *do not* take victory laps in the press."

He looked at the floor, shamefaced. "I screwed up."

Ridley let out a puff of air like a kettle releasing steam. "I'll call her and try to convince her to do the right thing." He turned to Lucy. "You and Austin get going. I'll be right behind you. We talk to the recent victims, then you two head out to see Benny and Sarah. I'm hoping his fresh eyes will bring something new to this thing."

CHAPTER TEN

"TELL me about the first victims, the Shreever family," Austin said. "Did you interview the parents?"

"Ridley led the interview," Lucy said, flicking on the windshield wipers, "but I was there. He and I are partners, normally."

They were halfway across the Agate Pass Bridge, an old steel truss bridge that had replaced a ferry service that had run people from the Kitsap Peninsula to Bainbridge Island from the 1920s into the 1950s. Despite the light drizzle, the views to the southeast were stunning: blue-gray water, evergreen western hemlocks and Douglas firs dotting the misty shores. The area was an endless maze of inlets, bays, pebbly beaches, and view after view that looked like it belonged on a postcard.

"How hard did you look at the Shreever family?" Austin asked. Every detective shared the first instinct when it came to both kidnapping and murder: work from the inside out. The inside was the circle closest to the victim: spouses, boyfriends and girlfriends, close family members, extended family, friends, and work acquaintances. Though most people feared random attacks and senseless home invasions, the truth was that most violent crimes were perpetrated by people already known to the victim.

"We were all over them," Lucy said. "Regular Bremerton family. Pretty well off. Mom was a JAG lawyer. Navy. Dad wasn't Navy, but he worked in the shipyard."

"What role?"

"Contractor. Well, he works for one. Painting, repairs, that kind of thing. My read on them was a negative right away, but we worked it pretty hard. Before the bones were found, we were treating it like a regular kidnapping, as if any kidnapping can be considered 'regular.'"

"Their marriage?"

"Shockingly good. They'd just had their fifth wedding anniversary, dozens of people came. Years of Facebook posts about each other. Kind of couple that posts gushy appreciation stuff about each other every day. Kinda gross, but also kinda sweet, depending on how sentimental I'm feeling."

"Staged, maybe?"

Lucy shook her head. "They handed over their cellphones within ten minutes. No arguments to speak of. Doctors and nurses in the hospital said he was supportive, caring. I'm cynical as hell, and even I ended up jealous about their marriage. I'd kill for a man like that."

Austin looked over. "What about Jimmy?"

She scoffed. "*No.*"

Austin waited for her to look over, then raised an eyebrow. "Seemed like—"

"Also no."

Austin smiled. "Touchy subject, huh?"

"We had a thing for about a month when he first started. He's five years younger than me. Ridley told me I should break it off if I want to be his boss one day."

"Do you want to be his boss one day?"

"Ridley should be Sheriff. He's five times the man Daniels is. When he's Sheriff, I could get lead detective." She smiled awkwardly. "Eventually."

Austin wanted to dig deeper, a welcome distraction from

thoughts about whether a seemingly happy couple would stage the kidnapping and murder of their own baby. It wasn't likely, but Ridley and his team had already looked at all the likely options. He'd been brought in to consider the unlikely ones.

His first thought had been that something could be wrong with the Shreever marriage, something that didn't show up in texts and Facebook posts. Maybe the father wanted out and didn't want the kid, so he staged it to look like a copycat serial killer. It was a stretch, though not impossible. Or maybe the couple had learned that Allie had a rare disease after she was born and didn't want to deal with it. As sick as that was, he'd seen it on more than one occasion. "So, in your mind, there is zero chance the Shreevers were involved?"

"Zero, and now with this new case—"

"Serial killers and serial kidnappers are a hell of a lot rarer than moms and dads who feel they have no other choice, moms and dads with drug and alcohol problems, moms and dads who accidentally kill their child, then try to cover it up."

Lucy gave him a frustrated glare. "I know that, New York, I didn't get my badge two weeks ago. All I'm saying is that two kidnappings this close together, with such similarities, and combined with the bones, makes me think we're not gonna find out a family member is behind this."

"Sorry, I wasn't trying to... just trying to go back to the beginning."

"Nah, I'm sorry. It's why Ridley brought you in." Her hands gripped the steering wheel tighter as she turned off the main road onto a winding side street heading east. "This one is really getting to me. I'm frustrated. I don't know if I can live through another meeting with a family where I show them a bag of their baby's bones."

"You have kids?" Austin asked.

"Nah, you?"

"No."

They rode in silence, the only sound the occasional splash of rainwater falling on the roof of the car after collecting in the branches of the evergreens that shrouded the road.

"I understand about the parents," Austin said. The horrors of this job were bad enough. Explaining them to innocent family members was worse. "Let's not let that happen."

Detective Calvin had mentioned that a woman had been spotted on the beach where the bones were found. That's where Austin's mind went next. "Anything on the woman who we believe left the bones?"

"Just the crappy sketch you saw."

"I assume you ran the sketch by the Shreever family to see if they recognized her? Family member? Nanny? Housekeeper?"

"We did. Nothing. After this interview, we'll talk to the witnesses. They've been helpful—or tried to be. Little hooligans never should have talked to a reporter, but... Well, all we have is a woman between fifty and seventy, light brown or dirty blonde hair. Kinda hard to tie that to the Shreever family, though we did comb through all their social media. Don't have a housekeeper or nanny. One aunt fit the description, but we placed her in Connecticut at the time. She's Navy, too. Airtight alibi."

Austin saw a TV news van parked at the end of the block, then the police tape surrounding the house. Lucy parked and led Austin into the yard, where Detective Calvin was taking questions from a gaggle of reporters that included one serious-looking Asian man with a *Seattle Times* badge, a couple younger reporters who looked like bloggers, and Anna Downey.

"We're not ruling anything out at this time," Ridley was saying when they stopped next to him.

The reporter from the *Seattle Times* followed up. "Would you say the similarities between this case and the Shreever kidnapping and murder concern you?"

"Everything concerns me," Ridley said, voice calm and direct. "And, like I said, though we do not have evidence the cases are connected, we are certainly looking at that angle."

Movement caught Austin's eye and he turned to the side of

the house, where a large peacock was prancing toward them. It strolled across the lawn like it owned the place, watched the reporters for a moment, then let out a long, shrill noise, halfway between a cat's meow and a baby's cry. Austin leaned over to Lucy. "That normal here?"

"Normal?" she whispered. "No. Unheard of? Also no."

The peacock proceeded to walk up to the crowd and spread its magnificent, shimmering tail, which spanned four or five feet and was covered in giant spots. Then it began to rustle and rattle its tail feathers, a sound almost like a drumroll.

"What the hell is happening?" Austin asked no one in particular.

Anna crouched down to get a closer look. "This is a male, he's looking for a mate. You interested?"

Austin frowned at her.

"Bird people call that noise the 'love rattle,'" Anna continued. "Vibrations can be felt in the tail of a female peacock."

Austin shook his head. "Learn something new every day."

As the peacock wandered away, Ridley declined to answer any more questions, then led Austin and Lucy into the residence.

Deidre Gailhammer and Damian Green sat on opposite ends of a beige leather couch. The space between them was only a single couch cushion, but it felt much, much larger. As Detective Calvin introduced Austin and Lucy, Austin studied them. Sometimes tragedy brought couples closer together. This was not one of those times.

There was a frostiness there, an anger. They wouldn't look at each other. Deidre's round face, freckled like Lucy's, was red and blotchy, possibly from hours of crying but possibly from drinking. Most likely, both. She passed an empty coffee cup nervously from hand to hand. Damian sat stone-faced, emotionless. To some detectives Austin had worked with, this was a red flag. If your baby son was taken from your house, wouldn't *you* be upset? But Austin had learned that victims respond to tragedy differently, and it was a mistake to leap to judgment too quickly. Still, it made him wonder.

When he'd woken up in the hospital after twelve hours of emergency surgery, numb from painkillers and desperate for news about his wife, he'd been similarly emotionless. When his captain had arrived to tell him Fiona was gone, he'd felt as though his heart had been hacked to bits with a rusty hatchet. He'd wished the gunmen had taken him, too. But he hadn't said any of that to his captain. Instead, he'd bitten his lip until it bled, trying to hold everything in. Then he'd proceeded to tell his commanding officer every single detail he could remember about the attackers. Only later, alone in the hospital bed in the middle of the night, had he allowed the emotions to come.

He knew what it was like to try to stay rational, stay sane, when everything was falling apart. So his first read on the father was that he was doing just that, staying calm so he could communicate with the detectives.

Then Damian Green glanced at his wife, stood slowly, and lunged at Detective Calvin like a drunk in a bar fight.

CHAPTER ELEVEN

BEFORE AUSTIN COULD REACT, Damian had his right forearm pressed into Ridley's chest. He was half a foot shorter than the detective, and probably sixty pounds lighter. Not a small man, but next to the half-giant Ridley, he was laughably outmatched. With his left hand, Damian reached for Ridley's throat. It never got there.

As Austin took his first step to intervene, Ridley deftly took a half step back, intercepted the hand coming for his throat, and twisted it so hard that Damian dropped to the floor, writhing in a ridiculous half flip and contorting his body to keep his wrist from breaking.

When Ridley let go, Lucy was all over the father, knee in his back, pressing his face into the couch. "You want me to cuff him?"

"Let him go," Ridley said.

Lucy patted him down, then backed off.

Ridley yanked Damian up and pushed him back onto the couch. "That was not wise, Mr. Green."

There were tears streaming down the man's face. His wife had inched even further away from him on the couch, a look somewhere between disgust and horror spread across her face.

"Another move like that," Ridley said, "and you'll be in jail when we find your son. You don't want that."

"You told my wife where I was that night," Damian said. He was trying to sound angry, but it came out more pathetic. "You did not need to do that."

"Yes he did!" Deirdre shouted, slapping him across the shoulder. "You selfish prick!"

Clearly, Austin had missed something, but their distance on the couch now made more sense.

Ridley said, "First of all, Mr. Green, I can't stress enough the extent to which it's in your interest not to come at me again. If you'd attacked Lucy like that, trust me, you would *not* get a pass. You'd be in the back of a police car with an assaulting-an-officer charge. But I have two kids. I can understand your grief, assuming that's what this is. I know how grief can flip to rage. It was important that I tell your wife that you were not, in fact, out of town on a business trip when your child was taken. Your initial alibi was a lie. Another poor decision. Another potential charge you now face. At this moment, every person on earth is a suspect, and it's crucial that we have a complete picture of everyone who's in Joshua's life."

"That bitch isn't *in* Joshua's life," Deidre spat. "She's in my husband's pants, apparently. And probably his wallet."

Damian grimaced.

Now it all made sense. Damian Green was having an affair. He'd lied to Detective Calvin about it and, likely on the ride over, his alibi had fallen apart and Ridley had called Deirdre. It's what Austin would have done. In his experience, people lied about sex more than anything else in the world. More than money and, shockingly, more than murder. He'd had hardened criminals who'd admitted to multiple murders lie about being bisexual. A father he'd arrested for drowning his teenaged son had denied dressing in women's clothing—despite reams of photographic evidence—because he thought it made him look bad. In short, sex made people crazier than anything in the world.

Ridley surely knew this as well. And when crimes were fresh, a lot could be gained by observing the genuine emotional reactions of the suspects, the victims, or the victim's families. Deirdre had found out her husband had been with another woman the night their son had gone missing, two weeks after she'd given birth. Ridley had wanted to put that pressure on their relationship right before they arrived to get the freshest responses possible. It was diabolical, sure, but good detective work.

Lucy knelt in front of the couch, between the couple, but she addressed Deirdre. "I've been cheated on. It sucks, I know. It hurts and—"

"I already *knew* he was having an affair," Deirdre said. "But two weeks after bringing our son home from the hospital." She glared at Damian. "You couldn't wait a whole month before... Bastard... You're such a bastard..."

She slumped back into the couch cushions like a deflated balloon. Then she sighed a long, weary sigh. "Can we just get on with this? We have to make this about Joshua."

"Exactly," Lucy said. "We're here to find out everything we can so we can find your son." She looked at Damian. "Find. Your. Son. You two need to grow the hell up right now." Her tone was commanding, but also compassionate, a good combination.

And it seemed to work because Damian glanced apologetically at Deirdre, who sat up a little straighter and finally made eye contact with Ridley, who said, "Thomas Austin is here consulting for us because he's an expert on infant abductions. He's going to ask you some questions."

Austin offered a reassuring smile, then said. "Take me back to the beginning. The night your son went missing."

Over the next hour, Austin got the whole story. Though Damian tried to interrupt a few times, he was mostly well-behaved. And Deirdre struck him as reliable and, though she obviously drank consistently, she came off as more of a wine-mom than a drunk.

Since bringing Joshua home from St. Michael's in Silverdale, Deirdre explained, she'd fallen into a reliable routine, one she'd followed the night he'd gone missing. That evening, she'd put Joshua to bed around 8:30 PM, texted her husband, who hadn't replied, watched TV for an hour, had a glass of Merlot, then gone to bed. She'd awoken around midnight when she heard Joshua crying on the baby monitor she kept on her nightstand. At that time, there was no sign of anything wrong, except that he needed a diaper change and a bottle. By 1 AM or so, she'd rocked him back to sleep and returned to bed.

The next thing she knew she was awake, the first light of pre-dawn creeping through the curtains. She knew something was wrong when she checked the clock on her phone: 6:30 AM. Joshua had never gone more than four hours without waking her up. Her fears were confirmed when she opened the door to the nursery and felt a cold breeze. Joshua was gone, along with his baby blanket. The window next to the crib was open. She was certain it had been closed when she went to sleep. Nothing else was missing from the house. Other than what might have been a foot imprint in the carpet, the kidnapper left no trace.

Within minutes, she called the police. Then she called Damian, who—she made sure to point out—hadn't answered. Detective Calvin arrived an hour later for the first interview.

"After that," she concluded, "everything was a waking nightmare."

Lucy asked, "Any family members you might have been arguing with recently, ex-boyfriends, that kind of thing?"

She glanced at Damian, who was shaking his head. "No, not that I can think of. My mom adores Joshua. Dad died when I was little, and my sisters live on the east coast."

Lucy pulled the sketch out of her pocket, unfolded it, and handed it to Deirdre. "She look familiar at all?"

Deirdre studied the picture. "No."

She handed it to Damian, who shook his head, then said, "Wait. I don't know the woman, but I recognize this picture. Is this... I can't remember where I saw it."

Detective Calvin said, "You may have seen this sketch on the news. This woman is a person of interest in another case. We don't know if they are related."

Damian looked like he was going to stand, but a cautioning glance from Lucy made him relax into the couch. "She's from the other kidnapping," he said. "The baby who... oh, God."

"The one who was killed a few days later," Deirdre said. Her face trembled, then she let out a sharp, anguished cry. Pure pain.

"Like I said," Ridley said sternly, "we *do not* yet have any reason to believe the cases are connected, but if you've seen this woman—a neighbor, a strange woman in the grocery store, someone at the hospital, a lady who delivers your mail—anything. Now's the time to tell us. Look again and think hard."

They did, both shaking their heads the whole time.

"I remember seeing the picture on the news report," Damian said. "That's it."

Austin stuck his hands in his pockets, letting out a long breath. "Can I see Joshua's room?"

Deirdre led them to the nursery, one door down from her bedroom. It was light blue, with yellow cartoon lions and bright pink elephants painted on the walls. As Deirdre had said, the crib was in the corner, next to the window, which remained open. The indent in the carpet wasn't visible to the naked eye, but it had been sprayed with a black powder and surrounded with little red flags attached to pins.

Ridley pointed at it. "Too faint to cast, but there was a partial shoe print in the mud outside, women's size eight, Adidas running shoes, consistent with the size of this indentation."

Austin crouched down to study it. It was probably irrelevant since she was behind bars, but Lorraine D'Antonia also wore a size 8. So did roughly thirty percent of the women in the country, so it wouldn't do a lot to narrow down the suspect list, even if they'd had one. The indentation was about three feet from the window, toe pointed to the center of the room, consistent with someone stepping in through the window toward the crib.

Austin asked, "What size do you wear, Ms. Gailhammer?"

"Six." She lifted a foot up as though to prove this.

"Do you have a housekeeper?"

"Yes, but she hasn't come since before he was born."

"I don't see what good this is doing?" Damian exclaimed from the doorway. "Why aren't you out looking for the bastard?"

Ridley took him by the arm. "You and Ms. Gailhammer, why don't you come back to the living room. Let our people work."

When they'd left, Lucy turned to Austin. "What do you think?"

Austin pointed out the window. "With the road right there, this is a good spot to nab a kid. First story bedroom. Bush blocks most of the view of the window. Perp probably left the car running, pried the thing open, one foot into the room, grabbed the kid. Gone in two minutes, tops."

Lucy gestured to the baby monitor, which sat on the changing table next to the crib. "Those things don't record, do they?"

"They can, but that one looks pretty basic. First impression is this was highly-targeted. Of all the houses on the block, this one is the easiest. The perp somehow knew enough about the house to know it would be an easy break-in and that it didn't have cameras, but it's not sounding like a family member did this."

Lucy nodded. "Exactly the same as the Allie Shreever case in Bremerton. First floor nursery, close to a road. Middle of the night. Family and friends cleared within a week. Feels targeted, but..."

"Damn." Austin shook his head. He'd hoped to find easy evidence showing this case was unrelated to the Allie Shreever murder.

"Damian's temper?" Lucy asked, holding up her phone.

"Email from Samantha, our intern. She says security footage from his girlfriend's apartment puts him in Seattle the night this went down. But still."

"It's concerning, but..." He shook his head. "I don't like him for this."

Of course, they'd have to look into Damian and his mistress more thoroughly. It was possible he'd hired someone to take his son. Maybe he'd wanted out of the marriage and knew he'd never get custody of Joshua, so he'd had the kid stolen, planning to disappear with him and his mistress. It was worth a look, but Damian Green struck Austin as a hothead, a bad husband, but not a sociopath. "Was Joshua born at the same hospital as Allie Shreever?"

Lucy nodded. "They did, and I had the same thought. Maybe Ridley can head out there next." Her phone dinged with a text. "You done here?"

Austin nodded.

"Then let's go. Our only witnesses are ready to talk."

CHAPTER TWELVE

AUSTIN CRACKED the window as they took the long hill down toward the water. The drizzle had died down, the sun creeping out from behind the clouds as they passed into Hansville. This was not uncommon as one drove north from Kingston into the tiny town at the end of the peninsula. When he'd moved to the area, Austin had learned that Hansville lay in a rain shadow—some called it a sun belt. Hansville received twenty-five percent less rain per year than the closest neighboring town only five miles to the south. In an area known for its rain, that twenty-five percent made a big difference.

After leaving Joshua Green's parents, Austin had huddled with Lucy and Ridley on the lawn, out of earshot of the reporters. While the peacock wandered around at their feet, they'd decided that Ridley would go to the birthing center at St. Michael's—the only known connection between the two victims —leaving Lucy and Austin to re-interview the teenagers who'd found Allie Shreever's bones on the beach at Point No Point.

Lucy's phone rang as they turned onto Point No Point Road, a one-mile stretch that led out to the famous lighthouse. "It's Jimmy," she said, tapping the touchscreen on the dashboard.

Jimmy's excited voice filled the car in choppy bursts. "Photos of... car that passed... Hansville road. 10... and... AM. In... inbox. Got plates on... few with... and add... Others... blurry, but I marked the type of car."

"Reception sucks out here," Lucy called loudly into her steering wheel. "But nice work, J-Cool. Anything leap out at you?"

"Only... dozen or so."

"You've got—"

"People heading to the addresses?" Jimmy's voice was clearer now. They'd hit a good patch of reception as they neared the beach. "Yeah. On it. Just got off the phone with Sherlock and he's got everyone he can on this."

"Thanks," Lucy said, "I'll take a look." She hung up as Austin spotted a pair he assumed were the witnesses. Teenagers, holding hands on a bench facing the water, both glancing around nervously. "That them?"

"Yup, this'll be my third interview with them. Pissed as hell they told Anna about the bones. They promised they wouldn't talk to anyone about it. When we made the announcement that Allie Shreever had been found deceased, we wanted to make sure the exact nature of her death was kept quiet, for now."

Austin shrugged. "I'm surprised they waited so long to blab about it. Most teenagers I've met would've had it up on Instachat before calling the police."

Lucy raised an eyebrow. "Instachat?"

"Snapgram, I meant."

Lucy laughed. "How *old* are you?"

He shrugged. "Do I not have it right?"

"It's *Instagram* and *Snapchat*."

"Are you sure?"

Lucy laughed again, then nodded at the teenagers, who'd started walking toward them.

"Their story been consistent the whole time?" Austin asked.

"Mostly. First time they left out that they were at the beach to smoke weed, but they've been forthcoming otherwise. We looked into them just in case, but they're basically good kids."

They met in the corner of the parking lot by the bathrooms. After chiding Sarah and Benny for talking to a reporter, Lucy introduced Austin as a "consultant helping out with the case."

When they were through with introductions, Austin said, "How about you walk me through it. Slowly. Exactly what you saw, heard, noticed, felt. Also, I want to know whether anything was different that day than the other times you've come here?"

"Got it," Benny said, flippantly. He seemed distracted, uninterested.

Austin waited until Benny met his eyes. "If a grain of sand was in a different spot than usual, I want to know about it."

Benny chuckled.

Sarah said, "Like, literally? Seriously?"

Austin offered her a tight smile. "Seriously, but not literally."

Benny led them down the beach, doing most of the talking. Since he'd already admitted to the other detectives they were there to smoke, he included that in his story from the beginning. From the beach they followed the trail up to the bench on the bluff.

When Benny reached the part about the woman appearing, Austin stopped him. "At what point were you aware she was carrying something?"

"Right away. I mean, I thought it was an umbrella."

"Was this before or after you started smoking?"

"Before," Benny said, looking at the ground. "I lit up after she left. And I know I'm underage, but c'mon."

"I didn't smoke anything," Sarah interjected. She was dressed in a dark blue dress with black leggings, the kind of outfit you'd expect to see at a chorus recital. It contrasted with Benny's greasy jeans and black hoodie.

"You two a couple?" Austin asked.

Benny said "yes" and Sarah said "no," then they both laughed and shook their heads.

"It's complicated," Sarah said, in a tone that communicated she didn't want to say anything more.

Austin pointed at the beach. "So she comes down the beach, leaves the bag, and how long was she there afterwards?"

"Maybe thirty seconds," Sarah said. "Snapped a few photos."

Like the size eight shoe, this was another similarity to the D'Antonia case. It had come out in the trial that Lorraine D'Antonia had also taken photos of her bags of bones. *Beloved memories*, she'd called them to Austin's disgust. "Was the woman facing the water when she took the photos? Or did she walk around the log so her back was to the water?"

Sarah thought. "She was facing the water, I think, um..."

"She was," Benny agreed.

"And did she take a long time composing the photos, or was it quick?"

"Quick," Sarah said.

Austin pointed across the water to the east. "And the sun was up, but not high in the sky, correct? 11 AM?"

"Right," Sarah said. "It was cloudy, drizzly, but still a glare coming through." She pointed east, across the water. "You know how it gets where it's raining but there's still a glare."

Austin knew. On the east coast, he'd grown used to clouds and sunshine, storms and clear skies, snow and heat, but here there were endless shades of gray depending on how thick the cloud cover was.

D'Antonia's photos had been well-composed, almost professional, then edited on her phone to look dramatic and moody. The woman who'd left the bones here seemed to have been in a hurry, like she didn't really care how the photos looked. If she'd cared, she would have stood with her back to the sun. The way she took the photos, facing the source of the light, would have made the bag look unnaturally dark.

Lucy asked, "Where are you going with this?"

He shook her off, not wanting to explain in front of Sarah and Benny. "Sarah, tell me about the noise you heard."

"I thought it was a gunshot," she said.

Benny shook his head. "Sounded like a car backfiring."

Lucy pulled her phone from her back pocket and opened the email from Jimmy. "Any of these cars look familiar to you? They were caught on a surveillance camera around the time you saw the woman."

Austin looked over their shoulders as they scanned through the document. Each car had its own page, some with license plate numbers, names, and addresses, others just photographs. All the photographs were from an odd angle, all were fairly blurry, but the general shape, size, and colors of the vehicles were clear.

"I didn't see a car pull in or out," Bennie said.

"Me neither," Sarah added. "And I know nothing about cars."

"But maybe you've seen them around town," Austin said, "or maybe you saw a car when you were on the bluff?"

"Sorry," Sarah said.

"According to Detective O'Rourke here," Austin said, taking the phone, "you heard a car pass soon after the loud sound. Is that right?"

They both nodded.

"How many seconds after you heard the sound?"

"Why does that matter?" Benny asked.

Austin gave him a hard stare.

"Okay, okay. It was like a minute."

"Wasn't that long. Like literally ten or twenty seconds after," Sarah said. "Maybe less, it was like right away almost."

Given that Benny had been high, he was going to trust Sarah's sense of time.

Austin scanned the document. A black BMW, registered on Bainbridge Island. A red Toyota Corolla, no plate visible. A green and brown Chevy truck, registered to a woman in Kingston. He stopped on that one. It was an older make, 1980. The rest of the cars were newer, and he scrolled back to the truck. "You sure you didn't see this truck?"

Newer cars were less likely to backfire unless the owners customized them to do so. He doubted a woman in her fifties or sixties would do that. Older cars in need of tune-ups were more likely to backfire in general, and specifically when they were in motion, rather than on the start. "Is it possible," he asked, "That the woman parked this truck, walked down the beach, left the bag of bones, returned to her truck, pulled out of the driveway, causing the truck to backfire, then sped past you up the road out of town?"

"Sure," Sarah said. "But I didn't see that truck."

"Same," Benny added.

Lucy was following Austin's train of thought. Tapping and swiping furiously on her phone, she said, "Give us a sec," to the teenagers.

They were happy to walk down the trail toward the beach.

Before Austin could ask what she was doing, Lucy held up her phone. It was open to Facebook and displayed a picture of a woman who appeared to be in her late-fifties. She had dirty blonde hair and a bony, well-worn face. She looked vaguely like the poorly-rendered sketch on the wall at the Sheriff's office. She also looked a little like Lorraine D'Antonia—around the same age, with the same hair color and skinny, angular face.

"Trisha Simone," Lucy said. "Kingston. Registered owner of the truck."

She jogged toward the teenagers, who'd only made it thirty yards down the path. "Could this be the woman you saw?"

They said "Yes" in unison.

A smile broke out across Lucy's face. "Keep your phones on. Both of you." Then she turned to Austin. "Let's go."

PART 2

THE CHASE

CHAPTER THIRTEEN

TEN MINUTES LATER, they pulled up in front of an apartment building a few blocks from the ferry in Kingston. It was a newer construction, five stories, holding twenty or thirty units, some of which looked out at the town's marina.

Austin threw open the door, ready to go.

Lucy put a hand on his shoulder. "Wait here. Ridley's orders."

Austin wanted to object, but he'd agreed to stay out of any situation beyond research, meetings, and interviews. He wasn't a detective, wasn't licensed as a private investigator, and Sheriff Daniels had insisted he sign a half dozen waivers just to act as a consultant. "If she's there—"

"You'll be in on the interview. I promise."

Detective Calvin had been at the hospital when Lucy called him. They'd agreed that she should head over to the apartment while he stopped to get a warrant for Trisha Simone's apartment and truck. A patrol car in the area had met them at the apartment building.

Austin watched from the car as Lucy hopped out and positioned one officer at the front door, waving another around the side of the building, presumably to stake out the back. Then she disappeared into the lobby of the apartment building.

Austin scrolled through the photos of cars Jimmy had sent earlier. They were low quality, but good enough for him to feel more certain than ever that Trisha Simone's old truck had backfired on the morning Benny and Sarah found the bones on the beach. All the other cars were much newer, and none had the look of a car that had been customized to backfire. He thought about trying to find the suspect on Facebook as Lucy had, but he didn't have the app on his phone and wasn't entirely sure how it worked. It wasn't that he didn't see the investigative value of combing through people's social media, but in the NYPD, he'd worked with a partner who'd handled that side of investigations.

He scanned the parking lot idly, then glanced up at the windows of the apartment building, then watched the officer out front, who paced in front of the door.

Letting his gaze fall again to the parking lot, his eyes stopped on a truck. He looked again at the document, then back at the truck. That wasn't *a* truck. It was *the* truck. 1980 Chevy, brown and yellow.

He really ought to let Lucy know, but Austin had learned in the NYPD that he could get a lot more done by asking for forgiveness, rather than permission.

He got out of the car and crossed the lot, glancing back at the apartment building every few paces. As he approached, he saw that the truck was empty. But even so, his pulse quickened, his breaths came a little louder, the hairs on his neck prickled, and he tasted the unmistakable tang of tart cherries. As much as he'd wanted out of this line of work, he couldn't deny that he loved the chase.

∽

Lucy had decided to take the stairs. Trisha Simone's truck was registered to apartment 4A, and Lucy figured that if she and Austin were spotted from the window, she might try to escape via the stairs. Plus, Lucy tried to always take the stairs—anything she could do to hit her 10,000 steps per day.

Two flights up, she wondered whether she was making a mistake. She could have left the officer off the back door and had him accompany her up. That might have been safer. After all, if Joshua Green was inside this apartment, Trisha would do anything to escape, including killing her. She should have waited for backup, but it was too late now.

After all, the chances were slim that she'd come out, guns blazing. Even if she was home, which she might not be.

She let out a long breath as she passed the landing on the third floor.

She was doing this.

∼

Pure excitement. The feeling that something big was happening. A piece of a puzzle falling into place.

Austin checked the truck bed—empty except for a few dead leaves, a little gravel, and an empty Starbucks cup.

He peered through dirty glass into the cab. More empty coffee cups, loose rolling papers, a couple ancient French fries wedged between the seats and center console. A sun-bleached ferry ticket from a few days ago sat on the dusty dashboard. If this was their copycat, she certainly hadn't copied everything about Lorraine D'Antonia. When Austin and his team had arrested her, they'd marveled at the spotless perfection of her apartment, the way her hair and nails were perfect even though they'd pulled her out of bed to make the arrest. Trisha Simone was a slob. The cabin looked like it would smell of wet diapers, moldy ketchup, and cigarettes. But there were no diapers in sight. Also no baby clothes, no baby blanket, no bottles. In fact, there was no evidence whatsoever that a child had recently been in the car.

~

Lucy started with a firm *knock-knock-knock*. She waited, ear close to the door, listening.

Silence.

She knocked again, louder this time, holding her breath, hand close to her gun. *Thud-thud-thud.* She'd closed a few big cases, but never anything like this. And she'd never felt like she was in true danger. She'd never once fired her gun in the line of duty.

From behind the door, she heard scratching, like nails on a hardwood floor. She tensed.

Then she heard the high-pitched yelping of what sounded like a tiny dog.

A door opened behind her and she swiveled fast, stepping to the side so she wouldn't have her back to Trisha's door.

An old man stood in his doorway, bathrobe half open revealing boxer shorts and a white tank top. "She ain't home."

Lucy took a deep breath. "Who?"

"The pothead. Her dog only barks when she's gone. When she's here, best-behaved dog you ever saw. When she's gone, that chihuahua's a terrorist."

She held up her badge. "Detective Lucy O'Rourke. Do you know the last time she was here?"

"Yesterday sometime."

Lucy sidestepped to have a better view of Trisha's door, just in case. "What can you tell me about her?"

The chihuahua was close to the door now, barking incessantly.

"Not much, she keeps to herself. Not real friendly. I assume you're here about the weed? I know the hippies in this state made it legal, but she's not allowed to smoke inside. Building rules." He shook his head. "Told the owner about it. He don't care."

"When you last saw her, did she have a child with her?"

He scratched at a wispy beard. "Child? Her? No. Can't imagine no one would want to have a kid with her."

"Have you ever heard a baby crying in the apartment?"

He pointed at the door, where the chihuahua was now clawing and yelping. "Not unless you count that little hellraiser."

～

Austin cast a furtive glance around the parking lot, then tried the driver's side door. Locked. He could easily jimmy it with a tool from Lucy's car, but, well, not only would anything he found be inadmissible in any future trial, but given that he was a regular citizen now, it would also be a crime. He shoved his hands in his pockets and scanned the area. The officer still paced by the front door. No signs of life from inside the building.

Turning back toward downtown, he noticed a line of people coming down the sidewalk. Looked like the ferry had docked and folks were making their way into town.

A woman caught his eye. She was about five foot five, with a skinny face and dirty blonde hair. He crouched next to the truck, watching as she sipped coffee from a white cup. A cold breeze tickled his ear and he tasted spice, cayenne pepper. Adrenaline.

It was Trisha.

She stopped across the street from the parking lot, raised a hand to her forehead as though blocking out the sun, then turned suddenly. She'd seen the officer out front.

Her eyes darted to the truck.

Austin stood.

Seeing him, she dropped the coffee, turned, and ran.

CHAPTER FOURTEEN

BEFORE AUSTIN COULD REACT, Trisha had taken off to the west. Her immediate reaction told him she'd been aware the police might show up, and she was faster than she looked.

Austin followed, fumbling for his cellphone. He had no gun, and no authority to use one even if he'd had one. But there was no way he was letting this woman out of his sight.

At a side street, she cut left, disappearing around a corner. Eyes darting between his phone and the sidewalk ahead of him, Austin pursued, catching a glimpse of her as he turned. He scrolled, looking for Lucy's number, heart racing, feet pounding the pavement in a way they hadn't in well over a year. He was still in pretty decent shape, though not as fit as he'd been in his thirties. And he'd never forgive himself if he got outrun by a frail-looking woman fifteen years his senior.

For a moment he thought he was gaining on her, but then realized she'd only slowed briefly to tug her sweatshirt back up as it slipped down her shoulder.

He called and Lucy picked up right away.

"Pursuing the suspect," Austin shouted between heavy breaths. "Norman Road. Heading south toward..." He wasn't sure. It looked like a park or a forest ahead of him. Then he saw the sign. "North Kitsap Heritage Park. I think she's going to try to lose me there."

Lucy said something he couldn't make out, and he stuffed the phone in the back pocket of his jeans without ending the call.

Breathing hard, he pushed forward. She was only about fifty yards ahead of him now, but if she made it into the heavily-treed park, it might be enough to disappear.

Pumping his legs as fast as he could, he locked eyes on the back of her head, trying to reel it in like a giant salmon flapping against his fishing line out in the Sound. Forty yards. Then thirty. He was all focus now, determined not to lose sight of her.

She was only twenty yards away. There was no way she could keep up this pace. He just had to stay with her until she collapsed, or until Lucy found them.

Suddenly, she veered off the sidewalk, weaving into traffic and cutting between two cars as though she'd decided against the park, which was now close. Austin followed, crossing more slowly and following a little further back. Then, just as quickly, she reversed course, veering back to the original side of the street and glancing over her shoulder.

Austin's eyes were dancing from the traffic to Trisha, from Trisha to the traffic, but they weren't on the motor scooter shooting out of a driveway to his right.

Trisha hit the park, looking back and stumbling as her sweatshirt caught on a tree branch. She hit the ground face first.

Austin tried to leap the curb, but the scooter clipped him. His hip screamed in pain and he spun, crashing onto the sidewalk and smashing his shoulder. Looking up, he saw Trisha on her hands and knees, patting around on the ground as though searching for something. He stood and limped towards her.

She saw him, leapt up, and jogged deeper into the park, disappearing into a patch of trees.

He collapsed, the pain in his hip getting the better of him, and slammed an open palm onto the sidewalk.

The driver of the scooter, an acne-faced teenager, had stopped. "Mr., I'm so sorry. I was... you were. Oh no!"

"I'm okay," Austin said, standing and brushing himself off. "Not your fault, kid."

Then something struck him. What had she been looking for in the leaves?

Limping, he made his way over to the spot where she'd fallen. The ground was a mix of wet, decomposing leaves, and drier leaves that had fallen more recently. He prodded them with his foot, feeling for something. His toe hit something hard. He knelt.

There in the leaves—its glass screen cracked, its case filthy, was an iPhone.

When he tapped the home button, it lit up. He wouldn't be able to break the password, but someone would.

He'd struck gold. He had their prime suspect's cellphone.

CHAPTER FIFTEEN

AN HOUR LATER, Austin sat on the curb outside the apartment building as a paramedic bandaged up a gash just above his right hip. "Gonna be a helluva bruise," she said. "But you'll be fine."

He flinched as she secured the bandage with adhesive tape.

When she'd finished, she patted him on the back. "The cut isn't too deep. You were lucky it was a scooter and not a car."

Austin nodded. "Thanks. I make sure to dodge vehicles over a quarter ton."

The paramedic frowned. Apparently she didn't approve of joking about getting hit by cars, but humor was the best way to distract himself from the rhythmic pulses of pain shooting from his hip down his leg.

"Sorry," he said. "Bad joke. Thanks."

She frowned again and returned to the ambulance.

He pulled out Trisha Simone's cellphone and the screen lit up with notifications she'd received. The first was a text from a woman named Mary:

How's Itsy doing? Give her kisses for me.

A notification from a local bank:

Low balance alert, account 111450892: $36.55 remaining.

As he held it, it vibrated in his hand:

TaskRabbit Notification: New Task Available in Seattle. $60.

He'd never heard of TaskRabbit, but it was something to look into when they returned to the office.

Lucy pulled into the lot. Austin looked up expectantly as she parked and got out, but she was already shaking her head. "She's in the wind."

"Damn." Just after he'd found the cellphone, she and the two officers who'd been on the doors had arrived. They'd fanned out around the park, but it was huge, eight-hundred acres of trails, logging roads, and dense forest. Austin had thought they'd find her. He was glad he'd gotten her phone, but embarrassed he'd been outrun. He told himself he needed to start jogging again the minute he was through with this case.

Lucy stood over him. "We've got three officers looking for her, but Sherlock is back with the warrant. We're gonna toss the place."

"How long will it take to get into this?" He held up the cellphone.

"Holy shit! Is that?" She nabbed the phone. "It'll take longer to get a warrant for this. And Apple is, well, their cooperation is hit or miss. Samantha can get us in, but it'll take a minute."

"A minute? I thought it would take a few days."

"It's an expression. You really don't get out much, do you?"

He ignored this. "Can I come up to—"

"No."

"You'll fill me in?" He held up his shirt, revealing the bandage. "I've got blood in the game now."

She smiled. "Every detail. And good work on this. You hadn't been there, she'd have taken her truck and disappeared."

~

Lucy was first into the apartment. The door opened into a small kitchen, which led to a living room that held a couch, a small table, and a treadmill too big for the space. Through the living room were a grimy bathroom and bedroom. The place was a mess, cluttered with too much stuff for the six-hundred square foot space and in need of a deep cleaning.

The dog was one of the tiniest—and cutest, and loudest— Lucy had ever seen. She had a cast on her left front leg, which was about the size of the leg of a Barbie Doll. She was a shivering little mound backed into the corner of the kitchen and her bark had gone from an "arf, arf, arf" sound to a more shrill, "oww, oww, oww" as though its leg were being broken all over again. Lucy picked up the dog and it stopped barking immediately and began licking any part of her it could reach. A loving but desperate gesture. Judging by the collar, her name was Itsy-Bitsy.

Photos of the tiny thing graced the fridge, the bathroom, and the bedroom. Framed, unframed, dressed up and natural, it seemed as though their suspect cared more for this dog than she did for anything else in the world. A pile of bills on the couch were marked in red with *Final Notice* warnings, and there was a half completed payment plan application for a veterinary bill on the couch indicating that she owed $6,000 for the surgery on Itsy-Bitsy's leg.

Tucked under the blankets on the bed, Lucy found a silver laptop. Combined with the phone, they now had access to Trisha Simone's entire digital life. Unless she was smart about digital forensics—which very few people of her age were—they'd be able to recreate much of her life. Lucy carefully packed it in an evidence bag and asked Ridley to start on the warrants.

They found multiple pairs of size-eight shoes and, after five minutes, Ridley came back from the bedroom holding up a single running shoe in his gloved hand. "Adidas, size 8."

"Boom!" It was the same size and brand found imprinted on the carpet in Joshua Green's nursery. A hell of a find, but Lucy couldn't escape a nagging thought. "I wonder: can you see anyone who cares for their dog this much killing a tiny baby? Boiling it and writing a poem on its bones?"

Ridley placed the shoe in an evidence bag. "Some serial

killers show early tendencies by harming animals. Others love animals. Their murders come from a different place entirely. Some of the worst killers are sickeningly sentimental about certain things." He labeled the bag and added it to the crate of evidence they would take from the apartment. "Buddy of mine in eastern Washington arrested a serial rapist who ran one of the best petting zoos in the state. By all accounts, he treated animals like kings by day and treated women like his property by night. He's doing life right now. Became a vegan in prison." He shook his head. "There's just no telling."

Lucy considered this. "Maybe, but..."

"Lucy!" Officer Johnson, whom she'd stationed by the front door earlier, stood next to the couch. Lucy turned to see him holding up a gallon-sized bag packed full of marijuana. "Intent to distribute?"

"Bingo," she said. "No evidence of any babies here, but this is enough to bring her in and hold her." She turned to Ridley. "Boss, you think she keeps the kid somewhere else?"

"The dog's water bowl is mostly full. So she's been here in the last day or two."

"Neighbor I spoke with across the hall said he thought she was here yesterday."

"Hmm." Ridley ran a hand over his bald head. "We've got enough to hold her, assuming we locate her. But..."

"What?" Lucy asked when he trailed off.

"I don't know. She looks kinda like The Baby Butcher. We know she's likely the one who left the bones on the beach. But why would you keep coming back to your apartment when you have a baby stashed somewhere else?"

Lucy pointed at a framed photo of Itsy-Bitsy, lapping at a Starbucks cup full of whipped cream. "They call it a puppachino. She loves this dog past the point of reason."

Ridley frowned. "Okay, then why not bring the dog with her?"

Lucy shrugged. "Could be a lot of reasons, but boss, this is a *good* day. We have our woman. Truck, eyewitnesses, fleeing from cops, a bag of weed the size of a ferryboat. She's our woman. And our guys are gonna find her out there. I'm just waiting for my phone to buzz with the good news."

~

Austin was growing impatient. He was fully invested in this case, and he wanted to be inside, executing the warrant. Across the driveway, another team was inspecting the truck, dusting for prints, and itemizing the various pieces of trash found therein.

"*Run Forest, Run.*" He recognized the woman's voice behind him. Turning, he saw Anna Downey.

"You stalking me?" he asked.

"Don't tell me you don't get that reference either?"

"Even *I* saw that movie," Austin said. "Shouldn't you be out snooping through people's trash or brainstorming salacious headlines?"

She laughed.

"Wait," Austin said. "How'd you know I was running? And who tipped you off to—"

"You literally ran past my house." She pointed down the block. "Little white dump with a busted picket fence. Like Dorothy's house *after* the tornado hit."

Austin shrugged. That one he didn't get.

Anna feigned a gasp, took off her sunglasses, and sat next to him. She put on an exaggerated reporter voice. "Mr. Austin, Anna Downey here, Kingston News at Five. The people need to know, did you *have* a childhood? Or did you come into the world as a jaded forty-something detective?"

He smiled. "The latter."

In her normal voice, she added, "It's from *Wizard of Oz.*"

He knew a good portion of his generation spoke in movie and TV references, but Anna was taking it to a new level. "Oh, yeah. I remember that witch terrified me when I was a kid. I must have blocked it out."

"Thank goodness." She swiped her hand across her forehead. "I was beginning to think you were born before television and books were invented."

He chuckled. "Clever. And listen, before you ask, I can't comment on what went down here."

"No worries, I already got it from someone else." She stretched her legs out in front of her.

Austin couldn't help but notice she had Adidas running shoes on. "What size do you wear?"

"Nine and a half. Why?"

He leaned back. She was tall, and her feet were definitely on the larger side. "Old habits die hard. Can't turn it off."

She pulled a thin notebook out of her pocket. "Are you saying one of your suspects has this kind of shoe?"

His lips formed a tight line.

"Then lemme ask something else," Anna said. "You were chasing that woman pretty damn fast for a guy who doesn't think the world can be saved."

Austin frowned. "That wasn't a question."

"More of an observation. Care to comment?" She tilted her head to the side, her look softening. "Not for a story. Just curious."

"Like I said, old habits die hard."

She considered this, then cocked her head to the other side as though flipping a switch. "I'm here to talk to Ridley, but I'll ask you first. Any thoughts on the fact that Joshua Green and Allie Shreever were born at the same hospital? As far as I can tell, it's the only connection between the two. And there's something else. Two nurses in the birthing center there haven't shown up for their regular shifts this week."

Ridley hadn't yet filled him in on what he'd learned at the hospital, but he had to assume that, if Anna knew this, so did he. "Could be a lot of reasons for that."

"Sure, but it's interesting."

"I'm sure Detective Calvin will tell you everything he cares to tell you."

She smirked. "Well, you're no fun, are you?"

She stood and handed him a business card.

Austin stuffed it in his pocket. "You already gave me one of these."

"I know. I assume you tossed it."

"I didn't."

She headed toward the apartment building, turning just long enough to call, "Then there's hope for us yet."

CHAPTER SIXTEEN

BACK IN THE OFFICE, Austin sat alone in the conference room, staring at the picture of Joshua Green taped to the wall. The missing boy had a chubby face, pink-beige skin, and a few straggles of brown hair. He was adorable in the way most babies were —cute and innocent without a lot of striking features yet, a generic cuteness that reminded him of the Gerber baby.

The week before she died, Fiona had told him she was ready to have children. He'd wanted to be a dad for years and they'd waited a long time, choosing to focus on their careers. Fiona was thirty-nine when she died, on track to be the DA of Manhattan. From there, the sky was the limit. Austin wouldn't have been surprised if she'd ended up as the governor of New York, or the Attorney General for the United States. She was that smart, that savvy, and that good at her job. But she'd decided to take a year off, maybe two, to have a child. She wanted to be as good at that as she was at everything else. Plus, she'd always talked about writing crime novels, and had gone deep into a fantasy about a new life. "You can keep fighting crime," she'd said. "I'll be a mom and *write* about crime. If that doesn't work out, the district attorney's office will always be there for me." In a moment of retro nostalgia, she'd even picked up a yellow Olivetti Lettera typewriter from the 1970s. Austin had teased her that *he* was supposed to be the luddite in the family, but she'd insisted she was going to write an entire novel on the thing. It now sat on a small rolltop desk in the corner of his living room, holding a single sheet of paper and the opening paragraphs of what was going to be her novel.

A lot of people talked about *having it all*—the job, the creative outlet, the family life. She was one of the ones who could have pulled it off. They'd had some rocky patches in the early years of their marriage, but the five years before she died had been better than he thought possible. Austin had been in awe of her, and happy to be along for the ride. It had been a year and he still couldn't believe that all he had of her now was a plaque, a typewriter, and his memories.

The door swung open and Detective Calvin strode in, followed by Lucy and finally Jimmy, who left the door open behind him.

"Nice work on that phone," Ridley said. "Sheriff is pissed at both of us, but damn, that's a helluva get." He made his voice higher and a little slurred, waving his arms randomly. "*Detective Calvin, DO NOT let that New York cowboy loose on Kingston again.*"

"I don't even have a gun," Austin said, cutting through the laughter. "Anyway, I'm just pissed I didn't catch up with her."

The tiny chihuahua burst through the door like a rat sprung from its cage, sprinting despite heavily favoring her broken leg. She looked around nervously, then bolted over to Jimmy, who reached down and cupped her in his hands as she tried to spring onto his lap. "Aww, Itsy-Bitsy, who's a good dog?"

Next to Jimmy's meaty hands and bulging biceps, Itsy looked even tinier. She curled herself into a ball and tucked away on his lap.

Ridley said, "We're waiting on Animal Control. They'll hold her until we track down Trisha."

"If she ends up in jail," Lucy said to Jimmy, "you should take her."

"You like a man with a puppy?"

"She's three years old. Not a puppy."

"She's as little as a puppy."

Lucy sighed. "And you're as smart as one."

Jimmy frowned.

"Actually, I take it back." Lucy cocked her head. "I wouldn't want to insult puppies that way."

Jimmy pet Itsy gently and she rolled onto her back, eyes closed. Austin missed Run.

Ridley rapped on the whiteboard with his knuckles. "Can we get back to it?" Before waiting for a reply, he continued. "Here's the deal: every available car in the county is looking for Trisha. We're watching her cellphone, hoping for some sort of notification that clues us into something. We're looking into Task-Rabbit—apparently they're a... Well, Jimmy, you explain it."

Jimmy handed Itsy to Lucy and tapped at his phone. A moment later, the screen on the TV popped on and a website appeared. *TaskRabbit* was written in big silver and red letters, below which were photos of happy-looking people staring at their phones.

"This is their homepage," Jimmy said. "Basically, it's an app where you sign up for random odd jobs, sort of like Uber, but for tasks. Sign up, get verified, then you're notified of tasks that need completing in your area. Like $40 to courier an envelope across town. Or $80 to wait for the cable guy from noon to four. Or $15 to take a dog on a half-hour walk. Everyone who uses it has to show a driver's license, and people get reviewed, so the users know who to trust." He tapped through to a different page. "This is her profile. Trisha Simone."

Austin saw a picture of the woman he'd chased through Kingston. In the photo, her hair was tied back in a ponytail and she had on a good amount of makeup. Her smile revealed crooked and yellowing teeth, but she looked friendly and professional enough. Her location was listed as "Kitsap and King counties."

Jimmy said, "We don't have any addresses for her in King County. My guess, she just ferried over there to do tasks sometimes."

Austin asked, "And we're in touch with the app?"

"Yeah," Ridley said. "They confirmed that she has an account and does tasks for them. Confirmed her name and whatnot. When it came to giving us a list of work she'd done, her clients, they stonewalled, said they'd have to check with their lawyers. 'Protecting the privacy of their valued customers.'"

Austin sighed. "This might be a place to get the FBI involved. Back in New York, when we had kidnapping cases, we sometimes coordinated with the FBI to get things moving. Three dudes in dark suits is more intimidating than a bunch of locals."

"Hey," Lucy said, petting the dog, "I can be intimidating. Yes, yes, yes... can't we Itsy-bitsy, can't we? We're *very* intimidating."

"No offense," Austin said.

Ridley tapped a marker on the whiteboard. "I'll talk to Sheriff Daniels about that. There's more on Trisha. She's got a record. Marijuana possession, back when it was illegal. Stole a car in the nineties." He set down the marker and tossed a file folder on the table between them.

Austin began rummaging through the file, which contained her police record. "Long way from stealing babies."

Ridley nodded in agreement. "We need to keep an open mind here. The fact that she dropped the bones at the beach and looks a little like Lorraine D'Antonia is too much to be a coincidence, but we still don't know what this is."

A young woman poked her head in the door. "New message on the phone. Thought you'd want to see it." She had a friendly round face, straight black hair, and a tattoo of Chinese calligraphy climbing up her forearm. From the look of her, she might have been only twenty. Like Lucy, her skin was fairly pale, like she didn't even go out in the small amount of sun the area offered.

Ridley waved in her general direction. "Austin, this is Samantha. Tech intern. She runs our social media and helps out with stuff even Jimmy is too old to understand. Samantha, Austin is—"

"I know." She smiled sadly. "Sorry about your wife."

"How did you—" He stopped mid-sentence. "Google?"

She nodded. "I do a cursory search on anyone before meeting them. Started doing it with dates, now, well, I like to be prepared."

Jimmy said, "She's an honors student in criminal justice at Olympic College. Taught me half of what I know about tech."

Samantha smiled. "Three quarters. And actually I'm doing forensic science with a self-designed minor in digital forensics." She noticed Austin's blank stare. "Digital forensics? Everyone knows that people leave clues based on their online activity, right? Facebook posts, location tags if they're stupid enough to leave those on while committing a crime. But the really good stuff you need access to their phone or computer to get. Emails, Google searches, and so on. I specialize in getting the good stuff *before* we get warrants for their phones and computers."

"Hacking?" Austin asked.

She shook her head. "That's illegal. Everything I do is one hundred percent legal. Using AI to comb through files and internet databases. Trends in public blockchain transactions, facial recognition and license plate recognition software on public photographs. You'd be shocked at how much evidence people give up in the background of their Instagram selfies. And, of course, when we do get into a phone, then it's on like *Donkey Kong*."

Austin could feel himself aging in real time. As much as he wanted to believe that his old-school ways were superior, it was hard to deny that people like Samantha were crucial to the future of investigations. "Good to meet you."

"So what have you got?" Ridley asked.

Samantha held up Trisha's phone. "New notification."

"Tell me something good," Austin said.

"Nothing major, but interesting. Text from someone named David: *How's Itsy? Can't wait to see her. Tomorrow at 5 PM. Kingston Waterfront.* Sounded kinda coded. I looked up every codeword for marijuana and no one has ever called it *Itsy*, not that I could find anyway. Figured maybe Itsy was Trisha's codename?"

Jimmy cupped his face in his hands.

Lucy laughed loudly. "Guess we should have told you." She held up the dog. "Meet Itsy."

Samantha stared at the phone. "*That* makes a lot more sense. Okay, back to the dungeon for me."

"Kingston waterfront at five tomorrow," Ridley said when Samantha had left. "We'll have someone there, though I doubt she'll show. Maybe this guy David will."

Jimmy said, "I've got something else." The TV screen changed to a news article from the *Seattle Times* dated three months earlier. "I've been running a series of searches, combing the internet for anything new on The Baby Butcher. In the last year, there were multiple mentions of her in articles about the agency that set up her adoption when she was a baby."

The headline on the screen read "Johnson Hill Adoption Agency Sued for Inappropriate Placements, Fraud."

Ridley said, "What's the point, Jimmy? Lorraine D'Antonia is behind bars. I appreciate the thoroughness, but what does it matter if her adoption agency is getting sued for some shady shit sixty years ago?"

"Well, the article says that two families are suing them for promising to put children with well-off families but leaving them in poverty. Something about collecting state money."

Austin tapped his foot impatiently. "Any connection to Lorraine or her birth or adoptive parents?"

"No," Jimmy admitted. "But I'm telling you, sometimes algorithms know more about what's going on than we do."

"Stay on it," Ridley said. "But our priority is getting into that phone."

Itsy sat up suddenly and yelped, as though waking from a bad dream.

"Looks like she doesn't want us getting into that phone," Lucy said.

"Luckily for us," Ridley said, "it's up to a judge and not a dog. I'll hear back by tomorrow. Cell phone warrants are tough, but I'll get it."

The woman who worked at the front desk came in. "Sheriff Daniels would like to see you," she said to Ridley. She turned to Austin. "And you."

"How does he seem?" Ridley asked.

She smiled. "I'd never say anything bad behind my employer's back, but if you've got Kevlar vests, I'd wear them to the meeting."

CHAPTER SEVENTEEN

"WHAT IN THE ever-loving-hellfire did you guys do?" Sheriff Daniels stood as they walked in, waving his hands as though swiping spiderwebs from a doorway.

Austin was careful to stay a step behind Ridley. When Ridley sat, he took the chair next to him.

Daniels stood, mouth agape, then slowly sat, eyes shifting between Austin and Ridley.

Ridley said, "I'm not sure what you mean, Sheriff."

"I got calls from two different business owners in Kingston saying there was some kind of chase scene happening? And you *didn't* catch the suspect?"

"I can address that," Austin said. He'd known tough guys. *Truly* tough guys. Sheriff Daniels was a bully, an insecure man who had failed upward and had to compensate for the fact that he was the dumbest guy in the room by lording his position over everyone else. He'd served under a guy like this once before, and he'd learned that the best way to deal with them was cordially, but without apology. Like it or not, Daniels could kick him off the case, and Austin didn't want that to happen.

"I'll get to you in a minute, but first..." he slid a printout across the table to Ridley.

Austin leaned over to read it with him. It was an article from the *Kitsap Union* by Anna Downey. The headline read: *Possible Connections Seen Between Recent Abductions.*

Daniels crinkled a paper loudly. He had his own copy. "I'll tell you what it says." His voice was an angry staccato, like he was biting off the last ten percent of each word. "Despite police assurances that no connection has yet been found between the recent kidnappings in Kitsap County—the first of which ended in the tragic death of Allie Shreever—the *Union* has learned that both babies were born in the birthing center of St. Michael's medical, and only two weeks apart. Further, the *Union* has learned that two nurses, both of whom may have been present during shifts that overlapped with the victims, have gone missing in recent days."

"Wait, wait, wait," Ridley said. "They missed shifts. They haven't 'gone missing.'"

Daniels slammed the paper down on the table. "How is it that I'm hearing about this in a local paper from a reporter who works part time, and not from my lead detective on this case?"

Ridley let out a long, slow breath. "Look. I was at the hospital, questioning the administrative staff and acquiring surveillance video when we located our prime suspect. I'll be following up right after this meeting."

Daniels and Ridley stared at one another silently for a little longer than necessary.

"Fine," Daniels said at last, turning to Austin. "Didn't I tell you, *no cowboy shit?*"

As flatly as he could manage, Austin said, "I've never ridden a horse, sir."

Ridley laughed, but Daniels was having none of it. "I told you to play by the rules, you signed paperwork saying you wouldn't put yourself in danger. If you get yourself killed, do you know how that would make me look?"

Austin held his gaze. Daniels' eyes were wet and bloodshot,

like he'd been up all night drinking. "It's nice to know I'm cared for."

"Your New York sarcasm won't play here, Austin. I've half a mind to terminate your contract."

"I need him," Ridley said quickly.

As much as Austin wanted to tell Daniels to go to hell, he wanted to see this thing through to its conclusion. Even more than that, he owed it to Ridley, Lucy and Jimmy. They were in this together now.

Austin tried to sound conciliatory. "Sheriff Daniels, *look*." He held up both hands in an *I-Surrender* gesture. "I saw the suspect and made a spur-of-the-moment call to pursue her. I called it in to Detective O'Rourke immediately, and at no time was I in danger."

"You got run over."

Austin patted his hip. "It's a scratch." He thought for a moment, then made his tone so soft it likely came off as patronizing. "I will try to be safe. I will play by the rules. But there's something you should know about me, Sheriff Daniels."

Daniels was fidgeting with a snow globe paperweight on his desk. "And what's that, New York?"

Austin stood and waited until Daniels looked up. He leaned in, meeting his eyes. "If I have the chance to pursue a suspect I believe to be a baby-murdering psychopath, the rules go out the window. When lives are in danger, I make the rules."

Daniels stood, pointing a finger at Austin's chest. "You're an arrogant prick."

"Maybe," Austin said. "But that's how I do things. If that doesn't work for you, then I'll see myself out. I've got a café to run. And general store. And bait shop."

He glanced at Ridley, then returned his gaze to Daniels, who seemed to be thinking. Austin was betting he'd cave, as bullies usually did when confronted.

Daniels sat heavily. "You can stay on. For now. Ridley, keep your New York cowboy in line, okay?"

Ridley nodded, stood, and moved to the door. "Before I forget, chief, can you get your FBI contacts to lean on an app called TaskRabbit? We're looking for a list of tasks, with details, performed by Trisha Simone in the last three months."

"I will," Daniels said. "But it'll just give them more reason to box us out. I was gonna tell you, FBI Task Force from the D'Antonia case, combined with a unit from the Seattle PD and—" he jerked a thumb in Austin's direction—"even one of *his* old colleagues from the NYPD, they're meeting tomorrow. Secure video call."

"What for?" Ridley asked.

"Discuss the case. FBI is helping us out with forensics on the Green house. Nothing so far. They assured me they won't swoop in, but if we don't get something soon, I can't justify keeping this thing local. I don't think I need to tell you, Rid, this is *the one*. For me, for you, for our department. You may think I'm an asshole, but we can both agree that the next forty-eight hours will make or break our little cop shop here."

Ridley swallowed hard. "Heard, boss."

Even Austin had to agree. Daniels was a bastard to be sure, but he wanted this thing solved as much as anyone, even if it was only out of self-interest. The case was already getting national attention, and now that Anna Downey had raised the possibility of a connection between the two kidnappings, that would increase. And if someone leaked details about how the bones had been found—the Thanksgiving gift bag—then the entire national media would descend on Kitsap County.

Austin paused at the door. "Heard, Sheriff Daniels. Don't worry. Keep the FBI off our backs for another day or two and I promise we'll find Joshua."

CHAPTER EIGHTEEN

AUSTIN CLAPPED his hands together to get everyone's attention. "Rule of thirds!" He'd taken the position at the front of the room, standing before the big whiteboard and passing a marker from hand to hand.

Lucy, Jimmy, Ridley, and Samantha sat around the conference table, all consuming their preferred varieties of caffeinated beverage.

"Basic stats in stranger abductions," Austin continued. "A third of the kids are never found, a third are found dead, a third are found alive. Of the ones who are found alive, the vast majority are found in the first seventy-two hours." He glanced at his watch. "It's six o'clock, December 22nd. Joshua Green was abducted roughly fourteen hours ago. If his abductor follows the same timeline as he or she did with Allie Shreever, we have roughly forty-eight hours. If the abductor follows the pattern of most stranger abductions, we have forty-eight hours. And, judging by what the Sheriff of Nottingham just spewed at us, we have forty-eight hours—possibly less—before he allows the FBI to take the lead on this thing. No shame in getting help from the Feds, but Daniels said one thing I agreed with. This is *the one*. It could be the biggest case you ever work. Do not take that for granted." He looked from Lucy to Jimmy, from Ridley to Samantha. "I firmly believe that the five of us have the best shot at bringing Joshua home. If the FBI comes in two days from now, chances are..." he lowered his voice... "chances are Joshua Green is already dead."

"Agreed," Ridley said.

"Then let's go get it," Jimmy added. "Where are we on the phone warrant?"

"Judge has been in court all day," Ridley said. "Should have it by late tonight. I don't know about you four, but I'm not going home."

Jimmy held up a plastic grocery bag, which rattled when he shook it. "Red Bull. Cold Brew. Monster Energy. Even the gum is caffeinated. Enough for everyone."

"I'll stick with coffee," Austin said. "The important thing is that we locate Trisha. I'm convinced she'll take us to Joshua, or to the person who has him."

Ridley stood and wrote two names on the whiteboard. *Myrian Brightstone* and *Mary Bonner.* "These are the two nurses who didn't show up for their shifts. I'm on a Board of Directors with the administrator of the hospital. Spoke with him personally. Neither of these nurses has a single mark on their records. He said that Brightstone is a known partier, but she doesn't let it affect her work. Both called in sick. They are not 'disappearances' as some reporters would like the public to believe."

Jimmy cracked a Red Bull. "Still. It's interesting, no?" He took a long swig, smacking his lips in Lucy's direction.

"How can you drink that stuff?" Lucy asked.

He held up the can. "Sugar free."

Ignoring them, Ridley said, "I've got officers heading over to their apartments now to question them."

Samantha had been typing on her laptop as though she wasn't listening, but stopped suddenly. "What do you want to know about them?"

"Whatcha got?" Austin asked.

"Myrian Brightstone is all over Facebook and Instagram. She's thirty-five, pretty, and flaunts it. Yoga poses, beach selfies, tequila shots with friends. She has a thing about taking pictures of her and her friends doing shots. No kids, is dating a woman named Diane." She glanced down at her laptop. "And possibly a guy named Samuel as well. Went to Mexico for a friend's wedding last year. Big partier, it looks like. No red flags when it comes to abductions. I'll have to get the metadata and geotags, but she was posting stuff late into the night when Joshua was taken."

"Can't you set up posts in advance?" Austin asked. "To create an alibi?"

Samantha nodded. "But it's a lot harder to fake location tags. She was in Tacoma, ninety minutes from Bainbridge, at midnight the night Joshua disappeared. Closed down a bar there with her friends. Still had time to make it to the island, but she also has a location-tagged post the next morning. Doesn't rule her out, but it's a stretch."

"Good work," Ridley said. "We'll verify with the bar. And Mary Bonner?"

"Rents an apartment in Bremerton. Been a nurse for a long time. She's got a 2014 Kia Soul registered in her name. No record. She's not on social media at all, at least not that I've found yet. Very little online imprint."

"Keep digging," Ridley said.

Itsy was chasing a fly around in the corner of the room, standing on her hind legs, snapping her jaw, swiping at it with her one good front paw, and missing by a mile.

"Excuse me for a sec," Austin said, heading out to the hallway and dialing the shop.

The phone rang for a long time before Andy answered. "Tell me it took you so long to pick up because the place is packed tonight."

Andy chuckled. "Does four customers count as packed?"

Austin smiled. "Not bad for three days before Christmas. Thanks for holding down the fort."

"Your new burger is literally *flying* off the menu. Made two already. One guy said you should bottle that tomato jam."

Austin paced the hallway. "Glad to hear it. Did you let Run out into the yard?"

"Yup," Andy said. "Fed her, too."

"Appreciate it. I didn't figure I'd be gone all day, but I may be gone all night."

"Anything on the missing kid?" His voice had turned somber. "Everyone who's been in has been talking about him."

"We're doing our best."

"Were you really a badass NYPD detective before?"

Austin smiled. He'd told Andy he used to work for the NYPD, but shared as little about himself as he could get away with. "I don't know about the 'badass' part, but yeah. Twenty years in the NYPD, ten as a detective."

"People are talking about it. An old lady came in and said she looked you up. Said you looked like Bobby Simone. She was thirsting big time."

"I understood only fifty percent of the words you just said."

"Bobby Simone, from *NYPD Blue*. Played by Jimmy Smits. Went off the air when I was seven, don't tell me I know more about it than you."

He'd heard of it, but TV had never been his thing. "Okay, and what does 'thirsting' mean?"

"You don't want to know, boss. One more thing, though, a lady came in, looking for you, kinda pushy."

Austin leaned on the wall. "Lemme guess. Above average height, blonde ponytail, holding a notebook?"

"That's her. Anna something. Don't worry, I didn't tell her anything. She ordered the French Dip sliders, extra horseradish. Left a thirty percent tip, so I can't complain. Not gonna lie, she seemed kinda thirsty, too."

Austin got it now.

He thanked Andy, promised to check in tomorrow, and headed for the lobby. The coffee was lukewarm, so he gulped it down like water and refilled it. As he opened the door to the conference room, he saw everyone hunched around Samantha, all staring at Trisha's phone.

"New message," Ridley said. "Could be big."

Austin leaned over and read: *Juanita's Mexican Restaurant has confirmed your DoorDash order. We'll let you know when your Dasher has picked up your food for delivery!*

Lucy leapt up. "Juanita's is in Bremerton. Fifteen, maybe twenty minutes from here."

"No way she'd be stupid enough to order food," Jimmy said.

Lucy punched his arm. "Twenty bucks says she is exactly that stupid."

Ridley said, "I've got twenty with Lucy. Cop shows make criminals out to be a helluva lot smarter than they usually are."

Austin was still stuck on the text. "How did she order food when *we* have her phone?"

"You can have the app on multiple phones," Samantha said. "And you can order from a computer, assuming you have your login info."

"How long 'til the food's delivered?" Ridley asked. "How does it work?"

Samantha shut her laptop and placed the phone on top of it. "Most places, it's twenty to forty minutes. But it depends on where you get the food delivered."

"Even if she's dumb enough to order food," Austin said, "she's not getting it delivered to the apartment she'd just fled."

Samantha nodded. "And it's unlikely DoorDash delivers from Bremerton to Kingston. Too far. You can put in any address you want. A hotel, for example."

"There's no way for us to tell where the food is headed?" Austin asked.

Samantha picked up Trisha's phone. "Not without unlocking this. Three ways to find out. One: ask Trisha. Two: get Door-

Dash to tell you, and good luck with that. Three: trail the delivery person."

"What about the restaurant?" Ridley asked.

"They don't see the address on the ticket. Just the order and a name. Only the Dasher sees the actual address."

Ridley was already throwing on his jacket. "Samantha, ride with me. I need to understand everything I can about how this works. Lucy and Austin, follow me in Lucy's car."

"Jimmy, you stay here. Get DoorDash on the phone and get that address, no matter what it takes."

CHAPTER NINETEEN

THE LITTLE CABIN smelled of sugar, butter, and vanilla. Christmas cookies.

She had no happy memories of the holidays, but she imagined this is what houses were supposed to smell like at Christmas. Some people liked ginger and cinnamon and other spices, but she thought little Joshua would prefer the classics.

Not that she would give him a cookie. He was far too young for that. But still, this was his Christmas, *their* Christmas, and it was important that it be perfect. It was important to make memories now.

After all, they only had another day or two together.

The old wooden floor creaked as she made her way across the kitchen. On a changing table next to the stove, Joshua lay, sleeping on his stomach. She stood over him, admiring his outfit. She'd dressed him in a red and white onesie with a patch across the back that read "Santa Baby" in cute green cursive. His tiny feet were covered in green elf booties she'd made herself and his head was nestled snugly in a mini Santa hat.

She frowned. She'd forgotten to get him a present. Not that a three-week-old baby needed a present, but it was important to make these memories perfect. She considered running out to the store while he slept, but that would be neglectful. The cookies would have to do.

Joshua was a big eater, and it had taken forever to get him to sleep. The website said that a boy his age would need a maximum of four ounces of formula per feeding. He'd finished off six without coming up for air.

"That's my big boy," she said, but not loud enough to wake him.

Her voice sounded odd in the little kitchen—thin and airy like the wind whistling through the cracked window.

With an old-fashioned Polaroid, she snapped a photo of the sleeping little angel. She shook out the photo with one hand, checking on the cookies in the oven with the other. They needed a few more minutes.

She examined the picture. It was her third of Joshua, but definitely the cutest. In the first one he was crying—what a fussy little treasure!—and in the second his Santa hat had slipped down over his eyes. This new one was perfect.

A clothesline ran across the kitchen and she clipped the polaroid in the very center, next to her favorite photo of baby Allie, dressed in a turkey onesie, surrounded by a cornucopia of squash, pumpkins, and cranberries.

Joshua let out a tiny squeal, but didn't wake. "Hush little baby," she said, sitting at the kitchen table.

She picked up a pencil and studied what she had so far.

Christmas is
A time for joy
Let's gather together
Every girl and boy
Stockings and cookies
And presents for all
Bring good cheer and wonder
As winter does call

She let the words roll through her mind and off her tongue in a gentle whisper. Why did her voice sound so strange? Maybe it was because of Joshua. It was as though he might condemn her, criticize her, as silly as that was. What if the poem wasn't good enough? He was less than a month old; surely he wouldn't judge her mothering skills. After all, she'd done everything she could to make Christmas perfect.

Her eyes wandered across the kitchen. Through the window, she saw a pair of eagles, looping and gliding around each other as though engaged in a secret aerial dance. She wondered whether they were potential mates, brother and sister, or father and son. She didn't know, but they struck her as family. Just like her and Joshua had become.

She considered rhyming *eagle* with *regal.* What holiday was more regal than Christmas? But she didn't think eagles were especially Christmassy, so she dismissed the idea.

Her eyes landed on the giant canning pot covering both burners on the two-burner stove. That made her think of jam and holiday-spiced apple butter. One year she'd canned a holiday salt scrub scented with ginger and cloves. Maybe there was a way to work that into the poem.

She had so many wonderful Christmas ideas, and so little time.

CHAPTER TWENTY

LUCY SCREECHED to a stop in the parking lot of Juanita's, a hole-in-the-wall joint with a tiny sign that couldn't be seen from the road. In Austin's experience, this was the type of place most likely to serve authentic food. As he got out of the car, the savory aromas hit him right away and reminded him that he'd been surviving on black coffee all day.

Samantha and Ridley had yet to arrive, but Lucy charged through the parking lot, Austin right on her heels as she burst through the door of the packed restaurant. It smelled of cumin and grilled meat, of corn tamales and rich mole sauces.

Lucy yanked out her badge and held it in front of the hostess's face. "Detective Lucy O'Rourke, Kitsap County Sheriff's Department. I need to speak with a manager."

The young lady took a step back, thought for a moment, then hurried into the kitchen without saying a word. Lucy was generally mild-mannered, but could be pretty damn commanding when she wanted to be.

A moment later, a short, squat woman emerged, wearing a white apron, her hair tied into a messy bun. She wiped her hands on a rag, then hung it over her shoulder with an efficient flick of the wrist. "I am Juanita." She looked to be in her late fifties and had a thick accent, her words a little forced and searching, as though English was her second language.

Lucy said, "You received an order from DoorDash about thirty minutes ago. We need to know where it went."

The woman blinked, confused. "Ten or twenty orders we received tonight already."

"Can you show me?"

The woman eyed her skeptically. "Orders no have addresses. Only delivery person sees."

Austin cursed under his breath. He'd hoped Samantha was wrong about that, but he wasn't surprised to learn that she was right. Like most people under thirty, she seemed to live in a different world, one with rules and systems he didn't understand.

"Show us, please," Lucy said. "This is a critical police matter involving a missing baby."

Juanita squinted at Lucy. "*El bebé de la isla Bainbridge?*" In Spanish, her words came lightning fast. Her look shifted to genuine concern, as though the idea that her restaurant could have anything to do with the kidnapping horrified her.

"*Sí*," Austin said. "The baby from Bainbridge Island." He'd picked up a little Spanish on the job in New York. "We know you have nothing to do with it. It is a customer we are looking for." He gestured at a tablet terminal next to a cash register, where he assumed orders came in. "*Por favor.*"

She hurried over to the counter, studying the screen for an aggravatingly long time between single-fingered taps. Austin had worked in restaurants to put himself through college. In that business, there were front-of-the-house people and back-of-the-house people. Like Austin himself, Juanita was definitely more comfortable in the back of the house. Finally, she gave up and waved over the hostess, spoke rapid Spanish—incomprehensible to Austin—and moved aside.

Seconds later, the young woman said, "Okay," and returned to the dining room.

The screen displayed a list of orders from the last hour. Sure enough, right in the middle, was an order from "Trisha S.," placed at 6:05 PM. A chicken burrito, rice and beans, and a Mexican soda called Jarritos, mandarin orange flavored. There was no address listed and only half a phone number, the second half blacked out.

Austin pointed at the order. "Can you click it to get more information or something?"

Lucy shook her head.

Juanita said, "No."

Austin pointed at the screen. "It says that Dasher's name is Mark. Who is Mark?"

"Delivery man."

It said the order had been picked up at 6:31. It was now 6:38. Austin cursed under his breath. Seven minutes. They'd missed him by seven minutes.

"Can you call?" He tapped on the phone number listed for Trisha S., the second half of which was blacked out.

Lucy said, "They make it so you can call without seeing the whole number. Privacy."

"*Sí*," Juanita said. "Only through the tablet." She tapped twice, picked up the tablet and handed it to Austin. He felt ridiculous holding the thing up to his head like a phone, but after three rings, a woman's voice said, "Hello?"

It was a voice he recognized. "Samantha?"

"Austin? Why are you calling me on Trisha's phone?"

"Damn." He'd hoped Trisha had added a different number to the account.

"We're only a few minutes out," Samantha said. "And Trisha got another text—'Dasher is on the way'—something to that effect. And Ridley got the call. Search warrants have been approved for the laptop we found in Trisha's apartment."

"Good," Austin said. He ended the call and scanned the tablet again, scrolling down in hopes of finding anything else that might help them.

Lucy pointed to the "Notes" section and read it aloud.

"Knock twice. Leave bag outside. Any problems, have dasher text 360-555-1290."

Jackpot. Austin grabbed the land line and dialed. A man's voice came on the line. "Hello?"

The voice was loud, somehow the thing was on speaker phone, and Austin stepped back into a supply closet off the lobby, carrying the phone and tablet with him. Lucy and Juanita followed him.

Thinking fast, he said, "This is Brian from Juanita's. May I speak to Trisha? It's regarding her order."

"She's not in."

He glanced at Lucy, who shrugged. "Um, have you received an order yet?"

"No. App says it's three minutes away."

"We're concerned the dasher may have picked up the wrong order, can you confirm the name and address on the order so we can check it against our order history?"

The man didn't reply.

Austin held his breath. All he heard was breathing, and possibly a cat's faint meow in the background.

Finally, the man said, "I'm sorry, who is this again?"

"Brian. From Juanita's."

"*No suenas como un Mexicano.*"

Austin wasn't certain, but he thought that meant something like, "You don't sound Mexican."

"I'm new," he said.

"I eat there three times a week, bro, every single person there is Mexican, Juanita's sisters and cousins and nieces. Who is this?"

Austin thought fast. He considered telling him the truth and demanding the return of Joshua, but that would likely cause the man to flee if in fact he had anything to do with the kidnapping. "I'll get the manager." He handed the phone to Juanita, who looked like she had little idea what was going on. Austin whispered, "Tell him there's a problem with the order."

"This is Juanita," she said. "You ordered chicken burrito, soda?"

"Yes."

"We were out of shredded chicken. Substitute grilled."

She was a better liar than he expected.

"That's fine," the man said.

"If it's a problem I will send you five dollar coupon. *Cinco dólares.* Just tell me home address and I send."

She was a *much* better liar than he expected.

The man said, "Really, it's fine. You guys are the bomb, and the order is here now anyway. Bye."

The line went dead.

Ridley and Samantha burst through the door. Ridley looked pissed.

"Wrong turn," Samantha said, apologetically and to no one in particular.

"We got this," Lucy said. Then, turning back to Juanita, "Mark, the dasher guy, do you have a number for him?"

Juanita smiled proudly, hands on her hips. "He's my grandson."

Austin let out an exasperated sigh, his eyes nearly bulging out of his head. She couldn't have mentioned that earlier? "Cell phone number. Quickly. Please."

"He can't tell you the address. Against the rules. Get our account canceled with DoorDash."

Lucy put her hands on her hips, about to go at her. Austin pulled out his phone, found the photo of the bag of bones Ridley had sent him, and held it up to her. "In this bag are the bones of a tiny baby. Another baby is missing. *El bebé de la isla Bainbridge.* Call your grandson. Get the address where the burrito was delivered. You can help us save a child."

Juanita looked at the photo, pulled the rag off of her shoulder, and wiped her hands again, even though they still seemed perfectly clean.

She picked up the landline and dialed.

CHAPTER TWENTY-ONE

DETECTIVE CALVIN POUNDED the door like it had insulted his sister. "Kitsap Sheriff's Office, open up please." The way he spoke, even the "please" sounded like a direct order one ignored at his own peril.

The dasher had given them an address only ten minutes away, a two-story apartment complex that looked like it had once been a motel. External staircases led to outdoor walkways that ran the length of the building, with five or six apartments on each floor. From the doorway, Austin could see down into the parking lot, where Samantha waited in the car.

When there was no answer, Lucy gave the door a pound as well. "Detective Lucy O'Rourke, open up. Now." She didn't bother with the "please."

A series of odd noises came from inside the apartment: a muffled clang, a shifting and swishing, a dull thud. When the door swung open Austin was struck by the sickening stench of cat urine. But not just any cat urine. It was the kind that had sat for days, possibly weeks, developing into a sick ammonia smell that caused all three of them to step back a pace into the fresher air of the walkway.

The man, dressed in white boxers, a stained t-shirt and a half-open robe tied loosely around his waist, didn't look surprised to see them. "May I help you?" He held a foil-wrapped burrito out in front of him as though offering it up for his guests.

"I'm Detective Calvin. We're looking for Trisha Simone."

"Who?" When he took a huge bite of the burrito, a few grains of rice escaped onto the carpet.

"We know you know her," Ridley said. "I'll give you one shot to tell the truth before your day goes from bad to worse."

"Never heard of no Trisha." As he spoke, flecks of chicken and tortilla sprayed out through the doorway, landing at their feet. Austin thought he was going to be sick.

When he'd finished chewing, he eyed the burrito as though choosing the perfect bite, then lowered it to his side. "Why do you think I know a Trisha?"

Lucy stepped toward him, swatting the burrito onto the ground. "Detective Calvin asks the questions. You answer them."

"Hey, that cost ten bucks plus tip."

Austin could see Lucy's fists clenched by her side, her knuckles turning white.

"Where is she?" Ridley demanded.

"Dunno."

Ridley stayed composed. "You don't know her, or you *do* know her but don't know where she is?"

"I ain't got nothing to do with whatever she has going on."

Ridley leaned in. "So you *do* know her?"

He nodded.

"And what does she have going on?"

"Weed, I guess. I mean, right? That's why you're here, right?"

That was quick. Ridley had broken him in under two minutes.

"And what else?" Ridley asked.

"Else?"

Ridley stepped a little closer. "An order was placed on her DoorDash account with this address."

He swallowed. "Don't mean I know where she is."

"Does she live here?"

"No."

"What's your name?"

"Frank Baxter."

Ridley whipped out a notebook and jotted down the name. "Why are you using her account, Frank Baxter?"

"She in some kind of trouble?"

Austin's read on this guy was that he was clueless, likely a deadbeat, but he doubted Frank Baxter had the inclination—or the intelligence—to pull off two kidnappings without leaving a trace. After all, he couldn't even eat a burrito without leaving DNA evidence all over the place. If Trisha was behind the kidnappings, he was pretty sure Frank Baxter wasn't an accomplice.

Austin caught Ridley's eye, asking with a look whether he could take over. Ridley nodded. "Mr. Baxter, right now, you're not in any trouble. Trisha sells weed without a dispensary license. We know that. Maybe you're part of that, maybe you're not. Here in Washington State, that might get her—what?—a month or so in jail, maybe a year on probation. I honestly don't give a damn if she rolls up a joint the size of the Empire State Building and smokes it on the beach with every single person of legal age in the state of Washington. Right now we're trying to find a missing baby." He stepped forward, eyes hard, mouth and nose unbreathing. "Tell us everything about her, now, or we'll haul your filthy ass in as an accomplice to kidnapping and murder."

Austin held his gaze. Frank Baxter's eyes were light blue, wet, and a little bloodshot. This wasn't the first time he'd been under police scrutiny, Austin thought. When Baxter's gaze dropped to his burrito, which was scattered all over the carpet—Austin stepped back.

Baxter closed one eye and cocked his head to the side, like he was trying to focus hard enough to tell the truth. "Trish and I bang sometimes." He said it casually, shooting a lewd look at

Lucy like he wanted to see her reaction. "It's not serious, but...
well, like I said, we bang sometimes. Met her on an app."

"Why are you using her DoorDash account?" Austin asked.

"She put the info into my computer last time she was here.
Or maybe the time before. Phone was dead or some shit.
Anyway, we bang, then we order food and watch Netflix. Just like
the kids say, Netflix and chill, right?"

"Where is she?" Ridley demanded.

He shrugged. "I swear, I dunno." He picked up what was left
of his burrito, a limp tortilla with bits of rice, beans, and chicken
clinging to it for dear life. Inspecting it for carpet fuzz and dirt,
he said, "I'm gonna report this, get the county to buy me a new
burrito."

"When you meet up to have sex," Ridley said, "who usually
initiates it? Does she text you first, does she just show up? How
does it work?"

"Different ways. Usually she texts. Couple times she's just
showed up when she needs the secret sauce, ya know?" He
winked at Ridley, who grimaced.

"You're a pig," Lucy stated, matter-of-factly.

He shrugged. "She's the one making the booty calls."

Austin asked, "If she was in trouble, would she come here? If
not, where would she go? Think hard."

"I know she works over in Seattle sometimes, *Task-something*.
But she doesn't stay there unless she's got another booty call
over there I don't know about."

"What else?" Austin asked.

"I don't think she'd come here. Like I said, we're not real
close. Other than the secret sauce, I don't give her nothin'.
Other than the honeydew pudding, she don't give me nothing."

The urine smell was somehow intensifying, mingling with the
spices and chicken from the burrito, creating a new smell unlike
anything Austin had ever experienced. He stepped back and
leaned over the railing, his stomach turning like he was going to
vomit.

He saw a woman. Thin, with dirty blond hair. She was walking across the parking lot, carrying a plastic shopping bag. "Ridley, Lucy." They turned and he pointed. "That's her."

Ridley said, "Lucy, take the staircase on the left. I'll take the right. Austin, stay here and keep an eye on this guy."

Trisha still hadn't looked up. Lucy and Ridley took off, leaping down the stairs two and three at a time. When they reached the lot, they were only thirty yards from Trisha. She had no chance.

"Trisha!" Baxter screamed. "Ruuuuuuunnnnnn!"

She glanced up and saw Austin. For half a second, she seemed to inspect him, trying to place him. Then she pivoted, saw Ridley coming for her, and bolted back in the direction she'd come from.

Austin turned back to the doorway. Frank Baxter was gone. He poked his head into the apartment, holding his breath.

The last thing he saw was a brown clay pot coming for his head.

CHAPTER TWENTY-TWO

FACE DOWN ON THE WALKWAY, Austin kept his eyes closed even after he'd regained consciousness. How the hell had he gotten himself into this? Yesterday morning he'd been in his kitchen, trying to make the perfect hamburger. Now he was lying face down on a sticky walkway, blood running down his cheek, surrounded by potting soil, flecks of Mexican rice and chicken, and broken shards of a pot that had left a gash in his head.

He slowly opened one eye. The blow had spun him around so he was facing the railing, where he could see down into the parking lot. Despite the sharp pain in his head, he cracked an involuntary smile when he saw Lucy pressing Trisha Simone face first into her cruiser. The smile disappeared just as fast as he took a deep breath. Cat piss, ammonia. Then he remembered Frank Baxter.

Leaping up like a dead man coming back to life, Austin spun on Baxter, who stood in the doorway holding a small piece of the pot he'd broken over Austin's head. The look on his face told Austin that not only was Baxter not a threat, he was re-thinking every life decision that had brought him to this point. An hour ago he'd been anticipating a lovely burrito, probably a joint and a beer, maybe a movie. Now his "girlfriend" was under arrest and he'd just assaulted a man who had six inches and fifty pounds on him.

Austin wiped blood from his cheek with the back of his hand, then raised his fists, poised to strike. "You're having a *very* bad day, Baxter."

For half a second, Baxter raised his fists, a tough-guy look painted across his face like he'd just watched *Raging Bull*.

It only took the slightest movement—Austin cocking his right hand back two inches—for Baxter to fold. In one motion, he threw his hands straight up and allowed his legs to collapse out from beneath him, dropping into a cross-legged posture on the ground, arms to the sky. Austin thought it looked like the most ridiculous yoga posture he'd ever seen. He decided to call it *The Surrendering Loser* pose.

Austin showed the back of his hand to Baxter. "See the blood? Like I said, this is a very bad day for you."

"I swear I don't know anything."

"Why'd you hit me with a pot?"

Baxter hung his head. "I'm a frigging idiot. I saw Trisha, thought she was in trouble." He closed his eyes tight, as though pinching his face into a ball of remorse could somehow get him out of this situation. "I swear to God I've never done anything like that."

In general, Austin wasn't a vengeful guy. As much as he wanted justice for victims, as much as he wanted genuinely bad guys off the streets, he was quick to forgive when someone wronged him personally. With one exception, he didn't seek out vengeance. If he ever got twenty-minutes alone in a room with the men who'd killed Fiona, well, that would be different. Very different. But Frank Baxter? Austin had always had a soft spot for guys like Frank Baxter. A sort of *there-but-for-the-grace* kind of pity. Without knowing any of the details of this man's life, he knew it hadn't been easy. And if he was reading Baxter right, he wasn't involved in any of Trisha's schemes.

Austin loomed over him. "In a minute or two you'll be in the back of that police car." He pointed down to the parking lot. "I'll make you a deal. When we get back to the office and I ask you questions, tell me the exact truth, the whole truth, the first time I ask you a question. If you do..." he pointed at the gash in his head... "we'll forget about this. You could be home by late tonight, maybe even in time to order another burrito." He squatted, meeting Baxter's flighty eyes. "If you don't, we're gonna have to assume that you're involved in Trisha's dealing." He held a shard of the broken pot right in front of Baxter's eyes. "And I'm gonna have to tell the detectives down there about your assault with a deadly weapon."

～

Ridley had agreed to let Austin take the lead in the interview, hoping his knowledge of the D'Antonia case would allow him to twist the questions in the right direction. But first he'd forced Austin to take care of his head. There was no way he was going to the hospital and risk missing the interrogation, so after popping a couple aspirin with another cup of lukewarm coffee, he'd used the mirror in the men's room to clean up and apply pressure to the wound with a neatly folded paper towel.

The interview room was an eight-by-eight box in the back corner of the building. It had been painted a thin white, like nonfat milk, as though someone had thrown on primer then forgotten to finish the job with a coat of interior paint.

Austin sat in a plastic chair across from Trisha. Ridley leaned on the wall.

Trisha sat in a ratty old loveseat in the corner, her chin poking out above a thin blanket she'd pulled up around her neck.

Across the hall, Jimmy and Lucy were in an identical room with Frank Baxter. Though all agreed that he seemed to be a passenger on Trisha's bus of criminality, she'd probably let details slip in the past. Loose pillow talk, Austin knew, had brought down as many criminals as forensic science.

"Trisha," Ridley began, sitting down next to Austin, "this conversation is being recorded." He pointed to a small camera pointing down from the corner.

She nodded.

He read her the standard Miranda rights and she nodded along, only acknowledging them verbally when Ridley asked twice. Thankfully, she did not request a lawyer, which would have ended their conversation before it began.

When he'd finished with the preliminaries, Ridley leaned back in his chair and laced his hands behind his head. "Thomas Austin is a consultant on this case. He's going to ask you a few questions."

She glanced in Austin's direction, then continued to stare blankly ahead. "You were at my apartment. My truck."

"I was."

She opened her mouth right away, then thought better of whatever she was about to say. Finally, she said, "I've never been arrested." Her voice was weak, kind of raspy. She sounded tired.

Austin handed her a photograph. "Where's this little boy? Where's Joshua Green?"

She looked down for only a moment. "No idea. Never heard of him."

Austin held his head stone still. He'd learned that a total absence of movement was sometimes a better way to get someone's attention than a gesture, because it was unexpected. When Trisha looked over, Austin said, "I promise you, we can be here for a long, long time. You can go to jail for a long, long time. But everything in your life will end up better if you tell me right now everything you know about this boy."

She looked at the photo again, her lip quivering slightly. " I swear I don't know about *that* child."

Austin almost smiled. "Interesting phrasing. So you know about *a* child?"

"That's not what I said, not what I meant."

"Why'd you say *that* child'?"

"I didn't."

Austin made a quick pivot. "When was the last time you were in Hansville?"

She let her eyes wander up and to the left. "I don't know. Few months ago maybe."

"Then why do we have video of your truck entering Hansville three weeks ago?"

"Damn."

"Yeah," Ridley said angrily, "*damn* is right."

"Why were you in Hansville?" Austin demanded.

"I wasn't. Maybe someone stole my truck."

"And then brought it back and parked it in your spot? Without you noticing? That would be remarkable." Austin pulled out a fresh paper towel from his pocket and blotted his wound. He felt an overwhelming sense of urgency to get everything out of her as fast as he could, but his read on Trisha was that an aggressive approach would just make her clam up, possibly demand a lawyer. "Trisha, you might want to accept the fact that Detective Calvin and I are both pretty good at this. And, no disrespect, you're one of the worst liars I've ever interviewed. How about you tell us where Joshua is?"

Suddenly she stamped her feet like a toddler. "Did you hit your head or something? I told you I've never heard of *that* kid."

"There it is again," Ridley said. "'*That* kid.' There something you want to tell us?"

She folded her arms.

"When was the last time you were on Bainbridge Island?" Austin asked.

She shrugged.

"Do you wear size eight shoes?"

"Yeah, sometimes seven and a half, but yeah. So what?"

Austin reached down and swiped the blanket away from her feet. Adidas, same as the ones they'd pulled from her apartment.

"When the FBI compares these—or the pair we found in your apartment—to the size eight imprint next to that little boy's crib, what do you think they'll find?"

"I work out a lot," Trisha said. "I have a lot of shoes."

Austin turned to Ridley. "The FBI, I've heard they're pretty good at fingerprints, shoe prints, that kind of thing. You heard that?"

"If that shoe was in Joshua's room, we'll know by tomorrow morning. And if it was," he paused, shaking his head as Trisha stared at him, "that's the ballgame. Life in prison."

Ridley handed her a photograph of the Thanksgiving gift bag Sarah and Benny had found on the beach. "Recognize that?"

Trisha was trying to hold her face tight, but Austin noticed the slightest twitch around her eyes. "It's a bag, a Thanksgiving bag."

"And what's in it?" Austin asked.

"No idea."

Austin handed her another photo. The close-up inside the bag. The bones. The skull.

She stared blankly. "Bones?"

"Right again," Austin said. He handed her another photo. A picture of Allie Shreever. "*Her* bones.*"

Trisha looked back and forth between the photo of the bones and the photo of Allie Shreever. Her face trembled slightly. "Oh, God."

Her shock appeared real, but that didn't mean much. Some types of killers were so deranged they could convince themselves they hadn't done it, so proof of their actions often evoked genuine surprise.

Austin pointed at the picture of Allie Shreever. "That's right. *Her* bones. I worked in New York City for a long time. I saw a lot of horrible things. Things that would make your skin crawl. Things that would haunt you." He tapped the photo of the bag of bones. "This is the worst thing I've ever seen. And you did it." His tone was still relatively cool, relatively neutral.

She dropped the photos on her lap. She stared into Austin's eyes, her voice a whisper. "I swear I didn't kill her."

There was a quick knock at the door and Lucy poked her head in. "Boss, Austin, can we grab you a sec?"

Austin held Trisha's stare for a moment more, then followed Ridley into the hall, where Jimmy joined them from the other interview room.

"We're nowhere with Frank Baxter," Jimmy said. "Either because he's actually got nothing to do with Trisha besides giving her the—"

Lucy held a hand in front of his mouth. "Don't say it."

Jimmy brushed her hand aside. "The secret sauce. Or because he's a damn good liar."

"He's *not* a good liar," Austin said.

"All he has is the weed dealing. Says she buys in bulk from a guy in Seattle, then breaks it into twenty sacks and sells it to high schoolers. I believe he doesn't know much more than that."

Ridley nodded. "Trisha was definitely involved with Allie Shreever. Still saying she doesn't know where Joshua is. Lucy and Jimmy, keep pressing Baxter. Anything about Hansville, anything strange she's said about babies. Anything. Austin, what's your read on her?"

Before he could answer, Samantha appeared, walking down the hallway briskly and carrying a silver laptop. "I've got something. Something huge."

She turned the laptop around so they could see the screen, then held forth like a college professor. "Trisha erased her search history, but pieces of it were still cached. Look."

It was a screenshot of a Google search history. Trisha had run searches for "The Holiday Baby Butcher," "Seattle baby murders," and "baby bones in holiday sacks."

Austin smiled. Evidence this damning didn't often show up halfway through an interview. It was almost too good to be true.

Ridley patted Samantha on the back. "Nice work."

Austin took the laptop and returned to the interview room.

When Ridley joined him, he held it up like a proud parent showing off a newborn. "Recognize this?"

Trisha frowned. "That's mine. You can't just—"

"We can," Ridley said, firmly. "We did."

Austin sat, placing the computer where she could see the screen, see her own search history. "Look at the screen, then look at the pictures in your lap. Would you care to tell us anything about those two babies?"

"I didn't *do* anything."

Austin let out a long, slow, disappointed breath. "I'm trying to help you, Trisha." It wasn't a *total* lie, but it was pretty damn close. He was trying to help Joshua Green and his parents. It was too late to help Allie Shreever, but he was trying to help her parents. "Why did you run those searches? Telling the truth always feels better in the end."

She stared at the screen for a long time, then closed the computer. "Screw you, Google."

"Not a huge fan myself," Austin said. "All those ads, right? Where's Joshua?"

Trisha crossed her arms. "I don't know who that is. I swear it."

Ridley moved suddenly across the room and crouched to get right up in her face. "With those searches and the video of your truck, and the eyewitnesses putting you at the beach, we have you on the kidnapping and murder of Allie Shreever." His voice had turned angry, even a touch maniacal, like he was doing a Samuel L. Jackson impression. "When that footprint comes back from the FBI, we have you on another kidnapping. I urge you in the strongest possible terms: stop lying."

She looked at the floor, stacking and restacking the pictures in her lap. When she finally looked up, she had tears in her eyes. "Lawyer," she said softly. "I want a lawyer."

CHAPTER TWENTY-THREE

TWO HOURS LATER, Austin sat on the floor in the corner of the conference room, tossing a balled-up piece of paper for Itsy. She was well-trained; she knew her name, knew how to sit, and had ceased the high-pitched yelping. All in all, she was a lovely dog once she'd had the chance to calm down.

Itsy dropped the slobbery paper by his feet. He balled it up tighter and threw it to the other side of the room. Itsy ran to fetch it, still limping, then lay down in the corner to gnaw it to shreds.

Ridley was taking a statement from Baxter, who'd declined a lawyer and was being forthcoming, though he still claimed to know nothing beyond Trisha's low-level dealing. Baxter had turned over his cellphone, showing a long record of texts with Trisha indicating that he'd likely been telling the truth—booty calls, burritos, and Netflix. The occasional raunchy photo. Nothing to indicate he was involved in her dealing, or that he knew anything about the kidnappings.

Trisha was a different story, and Austin couldn't stop thinking about the interview. She'd obviously been lying. The question was, was she lying about *everything*?

What he couldn't understand was why she'd gone to Frank

Baxter's in the first place. If she had Joshua stashed somewhere, she would have returned to him the moment she fled from her apartment. She would have wanted to move him on the assumption that, if police had found her apartment, they'd soon find her stash house. It was possible she'd gone to try to borrow Baxter's phone, or borrow money. But she'd had $900 in cash on her when they'd arrested her. So why hadn't Trisha hopped a cab back to wherever Joshua was stashed after she'd disappeared into the park? It had only been a few hours between the time she'd ditched Austin in Kingston and the time she'd arrived at Baxter's. So if she *had* gone to move Joshua, she'd been quick about it, which meant she had another place nearby.

Another issue nagged at him. Austin knew Lorraine D'Antonia better than any other law enforcement officer in the country. She wasn't a jilted lover who got enraged and shot her ex. She wasn't even an overwhelmed mother who'd drowned her children in a lake. He'd arrested women like that before and, as horrible as they were, Lorraine D'Antonia was in a different category altogether. She'd taken children from their homes, played holiday dress up with them for three days, then administered lethal doses of poison. Afterwards, she'd boiled the flesh off their bones, then Dremeled cheesy poetry onto them. She was a psychopath on a level all her own. As much as he wanted to believe they had their woman, he simply didn't think Trisha Simone capable of that sort of inhuman behavior. Like Frank Baxter, she came across as a down-on-her-luck sad sack. A low-level criminal lacking both the intelligence and the psychopathy to pull off elaborate kidnappings and murders. And if she wasn't behind the kidnappings, why did she keep lying?

Itsy returned, offering up a moist scrap of paper, then curling up by his feet. He missed Run. He'd called Andy to make sure he'd be in early to feed her and toss the ball around, but he felt guilty for leaving her. He told himself he'd take her on an extra-long beach walk when this was all over.

Jimmy and Lucy came into the room and Austin joined them

at the conference table. "I've been thinking," he said. "What else do you have on those two missing nurses?"

"Don't think Trisha is our gal?" Lucy asked.

"Maybe an accomplice, but..."

"I'm with you," Jimmy said, squeezing a rubber ball in his left hand over and over. On the release, it let out a tiny squeak that made Itsy perk up her ears. "She doesn't have the evil in her."

Lucy gave Jimmy an annoyed look. "What *is* that ball?"

He held it up, squeezing it aggravatingly close to her face. "For forearm and wrist strength. Missing my workout tonight and gotta stay swol."

"Swol?" Austin asked.

"Jacked," Jimmy said. "Strong."

Lucy raised an eyebrow at him. "You sure that's what you want to be saying?"

He gave her a puzzled look.

She smirked. "You're strengthening your wrists and forearms to stay *jacked*? Sometimes I think you have a muscle mass where your brain should be."

Jimmy gently wrapped his knuckles against the side of his head. "Nope. One-hundred-percent community-college educated, grade-a brain matter."

Austin wanted to tell them to get a room.

Ridley came in, a weary look on his face. "That Baxter is a real shitheel, but he's no kidnapper."

Austin asked, "Jimmy, were you able to get dates on those google searches?"

"Samantha found them, but why does it matter?" Jimmy shrugged. "She ran the searches about a week after she left the bones on the beach."

Austin considered this. "She could have been googling to see what kind of coverage she was getting in the media. But also... hmm... it's possible she was actually trying to learn something." He turned to Ridley. "Did Sheriff Daniels have any luck with TaskRabbit?"

"Nothing yet. FBI is leaning on them, but... no. What are you thinking?"

Austin walked to the whiteboard, then traced a line with his finger from the picture of Trisha Simone to the photo of Allie Shreever. "So we know Trisha dropped Allie's bones on the beach, but so far we have nothing tying her to the Shreever crime scene, correct?"

"Correct," Ridley said.

"And we have the shoe print in the Green house, which could be a match. But it's not like women's size eight are especially rare."

"Correct."

"What I'm thinking is, why would Trisha search for the bags and The Holiday Baby Butcher *after* she'd already left the bones on the beach? I'm thinking TaskRabbit. Maybe someone hired Trisha to drop off the bones? What if she knew it was shady but did it anyway? Then, when she heard about the discovery of the dead baby in Hansville, and then the second kidnapping, she started googling and found the Lorraine D'Antonia case? Then she realized, 'Oh no, *I* left a Thanksgiving bag.'"

"It's possible," Ridley said, "But if so, she knows who hired her and is still withholding info."

Austin nodded.

Samantha burst through the door. "Holy freaking hell, bros and brodettes." As usual, she was carrying a laptop, but this time she had it cradled in her palms as though she was carrying a delicate Faberge egg on a velvet pillow.

Before she'd said another word, she turned her laptop around. Austin stared blankly. It appeared to be a Facebook post.

"So, remember how I said that Mary Bonner isn't on any social media?"

Austin nodded. Mary Bonner was one of the two nurses who'd missed work at the birthing center where both Allie Shreever and Joshua Green had been born.

"You found her?" Jimmy asked.

"Not exactly. But occasionally people are on a platform, get tagged in a post or photo, then *leave* the platform. The tag linking to their profile disappears, but their name is still there. On Facebook, it turns from blue to gray when this happens. In search, I didn't find a single reference to Mary Bonner—other than ones out of state—but I also got a list of all the nurses she'd worked with. So I searched for Jessie Johnson. She's another nurse at St. Michael's."

Austin was confused. "Why'd you search for her?"

"Ridley got me their work schedules. In the last year, Jessie Johnson shared more shifts with Mary Bonner than anyone else. Thought maybe I'd find a mention of Mary in Jessie's social. This post is a photo from the nursing party last Christmas. Only a year ago. It's captioned 'St. Michael's Birthing Team, Christmas Party.'"

Ridley sidled up next to her. "Please tell me Mary Bonner is in that picture."

"She's not, but she's in a grayed-out tag. She was tagged in this photo—probably because she was at the party—then left Facebook."

"Okay, so what's the big deal?" Austin asked.

"Look." Samantha pointed at the section below the photo.

There were dozens of comments, replies, and replies to the replies. Austin scanned the comments, shaking his head, wondering why this was so important. His eyes stopped suddenly on a comment from Myrian Brightstone, the other nurse who'd missed work in the last couple days.

Actually, they stopped on four words in the middle of a long comment: *The Holiday Baby Butcher.*

CHAPTER TWENTY-FOUR

EVERYONE HUNCHED around the small screen to read. For half a second, Austin wondered when reading year-old Facebook comments had become so relevant to detective work, but denying it would be like pursuing a fleeing suspect in a horse-drawn carriage.

The exchange under the photograph started out fine before descending into what read like high school gossip and bullying. Austin had a pretty good understanding of the dark side of human nature. It had been his job for two decades. But he'd never be able to understand a world where otherwise normal people treated others like this, in writing, in public.

Jessie Johnson: Ooh, I love this photo. Fun night!

Myrian Brightstone: Samesies! We gotta get the girls together more often.

Keeran Smith: Girls? What about me?

Myrian Brightstone: Sorry, Keeran, you're one of the girls now. You can take Mary's place.

Keeran Smith: Where'd she go, anyway?

Jessie Johnson: Left early. Doesn't drink.

Myrian Brightstone: Left early 'cause she's a weirdo is more like it.

Keeran Smith: Myrian, don't.

Myrian Brightstone: No, I'm sorry. Someone has to say it.

Keeran Smith: It doesn't have to be here, tho.

Jessie Johnson: Keeran, she's not wrong. That whole conversation was weird AF.

Myrian Brightstone: Weird? It was disturbing, and I honestly don't care WHO sees this. I was trying to have fun at a party and get my drank on. Talk about a buzzkill.

Keeran Smith: Not saying you're wrong, but she's literally tagged in this photo.

Myrian Brightstone: Wouldn't even be IN the photo, you think she's gonna look at Facebook? I'm sorry, but I'm so DONE with her. Creepy. Old. And WTF was that shit at the end? How do you spend five minutes of a Christmas party talking about a serial killer?

Jessie Johnson: I know, right? She was talking about it like of course we should all know already. I never even heard about it.

Myrian Brightstone: How dare you, Jessie!?! LOL. How dare you not want to discuss The Holiday Baby Butcher at your company Christmas party. LOLOL. And that schmaltzy poetry she posts in the breakroom before every holiday? GOD AWFUL!

For a long moment, everyone sat in silence. Stunned silence. It was Ridley who eventually spoke. "Samantha, excellent work. You may have just broken this case. But we don't have time for a victory lap. Who's this Keeran Smith?"

Samantha closed her laptop. "Another nurse who works there."

Ridley turned to Jimmy. "Get addresses for him and Jessie Johnson. Send patrol over there to question them about Mary Bonner." Jimmy nodded and raced out of the room.

Austin stood, shoved his hands in the pockets of his jeans, and paced. "Tell me if you're with me. So Mary Bonner is working at the hospital. Judging by this exchange, she's obsessed with the case, like most copycats. She meets the parents of Allie

Shreever, maybe she's working the night she's born. Likely, she gathers information at the hospital. Home address, and so on. Maybe she even scopes out the house while the parents are still in the hospital. Maybe she learns they're gonna have their child in a crib in a separate room. She'd confirm this *before* deciding on a child. She'd want to know for certain that this kid won't be co-sleeping with the parents. She kidnaps Allie—and we don't yet know what happened for the three days she had her—then kills her, does the poem on the bones, and then—"

"Then hires Trisha through TaskRabbit to drop the bones." Ridley was right there with him.

"Somehow," Austin continued, "she does all this without missing work or calling attention to herself."

"Or," Lucy said, "the entire ordeal—the three days—were days Bonner was scheduled to be off anyway. I'll have Samantha check her work records against the dates of Allie's disappearance."

"Good thinking," Ridley said.

"Right," Austin agreed. "A few weeks later, she figures she's gotten away with it, she repeats the exact same process with Joshua Green. But this time, something changes. Instead of continuing at her job, she disappears."

Lucy stood. "What changed was Anna's story about the possible connections between the cases. Once she saw that, she knew it was a matter of time before we knocked on her door."

Ridley moved to the door. "You two wait here, I'm gonna get us a warrant for Mary Bonner's place. This, plus what we already have, will be more than enough." He stopped in the doorway. "One more thing: you two think it's a coincidence that Trisha slightly resembles D'Antonia, or is that part of it?"

"Good question," Austin said.

Ridley shrugged and left.

Austin's head spun. He looked at Lucy, then at Itsy, who was sleeping in the corner.

Before he could convince himself not to, he leapt up, grabbed

Itsy, and raced down the hall to the interview room. Busting through the door, he saw Trisha talking to the public defender who'd just arrived to counsel her.

The lawyer stood immediately. "I'm in a meeting with my client." He was a young guy with a cheap suit and a buzzcut, no more than two years out of law school.

Austin waved a hand at him dismissively. "This'll just take a sec. Trisha, look at me."

She reached out pathetically and burst into tears when she saw her dog. Seeing Trisha, Itsy let out a series of high-pitched yelps and turned its head nearly backwards attempting to bite Austin.

"We know you didn't take any kids," Austin said. "I don't think you even knew what was in that bag. You're just a down-on-her-luck weed dealer who did odd jobs to pay for her dog's surgery."

"Don't say anything," the lawyer commanded her. Then, turning to Austin. "You're completely out of line. Detective, get this guy out of here."

Ridley had appeared behind him and Austin felt his large hands on his shoulders.

"Someone paid you to drop off that bag. We know who. Maybe she approached you first through the TaskRabbit app? I'm guessing you did a job for her, then later she reached out with a special job, extra pay?"

The lawyer now slid to the side, physically blocking his client from Austin. "Don't answer that!"

Austin crouched and let Itsy down. Immediately, the tiny dog sprinted across the room, through the lawyer's legs, and leapt into Trisha's arms.

"Trisha!" Austin blurted. "Answer me!"

She was in tears now, relief and pain all over her face.

"I'm betting she reached out to you outside the app, doubling, even tripling your pay. Probably by phone, nothing in writing. Tell us who paid you to drop off that bag and we can work with you." He scowled at the lawyer. "Get her to talk or that baby's blood will be on your hands, too."

He pushed Ridley out the door and slammed it behind them with a force that shook the walls.

CHAPTER TWENTY-FIVE

SHE NIBBLED the edge of a Christmas-tree-shaped cookie, cracking the crispy bits of sugar between her front teeth. The sound of crunching was loud in the tiny kitchen. Or maybe it only seemed loud now that Joshua had settled down for a nap.

The little angel slept so soundly. He radiated warmth and goodness.

Had she slept like that as a baby? She doubted it. Her home had not been filled with the smells of Christmas. She'd never been as loved as Joshua.

Outside, the wind howled through the cedar trees, battering the little cabin. But she was warm, so warm. And so was Joshua. She'd given him a wonderful home these last couple days. Memories that would last for the rest of her life.

And the rest of his.

She tensed suddenly, inadvertently.

A noise from outside. And it wasn't the wind. More of a thud, like a bird flying into the side of the cabin, which had happened once before. Or a tree branch falling onto the roof, which happened every time there was a storm.

It was probably nothing. But the article in the newspaper

had her worried. That bitch Anna Downey had gone snooping around at the hospital. She could ruin everything.

Hurrying out of the kitchen, she passed into the living room. The curtains were drawn. Creeping slowly, she reached the wall next to the front door and rested a knee on the arm of the couch. Carefully, she leaned toward the window, peeling back the curtain slowly, ever so slowly. Just an inch.

She saw nothing.

Another sound, a rumbling series of clicks. An engine starting up. Her mind raced to little Joshua. Had they found them? Had they come for her boy?

She heard tires over gravel.

Tires over gravel.

Getting fainter.

Fainter?

She peered out the window again. A van was *leaving* her house. An Amazon delivery van.

Her shoulders dropped. She let out a long breath and opened the front door. With a quick dip and grab, she swooped up the brown box.

Back at the kitchen table, she checked on Joshua. Precious angel hadn't noticed a thing. He shifted a little, moving his pudgy little arm onto his forehead like he was trying to block out the sun.

His present was here, but she was glad he was asleep. That way it would be a surprise.

She pulled open the box, busting through the brown packing tape easily with a long fingernail. The crinkle of plastic packaging always made her happy, and today was no exception.

She pulled out the bag and dumped its contents on the table. The description on the website had said it was "The perfect item for holiday gift-giving."

She agreed.

It was a small, felt gift bag. Mostly red and decorated with

little green Christmas trees, white snowflakes, and even a minia-
ture sleigh with a jolly Santa saying "Ho-Ho-Ho."

She brought the packaging to the garbage and set the bag
down in the middle of the table. It seemed small.

She wondered if it would be big enough. Little Joshua was
growing by the minute, after all.

Then she remembered Allie Shreever. She'd been about the
same size and had posed no problems. After all, a baby's body
was over seventy percent water.

She glanced at the large canning pot, silver and shiny, sitting
on her stove.

And most of the rest was meat.

CHAPTER TWENTY-SIX

IT WAS NEARLY midnight at the Kitsap Sheriff's Office, but no one was sleeping. After Austin's outburst, Trisha Simone's lawyer had huddled with his client for thirty minutes before appearing in the hallway and offering a single, weary sentence. "Against my legal advice, she's ready to come clean."

Now Austin, Ridley, Lucy, and a video camera watched Trisha's every move and hung on her every word.

"It started the week before Thanksgiving." Trisha stroked Itsy slowly as she spoke. The presence of the tiny dog had been a condition of telling the truth. "I got a message through the app. Hundred and twenty bucks to ferry some legal documents from Bremerton to Seattle."

"Where was the pickup?" Ridley asked.

Trisha hung her head. "Saint Michaels. The hospital."

Austin heard a thin stream of air whistling through Ridley's teeth. He was pissed, likely because he was thinking exactly what Austin was thinking: if Trisha had put two and two together when she'd heard that Allie Shreever had been found dead in Hansville, she could have prevented Joshua's kidnapping.

"Who gave you the documents?" Austin asked.

"Woman, white, maybe fifties or sixties."

"What else?" Ridley demanded. "Every. Single. Detail."

Trisha closed her eyes tight, trying to find the memories. "She was wearing sunglasses and scrubs. A nurse. Seemed nice and all. Documents were in a yellow envelope. I didn't ask her anything about them, but she said they were the final paperwork for her divorce. Said they had to be delivered that day. Something about a settlement."

"Name?" Ridley said.

"In the app it was Suzanne Brown."

"Did she ever refer to herself by another name?" Austin asked.

Trisha thought for a moment, then shook her head.

They needed to get back to the physical description, but first Austin was hoping they'd get lucky with an address or some other key detail that would lead them to Joshua. "Where was the drop-off spot?" Austin asked.

"That was the weird thing. The woman had written the wrong address on the envelope. When I got there, there was no legal office at the address. It was a grocery store. I got in touch with her through the app and I didn't hear from her until the next day. Brought the documents back with me. When she wrote she said it was her mistake—she'd written the wrong street name. But it was no big deal because she'd figured out how to file the paperwork online. I met her the next day, gave her back the paperwork, and she gave me a sixty-dollar tip through the app for my trouble."

Austin considered this, then turned to Ridley. "She was testing her. Seeing if she could be trusted."

Ridley nodded. "Please, continue. How'd you end up leaving that bag on the beach in Hansville?"

"About a week later, she contacted me again, saying she had a special job and could she contact me outside the app? Now, we're not supposed to do that—the app wants their fifteen percent cut, after all—but she seemed like a decent woman, so I gave her my cell."

"So you broke the operating agreement of the app?" Ridley asked.

Trisha's eyes flashed at Ridley. "Everyone does it. You really want to give me shit about *that* of all things?"

The lawyer held up the phone. "Ms. Simone has agreed to show you the messages she received in exchange for two things. Mr. Austin, she'd like you to decline to press charges against Mr. Baxter. And Detective Calvin, she'd like your word that you'll put in a good word should she face an intent-to-distribute without a license charge, or any charges related to the next phase of her interaction with the woman calling herself Suzanne Brown."

Austin and Ridley both nodded. Trisha entered the password and the lawyer handed Ridley the phone.

Itsy had fallen asleep and Trisha rocked her like a baby as she spoke. "It was a pretty quick thing. She offered me five hundred bucks to pick up a sack from one location in Hansville and drop it in another."

"Hansville?" Austin asked, surprised. "The pick up, too?"

She nodded.

"And that didn't seem odd to you?" Ridley asked, a biting tone creeping into his voice.

"Sure it did." Trisha laughed. "But it also sounded like rent money." She looked from Ridley to Austin, from Austin to Lucy. "Weed business sucks since they made it legal, and I'm guessing none of you have ever been poor. Like, really poor. Like, will-I-be-sleeping-in-my-truck? poor." She shook her head. "Anyway, that's what I did. Knew it might be sketchy, but honestly she seemed like a decent woman."

Ridley's eyes were on the phone. "And the pickup location was at the end of Northwest 360th?"

Trisha nodded.

Lucy's eyes were skeptical. "She was paying you five hundred dollars to pick up a bag and take it a mile away? And you agreed to that?"

"Read the texts," Trisha said, defensively. "Said it was one of those Instagram scavenger hunt things people do. She'd left the final prize in the wrong spot and had to pull a double at the hospital. Her whole family was in town and could I move it?"

"And you believed *that*?" Lucy asked.

"Honestly, I did. I know how stupid it looks now." She closed her eyes and sighed. "Maybe I just *wanted* to believe."

Austin shook his head. The things people would believe when money was on the line.

Trisha's lawyer raised a finger. "I'd like to highlight the fact that at no time did Ms. Simone take any action she thought illegal, or even immoral."

"C'mon," Lucy said. "I'd believe she thought it was a drug drop. That would at least make logical sense. No bleeping way she bought the scavenger hunt thing."

The lawyer shrugged, a smirk across his face. "We disagree."

Lucy glared at him, then at Trisha. "And you didn't look in the bag?"

Trisha shook her head.

"Why'd you snap the photos of the bag?" Austin asked.

"Just to prove I'd made the drop. Like package delivery drivers do."

Ridley held up the phone to Lucy. "Take down Suzanne Brown's phone number and check with Samantha. It's almost certainly a burner, but find out anything you can." Lucy jotted down the number. "While you're out there, get me a printout of every house back in the woods around 360th. And call around. See if you can convince any of our sketch artists to come in."

"It's midnight on Saturday, boss."

His look told her he didn't care. She nodded. She didn't care either.

When Lucy had gone, Austin turned to Ridley. "I've driven

past Northeast 360th a hundred times. Always noticed it. Never been down there, though." Austin had thought it odd that there'd be a 360th street in a tiny beach town where streets had names like Shoreview, Cedar Grove, Heron, and Sandy Cove.

"Dirt road," Ridley said. "Some gravel. Lots of little side roads, maybe thirty or forty houses altogether."

Austin made a mental note of this before asking Trisha, "At any time did she contact you by phone call?"

"No."

"Do you have another phone she might have contacted you on?"

"No."

"After she asked to contact you outside the app, did she ever again contact you within the app?"

"No."

Austin was growing frustrated. He could tell this wasn't going to get them where they needed to go. "Did *your* looks ever come up? The fact that you look a little like Lorraine D'Antonia?"

"What are you implying?" the lawyer asked.

Austin ignored him, eyes locked on Trisha.

"I don't think I look much like her. But no, it never came up."

"The five hundred bucks. Please tell me she sent that via PayPal or something?"

Trisha shook her head. "Cash, in an envelope with the bag."

A worried look crossed her lawyer's face.

He'd noticed the same hole in her story that Austin had. "You said you believed her story about the treasure hunt. That she was working and couldn't move the bag. And yet somehow she managed to leave five hundred dollars in cash with the bag, with your name on it?"

Trisha looked at her lawyer, who shrugged. She should have taken his advice and refused to speak.

"Okay," she admitted, "that lady cop was right. I thought it was a drug thing."

"And when you saw the police outside your apartment," Ridley said, "you ran because you'd figured out that you were an accomplice to the murder of Allie Shreever?"

She closed her eyes. "That, plus the weed I had in my place."

"We'll get back to money," Ridley said. "We want the bills she gave you. Forensics. Low priority at this point."

Austin agreed. They already knew the identity and home address of the suspected killer, Mary Bonner. Plus, bank notes were notoriously difficult to fingerprint, but it was worth a shot. It would be useful if this thing ever went to trial, but not much help achieving their number one priority: locating Mary Bonner and, they hoped, a living Joshua Green.

"To be clear," Austin said, "You had zero contact with this person outside the two meetings at the hospital, the texts we're now reading, and the exchanges you had within the TaskRabbit app?"

"That's right."

Ridley pulled up a chair beside her. "This next part is important, Trisha, and I want you to close your eyes and really think." His tone was warm now, fatherly despite the fact that Trisha had a dozen or so years on him. "I want you to think about what she looked like. Really try to picture her."

"She was wearing sunglasses." Trisha looked down at Itsy like the answer might be found on the top of her tiny head. "A face-mask, like she'd just come out of surgery."

"Tattoos, identifying marks? Scars on what skin was visible?"

"I really wasn't looking for anything like that. She seemed like she was in a hurry."

"Think," Ridley implored her.

"She was about my height, similar frame. Slight, like me."

"How'd she walk?"

Trisha considered this. "Quick. Purposeful. She wasn't some rickety old lady."

"What was her voice like?"

"I don't know. Normal?"

"Accent?"

"Nothing major," Trisha said. "Sounded like she was from here."

Ridley and Trisha went around and around about the woman's appearance for another five minutes before Ridley gave up. Trisha's story matched up with all the facts, but it hadn't brought them much closer to locating Mary Bonner.

Samantha had failed to find a single photo of Bonner online and was working on other sources. Officers were staked out at her apartment, and by morning Ridley would have a search warrant. But Austin didn't think that would do much good. He doubted she'd ever brought Joshua there, doubted she'd left any evidence about her location. Mary Bonner was in the wind, and she'd brought Joshua Green with her.

The one thing Trisha had provided that might bear fruit was the location of the pickup of the bones. That was the next lead to work.

Austin pulled Ridley into the hallway, where Lucy was leaning against a wall as though trying to catch a nap. "Northeast 360th."

"Way ahead of you," Ridley said. "Crack of dawn I'll be there with everyone I can get, knocking on doors."

"I'm with you," Lucy said, yawning. She handed Ridley a printout. "Forty-two houses in all. Addresses, names of owners. So far, no connection to Mary Bonner."

Austin said, "If we're lucky, she has a place there. Even if not, she *was* there, and maybe someone spotted her. Maybe she drove there and someone has a driveway camera."

Austin yawned. The coffee had made him jittery, but he was no longer the thirty-something detective who could pull all-nighters like a college student.

Ridley stretched his arms over his head, tapping the ceiling with a fingertip. "You've done a helluva job," Ridley said. "Go home. Get a few hours of sleep. Tomorrow's gonna be a long day."

"But—"

"You, too," he said to Lucy, ignoring Austin's objection. "I'm gonna finish up with Trisha and catch a few hours on the couch. Don't worry, Trisha's not going anywhere."

Austin reluctantly agreed, but only after Ridley had promised to call him the second they got into Mary Bonner's apartment.

CHAPTER TWENTY-SEVEN

AUSTIN FLICKED off his headlights and watched the tiny waves break on the rocky beach, foam gliding up the shore in the moonlight. He'd never been so happy to be home. The final mile of his drive into Hansville made him feel as though he was leaving the world behind and entering an alternate reality where things were smaller, simpler, and better.

Even after the longest day he'd had since moving here, his body relaxed as he came down the long hill into town, where the trees opened onto water, islands, mountains, and sky. Not that Silverdale, Bremerton, and Kingston were big cities—the closest big city was Seattle, a forty-minute ferry ride across the Sound— but compared to Hansville, any city was bustling.

His hand was on the door handle when a light glinted off his rearview mirror. He turned quickly, but could no longer see it. Studying the darkness, he watched for movement. The light flicked on again. A low glow in the shadows of his building, like a dim flashlight or, more likely, a phone screen. He watched closely, allowing his eyes to adjust to the darkness. Then he saw the figure.

He couldn't make out a face, not even a torso, but the person's white shoes caught just enough moonlight to be visible. He'd gotten his concealed carry permit when he moved to Washington State, but hadn't once carried a gun. After living in New York City, Hansville felt like the safest place on earth. But staring into the shadows, he wished his MR1911 was in the car, not locked in a safe at home.

But then again, whoever was standing there had seen him pull in. He was sure of that. So they wouldn't be looking at their phone if they'd come to do him harm. Not to mention, even if Mary Bonner knew he was working the case, she'd have no reason to come after him.

He was being paranoid. The last couple days had put him back into the mindset of a detective, a mindset in which killers and rapists were his daily companions, and danger lurked in every shadow.

He swung open the door and took three long strides toward the shadowed figure. The last of his fears disappeared as Anna Downey stepped out from the shadows. "Ridley said you were on the way home, and you weren't answering your cell."

Austin stopped halfway across the parking lot. "So you thought waiting in the shadows outside my place at one in the morning was a good idea? You're starting to make the hounds at the *Post* and the *Daily News* look like model citizens."

"I know cops have to hate reporters—it kinda comes with the badge—but you have no trouble using us when it suits your needs."

Austin couldn't deny this. He'd leaked stories to reporters often enough, but always with a strategic aim. "I'm not a cop. But when I was, if it would help get a case moving, freak out a suspect, or marshal the public to find a suspect, count me in. Difference is, I do it in service of solving crimes, you do it to sell papers."

"I'm personally offended!" Anna protested, a little too loudly. "We're online only. I do it for the *clicks*."

Austin said nothing.

"Oh, c'mon. I'm the one who has to rely on clicks to pay my

kid's college tuition." She stepped toward him. "I can't even get a pity laugh?"

"I'm too tired to laugh." He walked past her, heading around the side of the building. "And I know you didn't come here to tell jokes."

She followed him. "I have a scoop. It's big, and you won't like it."

He stopped and leaned on the gate, which led into a little fenced-in yard. "And I'm guessing Ridley wouldn't give you a comment?"

"Sure he did." She looked down at her notebook dramatically, though it was too dark to read. "He said, and I quote, 'No *bleeping* comment. And if you print that, you're blacklisted from my department.' End quote. And, as you can imagine, he didn't use the word 'bleeping.'"

"Sounds serious. Whatever it is, I wouldn't print it. And you already know I won't say anything, so why are you here?"

"Because it's my job." She stepped closer, a little too close, and he could smell her perfume. The scent was very northwest, like cedar and sea foam. "I'm here because, as much as you might not like it, as much as it might make *your* job harder, I have every right to do mine. And not only that, I'm damn good at it. Despite what my paychecks would indicate." Her tone wasn't angry, but it also told him she'd had this conversation with enough people to hold her own.

Austin was curious about any scoop big enough to have Ridley threaten to blacklist her. He didn't walk away, but he also didn't reply.

She took this as an opening. "I've noticed something about guys who work in law enforcement." She stepped back and put her hands on her hips.

"What's that?"

"You always assume that keeping every scintilla of information to yourselves is the best way to solve crimes."

Austin shrugged. "I'm really tired. I need to let my dog out.
What's your point?"

She pulled her phone out of the back pocket of her jeans,
tapped, and swiped. "It means that the Kitsap Sheriff department has been sitting on this photo for twenty-two days." A ball
of iron lodged in his belly—dread—and the taste of burnt toast
coated his tongue.

She held up her phone. The photo was the Thanksgiving bag
holding the bones of Allie Shreever, sitting on a driftwood log on
the beach.

His mind raced. Who could have leaked it. Lucy? Jimmy?
Samantha?

No. There was no way.

Then it hit him. Teenagers take photos of *everything*. "Was it
Sarah or Benny?"

"I'm not at liberty to reveal my sources, but it was Benny."

"That little shit. How much?"

She scoffed. "I don't pay for stories. I get them through
working my ass off. If you had kids, you'd understand."

Austin bristled. The mention of kids brought back Fiona and
he was way too tired for this.

She must have noticed his irritation. "I'm sorry. That was out
of line." She walked in a little circle, the only sound was the shuffling of her feet over the gravel driveway and the faint crashing of
small waves. "Look, the Sheriff's department hid from the public
for *three weeks* that the murder of Allie Shreever—the way her
body was discovered—was damn near *identical* to the murders of a
half dozen other babies. Hid the fact her killer has the *exact same
MO* as one of the most notorious serial killers in American history.
I know you've only been on this for two days. It wasn't your call.
Personally, I believe that decision made Kitsap County less safe."

"How so?"

"Maybe if the Green family knew that The Holiday Baby
Butcher had a clone out there, they would have put the crib in

their room that night. Maybe if..." she trailed off, kicked some gravel toward the beach, then turned back to Austin. "Look, there are a million woulda-coulda-shouldas here."

Austin's mind was racing. What would happen if the photo came out? The case of Lorraine D'Antonia had been one of the most talked-about of the last decade. Female serial killers were rare, ones who committed their atrocities in major media markets like Seattle and New York, even rarer. The fact that she'd targeted newborns—the most innocent among us—made the case even more disturbing, if that was possible. The last thing Austin had ever wanted was celebrity, but when he'd helped catch D'Antonia, he'd been drawn into a media circus that had taken months to die down, and only then because he'd done everything he could to kill it.

He'd been profiled against his will in a few magazines, and, at Fiona's urging, agreed to a couple segments on CNN, which had followed the story for months. In Fiona's view, he was a young, handsome detective, someone who made people feel good about law enforcement when most of the press they received was negative. She'd said, "It makes people feel safer to know guys like you are out there." He wasn't sure about that, but he'd figured out pretty quickly that TV was not his thing. He didn't like how little nuance the format allowed for, and he *really* didn't like putting on makeup.

If Anna's photo came out, the circus around the Holiday Baby Butcher would come back to town. The FBI would lead the charge into Kitsap County. They'd have no choice but to take on a larger role, and Sheriff Daniels would probably welcome them with open arms. It would get Daniels on TV and put his detectives in their place.

Next, the entire national media would descend. True crime experts, authors, amateur web sleuths. Every TV crime show would run a variation on the headline: *The Ultimate Copycat? Holiday Baby Butcher Back on the Scene, Despite Being Behind Bars.*

Or, even worse: *Holiday Baby Butcher Returns! Was Lorraine D'Antonia Falsely Convicted?*

Speculation would be all over the place. Had Austin blown the original case? Had D'Antonia falsely confessed? Had the real killer been free all this time? Hell, with the way nonsense spread on the internet, Austin might wake up to a blog post accusing *him* of the murders. After all, he'd recently moved to Hansville, where the bones were found. The internet had no limits when it came to stupidity.

He ran a hand through his hair. "We made a breakthrough today. We're close. Is there anything I can do to convince you not to run that photo?"

"I'm sorry. My editor already has the piece. The photo. Look at it from our point of view. It would be malpractice *not* to run it."

"Then I don't think we have anything more to say to one another." When he opened the gate, he heard Run's eager paws scrambling across the kitchen. She knew the sound of that gate and responded to it as though a juicy ribeye steak was making its way into the yard. She burst through the dog door and sprinted for him, rubbing her head and neck against his shins as he squatted. The motion-sensor light kicked on, bathing them in a soft glow.

"She's adorable," Anna said.

"Do you have a question for me, Ms. Downey?"

"C'mon, call me Anna."

He said nothing. She thought for a long time, Austin staring up at her as he pet Run's soft fur. He resented the fact that she'd ruined what would have been the best moment of his day. But what she'd said had him wondering: *what if she was right?* One thing he knew was that the behavior of killers was a lot less predictable than it looked on TV crime dramas. Even cold, calculating serial killers made mistakes, acted out of resentment, desperation, and sheer stupidity. And Anna was right that, on occasion, it was good for the public to know the details of a case in progress. Sometimes it led to tips that broke cases. So it was certainly possible that the photo would bring another break in the case. More often, stories like the one she was about to publish led killers to dispose of their victims and flee the state.

Anna leaned over the fence, her face half in the light, half in shadow. "You arrested Lorraine D'Antonia for the murder of Sonya Lopez in New York. She confessed to all the known murders committed by the so called Holiday Baby Butcher in Seattle. Johnathan Gruber, and three others, right?"

"Right."

"I guess my question is this: Is there any chance she was lying? Any chance you were wrong? Any chance the real killer has been on the loose this whole time?"

He stood and walked to the door. Run followed. In the doorway he paused just long enough to say, "No. There is no chance of that."

∾

Austin tossed and turned for an hour before falling into a restless, haunted sleep.

In his dreams, he saw bones.

First, the bones of Jonathan Gruber sitting in a bag next to Green Lake in Seattle. July Fourth weekend. Red, white, and blue, covered in stars and stripes, the bag floated through his mind like a ghost.

Next he saw the bones of Shaneequa Jackson. It was early April of 2015 and her bones had been found in an Easter Basket just south of Seattle's famous Pike Place market. He hadn't seen these bones in person, hadn't worked these cases. He only knew them from the photographs he'd seen when Lorraine D'Antonia emerged in New York a few years after going dark in Seattle.

Her victim was tiny Sonya Lopez, a premature baby who'd only been home from the hospital for six days when she went missing. The day after Christmas, a homeless man had found the bones outside a bodega in the Bronx, stuffed into a decorative holiday gift bag.

It was still dark out when Austin rolled out of bed and staggered to the kitchen. It was 5:30 AM, which meant he'd gotten maybe three hours of sleep. It would have to do. He put on a pot of coffee, watching jets of steam stream out from cracks in the plastic casing, and listening to the hisses and gurgles in the otherwise silent house. He needed a new coffee pot.

Run looked up at him expectantly. Her big eyes communicated an intelligence he'd never seen in a dog. He wasn't sure if it was because he'd grown more appreciative of animal intelligence, or if she was just a remarkable dog. Maybe both.

He knelt and gave her a treat, then nodded to the dog bed in the corner. "Bed."

She eyed the bag of treats, then reluctantly retreated to the bed and lay down.

He felt like he'd been gone for days, maybe weeks. He felt different, and yet Fiona's old plaque hung exactly where he'd left it on the wall.

Every single second,
Of every single day,
Every victim deserves my best.

He thought about her, about what she'd say if she knew he was chasing a clone of the Holiday Baby Butcher. Most likely, she'd tell him not to overthink it, to keep going to work, and to look up at the plaque whenever he got discouraged.

He wouldn't read the article, but by now Anna's story would have 'gone viral,' as Andy liked to say. The FBI would be on the line with Sheriff Daniels. National press would be on their way to Kitsap County. And, more importantly, if Joshua Green was still alive, his captor had a reason to become more unpredictable.

He poured himself a cup of coffee, watered it down with some cool water from the tap, and chugged it like a bottle of Gatorade after a long walk in the desert.

This was going to be a helluva day.

CHAPTER TWENTY-EIGHT

AUSTIN THOUGHT he'd be the first to arrive, but Ridley was already refilling his coffee cup when Austin walked in. Then he remembered that Ridley had slept in the office.

The first light of dawn had cut through the clouds, casting a dull gray light through the window and into the dingy conference room.

Ridley had texted Austin, Lucy, and Jimmy at six in the morning, telling them to get into the office as soon as possible. His plan was to get them all out in the field *before* Sheriff Daniels arrived and had the chance to slow them down or, worse, tell them to pass all their information to the FBI.

Austin had stopped into the café for five minutes before coming in, just long enough to chat with Andy—who was happy to be getting all the overtime hours, especially at such a slow time of year—and to set up Run's doggie bed behind the counter. He figured it was going to be another long one, and Run was well-behaved enough to hang out in the café while Andy worked. Most of the regulars knew her, and loved her as much as he did. Plus, she'd be the recipient of any special scraps he produced—a half slice of bacon here, a nibble of cheese there.

Without as much as a hello, Ridley began talking through

every lead, every angle, and dividing up the tasks for the day. He started with the address Trisha had been given in Seattle. As she'd said, it was a grocery store. Still, he'd asked a colleague in the SPD to head over there to ask some questions when they opened, in case there was some connection to the case.

A minor breakthrough had come from an early-morning call with Joshua Green's parents. When asked specifically about any nurses who might have struck them as odd, they remembered an older woman, late fifties or early sixties. Their description matched Trisha's, but came with a little more detail. The nurse they remembered was thin, with dark brown hair that looked dyed, and a sharp nose. They didn't remember the name Mary Bonner, but there was no doubt. They said she'd hovered a little too close, cared a little too much, asked a few too many questions. It had been the happiest day of their life, so it hadn't struck them as odd at the time. But in retrospect, she'd seemed much more interested in them and their child than the other nurses.

From the hospital, Ridley had received a photo of Mary Bonner, but it hadn't been a great help. They didn't store the ones taken for name badges permanently, so all they had was one their security team had pulled from hospital surveillance cameras. It was at a weird angle and, because she was wearing a face mask, not a lot of help. Still, it confirmed the description given by both Trisha and the Greens.

Lucy entered, carrying a massive Starbucks cup and whistling a tune.

"Lucy O'Latte," Austin offered, weakly.

Lucy offered a tired smile. "It's a mocha, but not a bad effort, New York."

Ridley's phone rang and Austin watched his face as he listened. Hopeful, then even more hopeful, then blank. Then a disappointed scowl.

Ridley ended the call. "TaskRabbit app finally came through. Once we gave them the name and address of Mary Bonner, their lawyers told them they could confirm that the account Trish was interacting with belonged to her." He paused, then suddenly struck the table with a single open palm, the sound echoing through the little room. "Bastards! If they'd told us that two days ago... just her name alone and we..." He squeezed his bald head together with both hands like he was trying to pop a watermelon in a strongman contest. "If Joshua Green dies..."

"He won't," Austin said. "We're close. Let's get back to it."

Ridley took a few deep breaths, then nodded in Austin's direction.

"Everything comes down to one thing," Austin said. "Location. We need to find Mary Bonner."

"I have something," Lucy said.

She paused when Jimmy came through the door carrying a Starbucks cup and one of those shaker bottles people bring to the gym. It was filled with some disgusting-looking liquid, greenish brown and slimy. "Sorry I'm late."

"It's 6:30 in the morning," Ridley said. "No one's late."

Austin noticed that Jimmy was wearing the same clothes as yesterday, khaki slacks and a blue jacket over a wrinkled white shirt. He also noticed that Jimmy didn't say anything to Lucy, didn't make eye contact.

Ridley waved in Lucy's general direction. "What do you have?"

"Five minutes ago," Lucy said. "Call from patrol outside Myrian Brightstone's house. She just got dropped off by an Uber."

"That's big," Austin said.

"I told them not to approach her, but not to let her leave. They said she was staggering like she was drunk—getting back from a bender—so she's probably passed out. I figure Austin and I head over there?"

Ridley nodded. "Jimmy, you're gonna head up the Hansville search. Every single house on or off NE 360th, then start spreading out from there. If we're lucky, we knock on a door and find Mary Bonner. Even if we're not, maybe someone saw her drop the bag of bones there for Trisha."

Jimmy nodded. "Speaking of Hansville. I wasn't going to bring this up, but Samantha emailed me this morning. It's a stretch, to be sure, but, well—"

"Spit it out," Ridley said.

"In the four hours since Anna Downey's article dropped, online discussion of the Lorraine D'Antonia case has exploded. Twitter, Reddit, Facebook, message boards, true crime sites, and so on."

Ridley waved him along like a man directing traffic. "As expected. So?"

"Right," Jimmy agreed. "But she ran a word usage AI, with an interesting result."

Austin stared at him. "What's that?" He couldn't help but notice what appeared to be the edge of a hickey barely visible when Jimmy turned and his shirt collar dipped slightly. Combined with the fact that Lucy, too, had a Starbucks cup, and that they'd arrived at almost the same time—spacing their entrances to appear as though they hadn't come together... Maybe their relationship wasn't as over as Lucy had made it sound.

"Ever seen those word cloud things?" Jimmy asked.

"No," Austin and Ridley said at once.

"Think of it like this: Samantha is able to use an AI to track common phrases and words in online discussions of the case, then compare it to word usages in known facts via the case files. Filtering out common words and phrases, like 'it' or the name of victims, for example."

"What's she looking for?" Austin asked.

"Anomalies. Words and phrases that don't belong. Essentially, it's using the wisdom of crowds to figure out if we're overlooking something."

Lucy took a loud sip of coffee. "'Anomalies' is a pretty big word for a meathead."

Jimmy ignored her comment, but gave her a raised-eyebrow look that confirmed Austin's suspicions. They were one of those on-and-off couples that were half passion, half derision.

"So," Jimmy continued, "no one outside this room, Trisha, and her lawyer know about the 360th Street thing yet. Everyone is talking about Hansville because Anna's story mentioned the location where the bones were found. But even when she *excluded* discussions posted *after* Anna's article came out, she found that Hansville came up way more than it should have, statistically speaking."

"What the hell does that mean?" Ridley asked, his annoyance matching Austin's. He knew the case as well as anyone, and Hansville had *never* come up. Before moving to New York, D'Antonia had kidnapped her victims in Seattle, killed them in Seattle, and left the bones in Seattle. As far as he knew, there was no connection between Lorraine D'Antonia and the sleepy little beach town he called home.

Jimmy stood up and pulled out his phone. "By itself, nothing. But when she started reviewing individual mentions... Here. Two years ago, a comment on a true crime message board: 'I went to high school with the Holiday Baby Butcher in Seattle and even spent a weekend at her parents' cabin in Hansville. Creepy AF.'"

"You're citing a random internet comment?" Austin asked, trying to keep the bite out of his tone. "There are no records of her parents having a cabin in Hansville. If there were, I would have found them."

Not to mention, he never would have moved there.

Jimmy took a big swig of coffee. "What about this, from September of this year: 'I met her parents, Maria and Mark D'Antonia, on a fishing trip in Hansville. Can't remember when, but they couldn't stop talking about their lovely adopted baby girl so it must've been right around the time they got her. I was fishing next to the parents of evil." He held up a hand before Austin could object. "On its own, it's not much."

"Not much?" Austin objected. "Maybe D'Antonia's parents

went fishing in Hansville once. Maybe they even had a little cabin there under a different name, or maybe it was a friend's cabin they used every now and then. How does that help us catch Mary Bonner?"

Ridley said, "It doesn't, but it's also not irrelevant, since the bones were both picked up and found in Hansville." He cocked his head to the side. "Hate to say it, but Jimmy's right." He stood and walked a slow lap around the conference table. "We need to find Mary Bonner. Today. Lucy and Austin, head out to see Myrian Brightstone." He waved in the direction of the bad photo of Bonner, which he'd taped to the wall. "Don't leave until you have either a good photo of her, or a sketch."

"Already have a sketch guy from the college on standby," Lucy said. "He said it's his kid's birthday, but he's ready."

"Jimmy, you and I will head out to Hansville. If Mary Bonner is there, we will find her. If she *was* there, we'll get her car, or something."

He looked at each of them, one by one. "We good?"

Austin tapped the table. "Let's do this."

CHAPTER TWENTY-NINE

ACCORDING TO THE GPS, they were five minutes from Myrian Brightstone's house when Lucy glanced at Austin with an odd look on her face, one he couldn't read. "Your wife was in law enforcement, too, right?'

"Assistant DA. So, not a cop, but yeah."

"A cop and a prosecutor. Quite the couple."

"Seemed to work for us. Why do you ask?"

"I know how she passed away, and I'm sorry, but can I ask you something?" She gripped the steering wheel nervously.

He thought he knew where this was headed. "About Jimmy?"

She smiled, embarrassed. "Can it work to have a couple in the same general line of work?"

Austin considered this. "Fiona and I never worked directly together. Same ballpark, but I only testified in her prosecutions a couple times. New York is a big town. Not like here."

Lucy swerved around a branch that had fallen onto the road. "What if you worked together every day?"

"Well, right now I'd take anything I could get. I'd spend the rest of my life dropping fries at McDonald's if she was standing next to me slapping pickles on burgers. But, I know what you're asking. And, no, I don't think it would've been good if we'd been working side by side."

"Why not?"

"My dad gave me one good piece of advice about women. He died when I was a teenager, just when I was starting to date. He told me, 'Find a woman who's as *different* from you as possible, while still sharing the same core values.'"

"So how was Fiona different?"

"She was more of a thinker—sometimes an over-thinker— I'm more of a charge-in-and-ask-questions-later kind of guy. She was a valedictorian, I lived by the motto: 'C's-get-degrees.' She liked to plan vacations down to the minute. I was fine to buy a ticket, throw some clothes in a duffel bag, and figure it out when we got there. I was impulsive, she was, well, not. We drove each other crazy for a while, but once we learned to appreciate each other..."

"Smooth sailing?"

Austin nodded. "Not that it was perfect, but we were lucky, and we both knew it. So, Jimmy?"

"He's... I don't know. What do you think?"

"Really can't say. Don't know him well."

She gave him a skeptical eyebrow raise. "You're a pretty good detective, and I've never met a detective who didn't take pride in getting a quick read on everyone they met."

Austin chuckled. "Well, let me ask you this: he slept at your place last night and—" when she held up a hand to object, he pushed it away. "Don't bother denying it. Like you said, I'm a pretty good detective."

She smiled. "We were together for a bit when he started. On and off since. We try not to make it obvious."

Austin chuckled. "You must not try very hard."

"So, what about him sleeping over?"

"Lemme ask you this: when you arrived, you knew Ridley wanted you in the office right away. You also knew you didn't want to come in at the exact same time. Part of your *ingenious* plan to hide your relationship?"

"Correct," she said, slowing long enough to wave at the guys in the patrol car sitting at the end of Myrian Brightstone's driveway, which was lined with mature trees. The house sat next to a small lake, its surface dappled by rainfall.

"So," Austin said, "who's idea was it for you to come in first?"

"What?"

"I mean, out in the parking lot, you got there at the same time after going to Starbucks together. You're nervous about your relationship being obvious. You had to decide who would go in first and who would wait a few minutes, then come in."

"What are you getting at?" Lucy parked the car in front of a gently-sloping lawn, which led toward the house.

Actually, toward the *mansion*. It was much too big for a single woman living on a nurse's salary. From the driveway, it looked to Austin to be around four-thousand square feet. A three-story Queen Anne with lake views, it looked like the setting for a cute bed-and-breakfast, not home to a party animal in her early-thirties.

He got out and caught Lucy's eye over the top of the car. "You're a good detective, what do *you* think I'm getting at?"

"I have no idea, but I remember, it was his idea for me to go in first."

"He knows you're a future leader," Austin said. "*Lucy O'Lieutenant*. He didn't want you to miss a moment. If someone had to be late, he wanted it to be him."

Lucy smiled and rapped the top of the car with her knuckles, then headed for the house.

"My read on him is that he's a decent guy," Austin said, following her. "I'm guessing you've had the thought that you're too smart for him at least once. Trust me, so has he. But I'll take a meathead with a good heart over a brilliant jerk any day. Plus, he seems to understand how technology works. If I ever date again, that'll be the number one quality I look for in a woman."

Lucy chuckled and, as they took the stairs to the wide porch, she pointed at the doorknob. It was polished bronze, and carved with an eagle. "Maybe we should be looking into her for money laundering or something."

"Family money?"

"Could be. Or house sitting."

Lucy rang the bell, which echoed loudly. Nothing.

Austin banged on the door. Nothing.

Lucy rang again. Still nothing.

Austin tried the door handle. Locked. "We know she's in there." He gave Lucy a wry look. "I have reason to believe she's in danger." He cocked his head, asking permission to bust through.

"Give it another sec," Lucy said, ringing the bell and pounding at the same time.

Austin stepped back, examining the door. He hadn't kicked one in for a couple years, and this one looked pretty damn sturdy. Five, maybe six inches of solid oak.

"You sure you can make it through?" Lucy asked.

He shrugged. "No, but there's only one way to find out."

"We've got reason enough," Lucy said. "Let's go."

Austin tensed, readying himself for the launch and kick.

"Wait." Lucy put her ear to the door. "Stairs."

Austin relaxed. Now he heard it. A creaking from the house. Then footsteps.

The creaking grew louder, then went quiet. The light behind the peephole changed just enough to let Austin know someone was peering through it. Then the door opened slowly with a long, sighing creak.

"Who the hell are you?" Myrian Brightstone's voice sounded like the croak of a sick bullfrog. A hoarse, throaty tone that Austin might've expected out of a chain smoking soldier on his deathbed, not the thirty-something that stood before them. She wore tight black pants and a sparkly red top, probably her clothes from the night before. Her makeup had been put on heavily, but had smeared over time leaving black lines on her cheeks near her eyes, and lipstick around her lips and across the side of her face.

Lucy said, "I'm Detective Lucy O'Rourke. This is Thomas Austin, a consultant on a case we're working. May we come in?"

"No." Brightstone swayed to the left, catching herself in the doorway before falling over. "I'm drunk as hell right now." She gripped the doorway with one hand and rubbed the heel of the other into her eye, further smearing her makeup. "Woke me up. What did you say you were here for?"

"We didn't say," Austin said. Under normal circumstances, he might have started with a slow build, striking a little fear into her by asking about why she'd disappeared from work. But time was not on their side. "Mary Bonner. Do you know where she is?"

"You're kinda cute," Brightstone said, her words barely comprehensible. Then she looked at Lucy. "You are, too, but I'm looking for a sugar daddy. Oh, I'm going to get fired alright." Then, as though her brain had finally processed the question, she said, "Mary? I know her. Yeah."

"Do you know where she is?" Lucy asked.

Brightstone shook her head.

"Do you know if she has a residence other than her apartment in Bremerton?"

"*Pfft*...I'm not friends with her."

"We know that," Lucy said, pulling out her phone. She held up screenshots of the Facebook post Samantha had found. "You bullied her online."

Brightstone glanced at the phone, shrugged. "I'm kind of a bitch. It's, like, my thing. I don't give a rat's ass." She leaned in closer, eyes moving heavily as though she was struggling to read the post. Then she laughed. "No lie detected. She's weird as hell."

"How so?" Austin asked.

She licked her lips in what was possibly the least-seductive gesture Austin had ever seen. "Listen, I broke up with my boyfriend last week. So, if you have any interest I..."

"That why you've been missing work?" Lucy asked. "Seems like you've been on a bit of a bender."

"I used to D.J. Parents made me go to nursing school. Only let me live here if I hold down a job." She scratched her head suddenly, forcefully, like some invisible fly had landed on it. "Act responsibly and all that."

"Mary Bonner," Austin insisted. "How was she odd?"

"Just distant. I mean, she's old enough to be my mom and too old to have her own children. Super-obsessed with the babies and—"

Austin's attention dropped to his phone, vibrating in his pocket. He had a new text from Anna:

I feel bad about the photo. So here's something, a tip: cabin on Heron Avenue in Hansville. You on that yet?

Brightstone wagged a finger at him drunkenly. "Um, excuse-a-*MWAH*, but it's kinda rude to read a text in the middle of a conversation, ya know?"

"Sorry," Austin said, "I... let's finish this up."

Lucy asked, "When did you last see Mary Bonner?"

"Whenever it was I last worked with her. Week ago, maybe."

"We noticed there are no photos of her online, none that we can find anyway."

"She didn't like to be photographed. Probably because she was..." Brightstone cackled. "*That's* why she was so weird. She had a head wound. Someone beat her with the ugly stick."

"Is this her?" Lucy held up the hospital surveillance photo. Brightstone nodded.

"Are you certain she's not on any social media?"

"I mean, I don't get all in her business, but she's old, right?"

Austin asked, "She's never mentioned a weekend house, a cabin, maybe Hansville, Heron Avenue?"

Brightstone just shook her head, humming some odd tune as

though they weren't there. Then suddenly, she said, "Wait here. I might have something."

She staggered back up the creaky staircase, leaving the door open.

Austin showed Lucy the text.

After reading it twice, she said, "Screenshot it, send it to Jimmy and Ridley, then write her back and ask for more details."

Austin did so and, by the time he'd finished, Brightstone was back, and she seemed to be holding a stack of photos. "Christmas party a couple years ago. I was in my ironic-retro Polaroid phase... anyway... Mary would come and, like, pretend to be a person for an evening. She didn't like to be in photos, but..." She sorted through the stack of photos, squinting at them as she placed one on top of another. "Boom! I knew it." She held up a photo.

Austin took it in. The shock hit him first, then the confusion, then the horror.

Lucy turned to him, eyes wide. "What the hell is going on?"

CHAPTER THIRTY

JIMMY WAS on his sixth house when he saw something strange. The rain was coming down in buckets now, filtering through the heavy tree cover and pounding the roof of his car with irregular splashes. A white SUV was parked halfway up a long driveway, maybe thirty yards from the house he was there to check out, the second to last on his list.

He pulled up beside it and rolled down the window. Empty. Why would someone park halfway up a driveway in this kind of weather? He checked the tires; they didn't appear to be stuck in the mud.

Continuing up the driveway, he parked beside a small raised-bed garden that looked like it hadn't been tended in a decade. The place was somewhere between a small house and a large cabin—a single-story of maybe eight-hundred square feet. It faced east and was only about twenty yards from a bank that dropped down to the beach fifty feet below. There was no other car at the house, though the attached one-car garage probably explained that.

When he stepped out of the car, his boots dropped into an inch of mud. "Damnit." He dragged them across a little patch of grass as he made his way to the porch, which was covered by a sagging vinyl awning. The place looked deserted. The curtains were drawn and no light shone through the little window at the top of the front door.

He knocked loudly.

Many of the houses back in these woods were only seasonally occupied, either by Seattle families looking for a summer getaway, or older snowbirds who lived in Arizona or California for the winter and came back for the gorgeous Pacific Northwest summers. In fact, half of the houses he'd checked already had been left vacant for the winter. The others had provided little help. One woman thought she might have seen Trisha's truck on the morning she left the bones on the beach, but not a single person knew Mary Bonner or recognized her photo.

Jimmy stood on his tiptoes and peered through the frosted window. No movement.

He listened carefully. Not a peep from inside the house. Just the whooshing of the trees above him.

He knocked again. Still nothing.

According to the records, the cabin was owned by a Mr. and Mrs. Houghton. Sounded old, Jimmy thought. No doubt they were golfing in Phoenix right now, or sipping Mai Tai's in Kona. He and Lucy had talked once about getting a little condo in Kona. Later—the third or fourth time she'd broken up with him —she'd dismissed that as pillow talk. But after last night...

He let his mind wander to the warm beach, sitting with Lucy in the sand, matching flip flops and margaritas. She'd have her curly red hair tied up into a bun. He'd swim every day. Hell, maybe they'd even learn to surf.

He shook his head. She'd probably break up with him again tomorrow. And he needed to keep his mind on the job.

He stepped away from the door, planning to head around back. He noticed something on the ground. It was just under the old vinyl awning that extended a few feet from the house. Mostly dry, its cover splattered with a little muddy rain, it was a notebook.

He crouched, opened it.

He read the words written in neat cursive on the inside flap of the cover:

Anna Downey, reporter. Reward if found and returned.

CHAPTER THIRTY-ONE

IN THE FOREGROUND of the polaroid, three women held up what looked like shots of tequila in a dimly lit bar, their faces illuminated by a camera flash that made them look unnaturally bright in the dark room. Austin recognized Myrian Brightstone, though not the two other women.

Sitting in a barstool to Brightstone's left, just outside the range of the flash, was The Holiday Baby Butcher. Her face largely shadowed, her hand was blurred, raised up to right under her chin as though she'd been reaching up to block her face.

It couldn't be her, but there she was. Her hair was a different color, darker brown and cut short. But it was the same lean, bony face that had haunted Austin's dreams. The same sharp nose and chin. And the eyes. He could have picked those cruel, dead eyes out of a lineup. If that wasn't Lorraine D'Antonia, it was a woman who'd had a lot of cosmetic surgery to look like her.

The covered porch protected them from what had become a heavy rainfall, and Austin turned away from the door to hold the photo in the little light that crept through. "How the hell—"

"I know, f'ugly right?" Brightstone said. "What did she do, anyway?"

"When was it taken?" Austin demanded.

"Christmas, two years ago."

"And *this* is Mary Bonner?" Lucy asked.

"Sure is."

Austin studied the photo, looking from the face of Mary Bonner to the two women doing shots next to Brightstone. "They are..."

"Jessie Johnson and uhh...." Brightstone scratched her head. "Marcia something. She only worked there like six months."

"Can we have this?" Lucy asked.

"Sure, but—"

Lucy stuffed a card into Brightstone's hand. "Call me if you think of anything else she's ever said to you that might be relevant to finding her." She grabbed the photo and leapt down from the porch.

Austin jogged after her, joining her in the car.

"What the hell is going on?" Lucy asked.

Austin looked again at the photo. It was odd, on first glance he'd been sure it was Lorraine D'Antonia. But the longer he looked, the more subtle differences he saw. The hair was the most obvious difference, but there was something different in the faces, too. Not in the shape or bone structure, those looked remarkably similar. But something about the complexion, the skin. D'Antonia had clear skin, not pale but not especially tanned. Like she'd spent a lot of time inside. Bonner, on the other hand, looked a little more worn, her skin a little more leathery, like she'd spent a good deal of time working outside or, more likely, under the bright lamps of a tanning bed.

When he didn't reply, Lucy said, "What I don't get is, what are the odds of having a woman who looks somewhat like D'Antonia drop the bones on the beach, then finding another woman who looks exactly like her working at the hospital where the missing kids were born? I mean, what the hell is going on here?"

"I don't know," Austin said. "Best guess, this is a woman obsessed with the case, and crazy as hell. Probably already looked like her and got cosmetic surgeries, then started copying her kidnappings, her murders. A lot of serial killers have had copycats. She's just taking it to a new level."

Lucy was dialing her phone. "Ridley, check out the photo Austin is sending you."

He snapped a picture and texted it to Ridley.

Lucy waited. "You get it yet?" She listened. "Right. We know." She tapped her phone, putting it on speaker.

Ridley's deep voice filled the car. "We've had two officers at Mary Bonner's apartment all day. Nothing. Hospital administrator says she still hasn't shown up for work. I'll send this to Samantha and have her edit for the clearest version we can get and spread it far and wide. I'll call Sheriff Daniels. This isn't something I can keep from him. Obviously, the FBI profile team needs to see it as well."

Austin asked, "Either of you seen a case where a copycat gets cosmetic surgery to look more like a perp?"

Lucy shook her head.

"No," Ridley said, but there are other options. "Austin, how sure are you that D'Antonia doesn't have a sister?"

"I went deep into her background. She was adopted, but no record of any sister."

Lucy asked, "And the other option?"

Ridley let out a long stream of air. "Ridiculous as this sounds, maybe that's not Lorraine D'Antonia in prison right now."

The thought had crossed Austin's mind in the same way a dozen ridiculous notions crossed his mind every week before he dismissed them. If Lorraine D'Antonia had escaped from prison, she'd somehow found someone who looked like her to take her spot. Not possible. "That was her on the video. You spoke with her. It *was* her."

"I know," Ridley said. "I know. It's insane. It's either the most obsessed copycat ever, or a sister no one knows about."

A long-buried thought about D'Antonia's upbringing wiggled from the edge of his brain to the center until it crowded out everything else. What if he'd missed something? Then he remembered the article about the adoption agency that Jimmy had mentioned.

"What about the Heron Avenue thing?" Lucy asked.

"No houses listed to Bonner, or D'Antonia, or any members of either of their families. Probably just Anna doing crazy Anna stuff. That woman is relentless. The house was on Jimmy's list to check out today, though. He may have already crossed it off the list."

Austin's phone dinged with another text from Anna Downey.

It was only a single word.

Help.

CHAPTER THIRTY-TWO

SHIELDING the notebook from the rain, Jimmy flipped through the pages. The first page listed Anna Downey's phone number, email address, and a mailing address for her newspaper.

Jimmy stuffed the notebook in his back pocket, then grabbed the radio on his belt. "Ridley, this is Jimmy, over." He waited. The crackling of the radio mingled with the sound of the rain as a cold breeze chilled his face. His eyes were on the house, darting from the door to the window. Not a single sign of life. "Ridley, this is Jimmy, over."

He checked his cellphone. No service.

He tried again. "Ridley, this is Jimmy. I found an abandoned vehicle and the notebook of Anna Downey at the Heron Street address. Requesting backup. Over."

"Ji-immy... I... what...." He was pretty sure that was Ridley's voice, but it was choppy and sporadic.

"Requesting backup at the Heron Street address. Off 360th. Over."

"Give... wait... the... over. I..."

Jimmy clipped the radio back to his belt. From Ridley's garbled reply, it seemed as though he'd heard him. Ridley and two other officers were also knocking on doors in the neighborhood and would be less than five minutes out. He had no special fondness for Anna Downey. But something was wrong. In fact— it hit him like a slap to the face—if Anna had shown up here and left her car and notebook, there was a chance Joshua Green was in that house. Alive. Right now.

He thought about Lucy. Lying in bed last night, she'd asked, "Why do you do this job, really?" He'd made a wisecrack of some sort, but finally admitted he really didn't know. His dad was a cop, his uncles were state troopers, his mom was a cop. He'd never really thought about it. But it was this right here. Moments like this. *This* is why he'd become a police officer. He couldn't wait for Ridley.

He crept around the side of the house, past the garage. The area had been cleared of trees, so the heavy rainfall pounded him, soaking him through to the skin in seconds.

On the back of the house, facing the Puget Sound, was a large picture window. The curtains were drawn. No light. No sign of life.

He heard something faint, a whistle, or maybe a bird. He spun around. Had it come from behind him? No, perhaps it had come from the house, but between the heavy rain and wind, it was difficult to tell.

He moved closer to the window. Leaned in. No sound from inside.

He crept around to the other side of the house, where a rusty screen door hung half off its hinge. He moved toward it. Another sound. Not a bird. It was a single, solitary squeal, like his baby nephews made seemingly at random, sometimes in delight, sometimes in discomfort. But he had no doubt: it was the sound of a baby.

He froze for half a second, unsure of what to do. Lucy would tell him to head back to the car, wait for backup. But Lucy herself would probably not follow that advice. He pulled back the screen and banged on the thin wooden door. "Kitsap County police, open up."

Nothing. No more cries. Not another sound.

He tried the doorknob. Locked.

It was a thin wooden door, likely the same one that had been installed when this cabin was built in the eighties. The paint had been worn away by rain and age, exposing a grainy pine that had seen better days.

He glanced back at his car.

Then he heard another cry, this one sharper, more pained. A different tone.

Not a baby. An adult.

CHAPTER THIRTY-THREE

LUCY FLOORED it down Myrian Brightstone's driveway and didn't slow as she raced past the officers staking out the house.

After forwarding Anna's second message to Ridley and Jimmy, Austin punched Heron Avenue into the GPS. They were thirty minutes away.

"Call her," Lucy barked, accelerating around a truck on the winding road and passing it in the left lane.

Austin dialed Anna, but it went straight to voicemail.

Next he called Ridley. His number went straight to voicemail as well. The cell reception in Hansville was spotty, but it wasn't non-existent. It was possible Ridley would hit a strong signal and the texts would come through even as the calls went to voicemail.

Lucy connected to Ridley's channel on the radio. "Ridley, it's Lucy, over."

Surprisingly, he was there in an instant. "Lucy. You heard from Jimmy? I just got a weird, garbled message from him. He requested backup, but I couldn't hear where he was. Even the radios are spotty out here."

Her eyes showed fear when she glanced at Austin. "Did you see the text? Over."

"No. Over."

"Heron Avenue," she said. "He's gotta be at the Heron Avenue house. Get there now. Over." Lucy swerved around a motorcycle and hit seventy miles an hour as she merged onto the highway.

Next Austin called the number of the *Kitsap Union* and, after a bit of a runaround, got connected to Anna's editor. After introducing himself, Austin said, "She might be in trouble. Do you know how and why she ended up at a Heron Avenue address in Hansville?"

The editor was skeptical. "She was working all kinds of angles on that story."

"You didn't answer my question."

"You served—what?—twenty years in the NYPD?"

"Yeah," Austin barked.

"And you think I'll explain one of my reporter's stories to you? Her sources?"

"She texted us for help, you jackass. She's in danger."

The editor seemed to consider this for a minute. The part of Austin that was inclined to think the worst of journalists assumed he was considering which would be better for sales: one of his reporters getting a scoop about the case, or one of his reporters dying in pursuit of that scoop. He'd known editors to make such calculations in the past.

"I'll tell you, but you have to send me screenshots of her texts. Just in case."

"Fine, fine," Austin said, impatiently.

"Now, please."

Austin spoke through gritted teeth. "Does it strike you as odd that when she needed help, she wrote to us and not you?"

He said nothing. He wasn't going to budge. Austin got his email address and quickly sent screenshots of her texts. After the editor had reviewed them, he said, "Can't believe she offered you the tip on Heron Avenue, but, well, nobody's perfect."

"Get to it!" Austin commanded.

"Early this morning, she said that she'd been poring over old property ownership documents through the night. She was working on a follow-up to the story with the photo, trying to answer the question, why Hansville of all places?"

"Okay, okay..."

Lucy performed a series of lane changes right out of a racing video game, swerving to the right to pass cars clogging up the left lane, then cutting back in front of them and passing a semi by veering off onto the shoulder.

"Told me it was just a hunch," the editor continued, "but in the 1980s, the Houghton family bought a cabin in Hansville, off 360th there. Heron Avenue. More like Heron Dirt Road, but still. Anna went to high school with a girl last named Houghton. Never saw that cabin, they lived over in Poulsbo, but a lot of people owned little cabins back then. Everything was dirt cheap."

Lucy hit the gas, topping ninety.

"And?" Austin asked.

"Point was, she said she looked into it on a few ancestry pages and Houghtons are cousins to the Bonner family in Seattle. Maybe second cousins. I don't know. Point is: Mary Bonner, one of the missing nurses, is related to a family that owns property on Heron Avenue."

Austin ended the call and slammed the phone down on his thigh. "How the hell did I miss it?"

The rain was coming in sheets now and, even with the wipers at top speed, the view out the front windshield was a watery mess. "We all missed it," Lucy said. "Where is Heron Avenue in relation to the street where Trisha picked up the bones?"

"Heron is a tiny dirt road that extends east toward the water. Quarter mile, half at most, from where she picked up the bones."

Lucy swerved into the left lane, passing a truck before cutting back into the right lane to pass an SUV. "So the chances that this is a coincidence are—"

"Zero. Mary Bonner kidnapped Allie Shreever, held her at the Heron Avenue cabin, killed her, and left the bones for Trisha to pick up. Then she kidnapped Joshua Green. My guess is that she's got him there now." He swallowed the burnt-toast dread in his throat. "If we're not too late."

CHAPTER THIRTY-FOUR

JIMMY STEPPED BACK and swung his size-twelve boot toward the door with a violent thrust. The heel struck just under the doorknob, cracking the frame but not breaking the door all the way open.

Leaping back, then lunging forward shoulder first, he crashed through the door, landing on a linoleum floor. He leapt up, eyes darting around the small, dark room. He smelled the sweet, buttery aroma of sugar cookies. The only light spilled in through the broken door, a soft gray glow revealing a little stove and a kitchen table. A few papers were scattered on the table, plus a notebook and...

Despite the cold, perspiration broke out on his forehead. Next to the notebook was a red and white Christmas gift bag.

Through the door next to the stove was a sofa, probably the living room. "Anyone there?" he shouted, pulling his firearm. "Police. Identify yourself."

Eyes on the door to the living room, he called again. "Kitsap County police. If anyone is here, get on the ground, arms and legs spread out."

Everything was silent. Had he imagined the sounds? Maybe they'd been here and left in another car. The wind had been racing through the trees, howling in its own way. Perhaps his ears had been playing tricks on him.

Eyes still on the door, he reached for the Christmas bag with his free hand. It appeared to be empty. Next to it, a folder caught his eye for half a second. It was labeled Johnson Hill Orphanage. The same orphanage that had handled the Lorraine D'Antonia adoption.

A sharp, pained cry erupted from the living room.

Then a muffled shout.

A baby's squeal.

"Kitsap County police. I will shoot you. Get on the ground, arms and legs spread out, and you will make it out of here alive."

He stepped slowly across the kitchen. Reaching the doorway, he peered into the living room. A blonde woman was tied to a chair on the far end. Anna Downey. He watched her eyes dart to her left, his right.

He turned, but it was too late.

The chef's knife was halfway into his belly by the time he looked up into the cold, vacant eyes of The Holiday Baby Butcher.

CHAPTER THIRTY-FIVE

AUSTIN AND LUCY were only ten minutes from the house when Jimmy's voice appeared on the radio. "Heron Avenue. Officer down." He sounded like a tired, ragged version of himself. His voice had lost all its usual confidence and vigor. "Stab wound to the belly. Anna Downey being held by... someone. Looked exactly like Lorraine D'Antonia. But dark hair. Heard a baby. Did not see. Repeat: Joshua Green likely alive but did not confirm. Over."

Lucy was speeding down Hansville Highway through sheets of rain, hands gripping the wheel so tight her knuckles were turning white.

After a bunch of cross-chatter, including Ridley ordering an ambulance and saying he was only a minute away, Lucy punched the radio button. "Jimmy, this is Lucy. You are okay. We will be there soon. Over." She waited. "Jimmy, say something. Over."

Austin said, "Jimmy, hold the wound edges together to control the bleeding, and try not to move, unless you can reposition yourself to help close the wound."

Ridley's voice came on next. "Jimmy, hold on. Ambulance was in the area for another call. Two minutes out. What else did you see? Jimmy?"

"Jimmy?" Lucy shouted.

They sat for what seemed like an eternity, radio silent. The rain stopped suddenly as they began heading down into Hansville.

Everything was silent except for the whoosh of the tires on the wet road.

Lucy had tears in her eyes. "Jimmy. Say something damnit!"

"Suspect fled. Heard ca- car start." A long pause. "Possibly white SU... SUV." Another pause. "Look on.. table. Ev- ev- ev... idence. Bag. Folder. Adoption ag- ag- a-. Oh, no."

A clatter, then silence. The radio dropping to the floor.

～

The ambulance beat them to the scene. When Lucy pulled to a stop in the muddy driveway and leapt out, paramedics already had Jimmy in the back. Before they could get a look, the doors slammed shut and the ambulance peeled away.

Ridley met them on the porch.

"Did you get a look?" Lucy asked. "How was he?" Austin thought she was trying to sound calmer than she actually was.

Ridley grimaced. "Puncture wound to the belly. Not good. If the ambulance wasn't nearby..." he shook his head. "Even so, the blood loss..." He looked at the ground. "He'd passed out. Didn't say anything."

"But he was alive?" Lucy asked.

Ridley nodded. "Barely."

"Out of our hands now," Austin said. "Best thing we can do is catch her so when he gets out of surgery—alive—we can deliver good news."

"We've set up a blockade at Eglon Road. No one is leaving Hansville without being stopped. Based on the timing, we think she's still on the peninsula. We've got every available officer on the way. They will knock on every door, talk to every resident."

Hansville was twenty-eight square miles, only a little bigger than Manhattan, but with a tenth of one percent of the population. He had no doubt they'd be able to find her if she was in someone's house, but... "What about the woods and beaches?"

"Should we involve the community?" Lucy asked.

Ridley sighed. "It's a tough one. If this were simply a missing person, then yeah. But do we want old ladies combing the forests for a murderer?"

"Teams," Austin said. "Teams of twenty or thirty, walking every park, every patch of forest. We can organize it at my place."

"Okay, but let's check out the house first." Ridley led them into the bloody scene in the living room. Jimmy had lost a lot of blood, assuming it was all his.

Austin's read of the scene said it was. "So, Jimmy approaches the house, sees Anna's SUV. He knocks and no one answers."

"How do you know Bonner didn't let him in?" Lucy asked.

"The chill in the air." He led her into the kitchen and pointed at the broken door. "Figured a door or window had been busted." Returning to the living room, he added, "Plus, Jimmy wrestled in high school, right?"

Lucy nodded.

"Six-feet, maybe a hundred eighty pounds of pure muscle? No way Mary Bonner overpowers him if they're face to face. No way she gets the jump on him." He pointed at the front door. "So, Jimmy knocks, no one answers. He hears something, sees something, or maybe figures out Anna is in there because of her car. He breaks down the side door, sees the kitchen, sees Anna through the doorway. She's likely had her mouth gagged so she can't warn him, he walks into the living room and..." he pointed at the empty crib next to the fireplace, "Joshua is there and Mary Bonner is hiding there, behind the door." Austin went back to the kitchen and slowly walked through the doorway, pretending to hold a gun. "As he walks through the doorway, he spots the crib. I'm guessing that's what distracted him. He sees Bonner out of the corner of his eye, turns and BAM, the knife is in his stomach." He dropped to his knees, holding his stomach. "Gun falls out of his hands and slides..." He crawled over to the couch. "Here." He lay flat on his belly and shined his cell phone's flashlight under the couch, revealing Jimmy's firearm.

Lucy knelt beside him and peered at the gun. "Damn, you're good."

Austin stood. "Done this a couple times."

"Don't touch it," Ridley said. "We'll bag it later. So we know what we're dealing with. Mary Bonner is older, but fit, strong, and not afraid to kill a cop. No knife here, so she has it with her."

"Probably used it to threaten Anna," Lucy said. "Get her to drive."

When they walked into the kitchen, Austin almost doubled-over, sick to his stomach. It wasn't the bag that did it. He'd seen that right away. What he hadn't seen was the canning pot, silver and glimmering on the small stove. In all his time investigating Lorraine D'Antonia, they'd never found physical evidence of what she did with the bodies.

Ridley was at the table. "Bag is empty. Poem in this notebook. On the radio, didn't Jimmy say something about a folder, something about the orphanage?"

"He did." Austin scanned the floor and kitchen counter. "Maybe she grabbed it when she bolted, but why grab that and not the bag, right next to it?"

Ridley flared his temples. "She made the transition. Her focus is no longer on her sick and twisted manner of killing. It's on not getting caught. Something in those papers would have helped us catch her. Either way, Mary Bonner is somewhere in Hansville."

"And we're going to find her," Lucy said.

Austin took one more look around the kitchen. The Christmas gift bag on the table, the notebook with the poem, the canning pot. Jimmy said he'd heard a baby cry, which meant Joshua was alive, or at least that he had been an hour ago.

He nodded to Lucy. "You're damn right we're going to find her."

CHAPTER THIRTY-SIX

THEY'D BEEN SEARCHING in vain for six hours when Austin returned to the café for a break. "Andy, coffee please."

Andy handed him a tall paper cup of black coffee. "You look like hell, boss."

Run bolted out from behind the counter, where Austin had set up her doggie bed that morning. It seemed like days ago.

Austin swigged the coffee, then sat on the floor, exhausted. "Calm down, Run. It's okay."

Run leapt into his lap, whined, then barked in his face. She jumped up and ran across the room and pushed the side of her body against the space where the floor met the wall, rubbing her nose and twisting her head as though she were trying to dry herself off. She hopped back from the wall, held still for a moment, then barked loudly before diving into Austin's lap, where she began whining softly and licking under his chin.

"What has gotten into you, you silly pup? I've not been around much the past few days, have I? Settle, settle."

He pet behind Run's ears and she finally calmed down, curled into a ball and let out a deep sigh, then yawned. It was an odd thing to think about, but Austin realized that the last few days were the most time they'd spent apart since he'd found her at the rescue shelter the week he'd moved to Hansville. It seemed like the day had been as stressful for her as it had been for him.

"Been going door to door," Austin said, "checking abandoned cabins and beach shacks. Safe to say I'm tired."

All he wanted to do was head back into his apartment, flop onto the couch with Run, have a beer, and turn on a game. There was no football today, but he didn't care. He'd take bowling or competitive darts at this point. But there was no time for breaks.

Andy had set up their commercial coffee maker near the entryway, along with hundreds of paper cups. He'd also set out a few dozen pre-made sandwiches, along with muffins and Christmas donuts they'd special ordered to last them through the holidays. The café was being used as a launching point for the search teams, which Andy had helped organize along with local residents who ran the town's Facebook group.

Andy filled the reservoir of the coffee maker from a large pitcher of water. "Anything yet?"

Austin shook his head. "They've talked to maybe a quarter of the houses in town. A couple joggers thought they saw a white SUV around the right time, but that's it. Say it was heading this way from 360th, but that ain't much. Lead detective wants me to go to the hospital, talk to Jimmy. Leave the hunt to them. With the volunteers, they've got a hundred people on it."

Andy walked around the counter, carrying another tray of sandwiches. "It's a small town. She's gotta be somewhere."

As Andy stacked the sandwiches, Austin grabbed one off the top. "Only way out is by boat or on the one road, which they had blocked within two minutes of Jimmy's radio call. Assuming Jimmy made that call the moment she left, there's no way she made it past the blockade. It's impossible. She's either in Hansville or she's on a boat. She's sixty, having to manipulate a younger, stronger captive, and a baby. I doubt she's in a boat." He shook his head. "I think she's close by. It's only a matter of time." He was trying to stay positive, but the fact that she was cornered was not necessarily a plus. Trapping a killer was usually a good thing, but when the killer held two hostages, it got more complicated. A lot could go wrong.

He gave Run one last pet, then shooed her away and headed for his car.

~

Austin hated hospitals. He'd spent three weeks in one after the shooting that killed Fiona. He received two different surgeries for his wounds and took enough pain meds to leave him numb. More than once, he thought the only way he'd leave the hospital was in a box. Once or twice, he'd wished it had been him who'd taken the fatal bullet instead of Fiona.

When he'd finally been rolled out into a cold fall day, he'd been awed by the simple beauty of New York City in the fall and he'd vowed not to enter another hospital until he was at death's door. And maybe not even then.

The smell was what got to him. Antiseptic, and somehow smelling of disease and death at the same time.

The presence of Sheriff Daniels standing outside Jimmy's door didn't make it any better. "Well," he said, arms crossed, blocking the door to Jimmy's room, "if it isn't our New York cowboy."

"How's Jimmy?"

"Alive. Barely." He let out a long breath. "He's going to live."

"Can I see him?"

Daniels scoffed. His cheeks were pale, not their usual red. It seemed even *he* laid off the bottle when one of his officers was wounded.

"You may not like me," Austin said. "But... look... Ridley sent me. He mentioned some evidence that may have been at the scene. And we couldn't find it. It could be important to locating Mary Bonner. I really need to talk to him."

"He *can't* talk. He was in surgery for five hours as they tried to put his intestines back together with duct tape, you arrogant asshole."

"I'm sorry."

"You *should* be. Whole time you've been telling us 'copycat, copycat.' Turns out Mary Bonner is *directly* connected to your Holiday Baby Butcher, and has been the whole damn time." The words were accompanied by spittle flying in Austin's general direction.

As much as Austin wanted to slap the guy, he was more confused than anything. "What do you mean?"

"Our tech intern—what's her name? Suzanne or something?"

"Samantha."

"She handed this to me on the way out the door." Daniels pulled a folded piece of paper from his back pocket and slapped it into Austin's chest. "You screwed up. This case, the original Lorraine D'Antonia case. Maybe both. And it almost cost Jimmy his life. Best case scenario, he'll be eating through a straw and shitting into a bag for months."

Austin took the paper.

Daniels gave him one last look of disdain, then sauntered down the hall. Austin watched him go, then slumped into an uncomfortable chair in the hallway and unfolded the paper. It was an article from the *Seattle Times*, printed off the internet.

The headline read:

Johnson Hill Orphanage Settles Case of Illegal Placements from 1970s

He scanned the opening paragraph once, then again.

Oh, No.

He'd considered what it meant for Mary Bonner to have had papers from the same orphanage as Lorraine D'Antonia, but figured it was another piece of her obsession.

As he read the article, it turned out it was something else entirely.

Something far, far worse.

PART 3

THE TRUTH

CHAPTER THIRTY-SEVEN

AS HE READ THE ARTICLE, Austin felt the walls of the hospital closing in around him.

Johnson Hill Orphanage Settles Case of Illegal Placements from 1970s

Only four days before the trial was set to begin, Johnson Hill Orphanage of Seattle settled a decades-old dispute with a group of plaintiffs who claimed the organization misled them in the 1970s. The case stemmed from three dozen placements of twins, and four placements of triplets, all occurring between 1971 and 1974.

According to court filings, the plaintiffs—who sought over $40 million in damages—alleged that the orphanage misled them when servicing their adoptions. Specifically, they were never told that the children they were adopting were parts of twin or triplet sets.

When revelations of separated twins and triplets began to emerge in the early-2000s, according to court filings, Johnson Hill claimed that it was difficult to place twins and triplets, which was the reason for the separation.

However, files discovered only recently show that, in fact, the twins and triplets had been intentionally separated in a controversial study conducted by psychiatrists Sandra D. Conrad and Mark Voohrees.

The study involved placing the separated twins and triplets with families having different parenting styles and levels of wealth and status. While one twin would be placed, for example, in an upper-class family, the other would be placed in a lower-class family. In one case, triplets were placed with three different families who had indicated wildly-varied parenting styles on their applications, ranging from "strict military disciplinarians" to "laissez-faire hippies," according to the unpublished study. And while the adoptive parents agreed to have their children studied, the full extent of the experiment was never explained to them, according to the lawsuit.

Byron Moskovitz, a researcher in clinical psychology at the University of Washington, believes the experiment—while perhaps not illegal in the 1970s—was a wild departure from the norms, and an egregious breach of trust. "In essence," Moskovitz said, "this was a nature versus nurture experiment on unwilling human subjects."

The plaintiffs, who sued in civil court, claim that Johnson Hill destroyed and falsified records for years to cover up the shared parentage of the separated twins and triplets. The true intent of the study—which was never published—only came to light recently when children of psychiatrist Mark Voohrees donated his papers to his alma mater upon his death.

The amount of the settlement has not yet been disclosed.

Austin stared at the article for a long time, his eyes soft and unfocused, turning the paper into a black and white blur. His mouth had gone dry as he read the article. The room had closed in around him. He couldn't believe it, and yet it explained so much.

Mary Bonner was Lorraine D'Antonia's twin sister.

His phone vibrated in his pocket. In a daze, he pulled it out.

"How's Jimmy?" Ridley's voice brought him back to himself.

"Couldn't see him." His words sounded strange, like he was observing himself from outside his body. The implications of the article were too big to take in all at once. "Five hours of surgery. Daniels was here. Sounds like Jimmy will make it."

"Good, that's good. If he hadn't made it..."

"I know. I... I screwed up."

"I know you had a run-in with Daniels, but he's just looking for someone to blame. This isn't on you."

"I appreciate that, but in some ways this *is* on me. Has anyone talked with the slip owners? Any boats missing? Or is it possible she had her own boat?"

"We checked the slip registrations," Ridley said. "Nothing in Mary Bonner's name, or in the Houghton name, the owners of the cabin. A boat is missing, though. We've got people looking for it."

He was going to tell Ridley about the article when he heard a commotion in the background of the call. It sounded like people were shouting, but more in excitement than in anger.

Ridley's voice came from faraway, like the phone had dropped from his face. "Right. Where? I'll be right there. No one touches anything." Then his normal voice was back. "Austin, we found the car."

"You did?" Austin perked up immediately. It was the first good news of the day.

But Ridley did not sound pleased. "At the boat launch next to Point No Point."

"So why do you sound like this is bad news?"

Ridley paused, and Austin could almost see him running a hand over his bald head. "Because it's six feet underwater."

CHAPTER THIRTY-EIGHT

THE BACK of Anna Downey's white SUV peeked out of the water as Austin pulled up to the boat launch. He watched from fifty yards away, leaning on a chain link fence as a burly tow truck driver steadily reeled it in with an electric crank.

The rear windshield slowly came into full view. Austin held his breath, trying to find the serenity he found sitting alone in the little church. A cold wind blasted his cheek and he pulled up the collar of his jacket, waiting as the car slowly, slowly emerged from the water.

He didn't pray anymore, but if he did he'd be praying that the car was empty. Praying that it didn't contain the drowned bodies of Anna Downey or Joshua Green.

The ride from the hospital had been hell.

He'd spoken with Lucy, updated her about Jimmy, and learned that teams had now knocked on two-thirds of the doors in Hansville. In addition, volunteers had swept through Buck Lake Park and Point No Point, finding no one. Now the teams were walking the beaches, which were bordered by barnacled rocks, bluffs of varying heights, and logs the tide had half buried, integrated into abandoned driftwood forts built during the summer season.

He'd also learned that the search of Mary Bonner's apartment was complete. They found reams of great material if the case ever went to trial—news clippings and printouts about Lorraine D'Antonia, more evidence that Bonner had been researching Johnson Hill Orphanage, even some photographs of the two women together as adults. Lucy had gone quiet for a moment before telling him about the most disturbing thing of all. Police executing the warrant had found a picture of Austin himself taped to Mary Bonner's wall. That, along with a notebook police had found, indicated that Bonner blamed Austin for the incarceration of Lorraine D'Antonia. Mary Bonner knew Fiona's name, knew Austin had moved to Hansville, even speculated that he'd moved to Hansville specifically to find *her*.

When they'd hung up, Austin began replaying every interaction with Lorraine D'Antonia in his mind. Every clue, every shred of evidence, every word of her confession. A lot more made sense about this case now, but it didn't make him feel any better.

At some point, Mary Bonner and Lorraine D'Antonia had figured out they were sisters. Most likely, this happened when all the news about the orphanage began coming out. He assumed that one of them had heard about the orphanage, then began looking into the past, eventually discovering the other.

Maybe it had taken some time to form a bond—or maybe the twin bond ran so deep that they were close the instant they met. But close enough to commit murder for the other?

The only plausible explanation was that Mary Bonner had been watching D'Antonia's case closely, only deciding to commit the first kidnapping when D'Antonia's most recent appeal was denied. The appeal had been based on what D'Antonia referred to as her 'false confession.' Perhaps Bonner believed that if more babies began disappearing and dying in the exact manner used by the Holiday Baby Butcher, prosecutors would have to admit that D'Antonia's confession had been false, that they'd jailed the wrong woman. She'd have to be a fool to think that's how it

worked, but Austin had learned never to underestimate the delu-
sional power of motivated reasoning.

As the back end of the SUV emerged completely from the
water, Austin passed through the gate that led to the boat
launch. Ridley was managing the process, and he stopped the
crew when the vehicle was high enough to get a clear view
through the windows.

Austin stepped to within ten yards. Close enough to hear but
not close enough to see. If they were in there, he didn't want to
see. He held his breath. His stomach tightened.

Ridley leaned in, then cocked his head back. "Empty!" He
shouted.

A few cheers went up from a small crowd. At least Bonner
hadn't drowned Anna and Joshua.

But then the next fact sunk in. If she'd abandoned the car at
the boat launch—or forced Anna to do it—she'd likely had
access to a boat, which meant she may have escaped hours ago.

Austin hurried over to Ridley. "Any word on the missing
boat?"

"No, but—" He stopped himself when a voice came through
his radio.

"Detective Lucy here. We have the boat. Washed up on the
shore at Twin Spits. Over."

Ridley grabbed his radio and began walking toward his car.
"I'll be there in two minutes. Secure it from twenty yards. Don't
touch anything."

Austin followed him to the car, but Ridley stopped on a
dime. "Not you. Not this time. There could be heat."

"Call me when you've searched the boat?"

Ridley nodded, then hopped in and sped away.

Austin shoved his hands in his pocket, mulling the thought
that had popped into his head. Not a thought so much as an
objection: he simply didn't believe that Mary Bonner had stolen
a boat. Maybe she was in good shape, but she was a small woman
in her sixties, with two hostages. Plus, it was winter. Most boats

were stashed away and winterized at this point. It was possible, but not likely. There was something he was missing, and he needed time to think.

Austin gave Anna's dripping SUV one last glance, then walked back in the direction of his house.

CHAPTER THIRTY-NINE

WALKING NORTHWEST, Austin took in the gentle curve of the beach that ran from the boat launch at Point No Point to his store. Across the Sound, beyond a lone fishing boat, the evergreens of Whidbey Island were lit by a soft golden light from the setting sun.

Something wasn't adding up, and he needed to figure out what.

The boat launch where Anna's car was found was about five minutes from Mary Bonner's house on Heron Avenue. After stabbing Jimmy, she must have forced Anna into the car and ordered her at knifepoint to drive down here. Then they'd ditched the car and either found another car, proceeded by foot, or stolen a boat. Problem was, the marina was on the other side of the peninsula, two or three miles from the boat launch at Point No Point. If Bonner had been planning to steal a boat, why wouldn't she have ditched the car at the marina, where all the boats were? The launch was for people bringing in boats from elsewhere, and in the winter that was very rare. On occasion, people left small boats unattended by the launch as they used restrooms or gathered supplies. But those were usually kayaks in the summer. No, Austin thought, she didn't steal a boat. After ditching the car, she'd escaped in a different car, or on foot.

The setting sun disappeared behind the hill to the west and the sky took on the dark purplish color of a bruise. Tomorrow was Christmas Day, and he could see the twinkling Christmas lights of his store in the distance. Other than those lights and the mini-tree in the store, he'd barely registered the holiday. He and Fiona weren't big into holidays, but Christmas was one they never missed. His family was small and spread out around the country, making gathering difficult, but hers was big and mostly in the northeast. She had brothers in upstate New York, a sister in Massachusetts, and parents in Connecticut, only forty minutes from New York City. Not to mention more nieces and nephews than he could count. So each Christmas meant a big gathering of Fiona's side of the family. He'd been invited to attend this year—Fiona's family tried hard to include him even after her death—but somehow it didn't feel right.

When he'd caught her, Lorraine D'Antonia had told him in an interview that Christmas was her favorite holiday. He wondered whether it was Mary's as well. Bonner was a copycat, but not a typical copycat. He was certain that Lorraine D'Antonia's failed appeal for a new trial had brought on the killings, but they may not have been the only motive. Likely, Bonner shared much of the mindset of her twin and might be motivated by similar things.

D'Antonia had maintained all the way through her trial that she gave those children lovely holidays. She seemed to genuinely believe that dressing them up, feeding them, loving them, then butchering them was what a good parent should do. Like a lot of killers, she used her own childhood as a justification for her actions. She was deranged, yes, but Austin had never questioned her sincerity. D'Antonia genuinely believed what she said. Holidays were important to her. The same likely held true for Mary Bonner.

If so, what would she want right now? It was Christmas Eve,

the day she would kill Joshua if she kept to the schedule. She'd want to move forward with that plan. When she'd fled her cabin, her plans had been disrupted. Her bag and her canning pot had been left behind. She'd want to regain that control, find a safe space. Holding Anna as a hostage, she'd want to dress Joshua up as Santa or a cute little elf, then murder him, boil him, and etch a poem onto his tiny bones. That wasn't possible unless she found another house.

She would know that her apartment was not an option. But what about friends? Austin flashed on his conversation with Myrian Brightstone. Would Bonner show up at her house or the house of another co-worker? Not likely, even if she could get off the peninsula, which was damn near impossible with the roadblock.

The beach had been combed, the surrounding homes and even the famous lighthouse itself had been checked. Possibly she had an accomplice who was hiding her in a nearby home, but she didn't seem to have many friends. It was also possible that she'd forced her way into a home nearby. In fact, that was the most likely option. The homes along the beach were a mix of large family homes and cute but expensive beachfront cabins. At least a handful would be vacant this time of year.

That was likely it. She'd ditched the car, wandered along the beach until she saw what looked like an empty house, then broken in, entering from the beachside. He thought of calling Ridley to see if the vacant homes had been searched but, as usual, he had no signal on the beach.

He studied the windows of the homes as he walked by. Some had big Christmas trees visible in living rooms, some were full of people cooking or playing board games. One seemed to have a holiday party in full swing. Others had drawn curtains, dark windows, their owners likely in Arizona or California, Hawaii or Las Vegas. He had to believe that Ridley and his team had checked every house.

The revelation that Mary Bonner and Lorraine D'Antonia

were twins was still reorganizing all past information in his mind. He flashed on the interview that Ridley had shown him. He had to assume that, the whole time, D'Antonia had known that her sister killed Allie Shreever. It brought a chill up his spine.

Her cold, dead eyes, the way she'd insisted that she'd been a good mother to those children. The way she'd mentioned him by name. What was it she'd said? Something like, "The handsome detective moved across country, just like me. New York to Washington State, though I think his new home is likely nicer than mine." She'd giggled after saying it, the wrinkles on her face jiggling sickeningly.

Austin stopped in his tracks.

His new home.

When she'd said it, Austin assumed she meant the town of Hansville. He'd moved to Washington state and settled in Hansville. She'd moved to Washington state and settled in prison. But what if she meant not his hometown, but his *home*? Bonner could have gotten his address from Anna, or perhaps the twins had somehow figured out that his apartment was connected to his business.

Then it hit him. Run's incessant barking hadn't been general stress. She'd been telling him that someone was inside their house.

He raised his eyes. He was a quarter mile from his store, from his house. Yanking his phone from his pocket, he took off at a full sprint down the beach.

CHAPTER FORTY

THE HOUSE WAS NICE, she thought. Nicer than her old family cabin. It didn't smell like cookies, but it would do for now.

The living room was spare, like a bachelor pad. A black leather couch, two cream-colored armchairs with a little table between them. Two photographs hung on the wall: an old black and white picture of the Brooklyn Bridge and a photograph of a woman in a Navy uniform. Probably Austin's mother. She had the same dark hair, the same nose, the same intelligent blue eyes.

No doubt she'd been a real mother, loved him and nurtured him every step of the way. Not like *her* mother. Not like *either* of her mothers. Hers had given her away to an orphanage that had offered her up to a fate worse than death.

Poverty. Violence. A dog cage when she misbehaved. "Good solid discipline," her mother had called it.

She'd had it rough. Rougher than her sister, by far. But still she'd made it through, and she'd turned out alright.

She checked on Joshua, asleep in the bedroom. She'd had to tape his mouth closed to keep him from crying, but he was smart. He'd learned to breathe through his nose. She peeled off the tape slowly. He moved a little, but didn't wake.

On the floor next to the bed, the reporter sat slumped

against the wall. She'd bound her wrists and ankles and gagged her mouth. "I'm going to take off your gag. If you scream, the people in the restaurant will hear you. They will come running, but the baby will be dead before they get here." She held up the long kitchen knife she'd used to stab the officer who'd come in her house without an invitation. "I will be captured and taken to jail, yes. But I will leave you alive to live with the fact that you are a selfish bitch who chose her own life over that of a helpless baby." She met the reporter's frightened eyes. "So, will you scream?"

The reporter shook her head no.

She removed the gag. "When will he come home?"

The reporter stretched out her mouth, adjusting to the new freedom. "I don't know. He's probably out looking for you with the police."

"Do you have a boat?"

"I already told you, no. I don't even *live* here. I live ten miles away."

"Do you have another car at your house?"

"No, and even if I did, I'm sure the road out of town is blocked." The reporter frowned. "Can I ask you something?"

She did not like reporters, but maybe this one could help her tell the truth, help her get Lorraine freed. She nodded.

"Are you Lorraine D'Antonia's sister?"

"Her twin."

"Do you really believe that killing like her will convince anyone to let her go?"

"They will have to."

"No, they really won't. All they will do is put you in jail with her."

"*With* her?" That sounded good, better than the life she was living.

"Not *with* her. Not in the same cell. But maybe you'd get to see her sometimes. Maybe they'd allow visits. I can help you. I know people at the prison."

"You're lying!" she spat. "Just like reporters lied about Lorraine."

"I promise that soon someone is going to find us here. Even if no one saw us come in, they are going to knock on that door. When they do, we might all die. They will not hesitate to shoot if they think it could save Joshua. Let me call someone I trust. You can get on the phone and they will take you out of here alive as long as Joshua is not hurt. I swear I will help you see Lorraine again."

She scratched her head, thinking. She didn't like this reporter. She returned to her side and gagged her again, tying the cloth even tighter than before. Tightening it until she squirmed in pain.

She walked to the doorway and turned. "They will let me live, let me go to Lorraine, even if I only have one hostage. We will call someone like you said. But it's Christmas Eve, and first there's something I need to do. For Joshua."

She walked to the kitchen and peered in the fridge. Ketchup, some carrot sticks and lunch meat, a few beers. Typical bachelor. If his wife was still alive, she probably would have done a better job of stocking it.

She cracked a beer and leaned on the kitchen table. On the floor was a dog dish. And yet, there was no dog. She hadn't known he had a dog.

Odd that the dog wasn't here while her master was out and about, and also a piece of good luck. If the dog had been home, it might have barked when she came in, alerting the folks in the adjoining café.

There was no dog cage. Just a nice fluffy dog bed in the corner. Nicer than the bed she'd slept in as a girl. Austin treated his dog better than her foster parents had treated her.

Scanning the room, her eyes stopped on a little plaque.

Every single second,
Of every single day,
Every victim deserves my best.

She pulled a big pasta pot out of the cupboard, filled it with water, and set it on the stove. With a rag from the counter, she polished the sides where it was tarnished.

It needed to shine.

In a hoarse whisper, she read the plaque aloud, "Every single second, of every single day, every victim deserves my best."

She couldn't agree more.

CHAPTER FORTY-ONE

THE VOLUNTEER SEARCH parties had gone home for the evening and the parking lot around his building was strangely empty. Run was sleeping in her doggie bed in the corner and Andy was just closing up the store when Austin arrived, slowing from his sprint and panting. "Landline... Call... Detective Calvin... Lucy. Anyone. I think... Bonner is here." He pointed at the wall next to the supply room, on the other side of which was his apartment. "In my house. I'm... gonna go check it out."

"Shouldn't you wait for—"

He was already out the door.

He crept around the side of the building, eyes on the living room windows. No lights were on. Nothing seemed out of the ordinary except for the sinking feeling in his gut. The wind had gone still, giving the evening a motionless, eerie quality. He smelled saltwater and heard the faint crashes of waves on the beach.

He stopped at the fence. He couldn't hear anything inside. He wouldn't open it. Not yet.

Instead, he crept around the building, moving slowly. Above the sink in the kitchen was a small window, visible from the west side of the building. Not a window, actually, but a section of old, metalized glass blocks, the kind that were designed to let in light while retaining some privacy from the outside world. No light through the glass blocks.

Maybe he'd been wrong. Paranoid. The only room that didn't have a window was the bedroom, so unless she was operating in darkness or had stashed everyone in the bedroom, Mary Bonner wasn't there.

Then he saw something. The glass blocks looked different. In addition to being wavy and opaque, they were damp, steamy from the inside. He'd seen that once before. When he'd boiled water for ravioli.

His first thought was to race through the front door. But that would take him right into the kitchen. Joshua Green weighed no more than ten pounds. If she still had the knife she'd used on Jimmy, a simple flick of the wrist could end him.

He hurried back to the store, shushed Andy as he walked through, and quietly entered the café's storage room, where an odd crawl space led into the apartment, into his bedroom.

Holding his breath, he crawled on his hands and knees, careful not to bump the sides in the narrow space. His eyes slowly adjusted to the darkness.

He reached the hatch at the back of his bedroom closet, which was covered by a piece of plywood that had been stuck up unceremoniously when the apartment was added to the building in the nineties. He could easily push it in, but he needed to stay quiet.

Prying with his fingers, he carefully lifted the plywood and peered through his small closet into his bedroom. The lights were off. He saw nothing.

Then he heard something. A muffled groan.

He let out a quiet breath as he leaned the hatch cover on the closet wall.

He crawled into the closet, head brushing up against hanging shirts, and looked to his left, where Anna Downey was tied up in the corner.

Still crouched, he duck-walked next to her, eyes on the door that led to the living room and kitchen. "Is she still here?" he whispered.

She pointed toward the kitchen.

Then suddenly he heard the gentle singing voice of Mary Bonner. He could not make out the words.

He took off the gag, a red bandana tied around her head and covering her mouth. He untied her feet. "Crawl through that space. It leads to the restaurant. Do not look back or try to help. Detectives will be here soon." He finished untying her hands, and met her look of defiance with one of his own. She wanted to stay, wanted to help, but she understood.

He waited until she was gone before inching toward the gun safe under his bed. Eyes still on the door, he tapped in the code and pulled out his MR1911. He'd hoped to never again use it outside a range, but he kept it loaded.

Quietly, he walked to the door and stepped into the dark living room. The only light came from the two burners that blazed on high in the kitchen. On top of them, his pasta pot steamed away.

Oh, God. He was too late.

Mary Bonner began singing again, and this time he could make out the words.

Christmas is
A time for joy
Let's gather together
Every girl and boy
Stockings and cookies
And presents for all
Bring good cheer and wonder
As winter does call

Her voice was a deep, throaty whisper, full of pain.

Then he heard the best sound he'd ever heard in his life. The gentle coo of a tiny baby. He peered around the doorway into the darkened kitchen. Mary Bonner stood next to the stove, cradling little Joshua Green in her arms, singing to him.

Christmas is
A time for joy

He raised his .45 and stepped into the doorway.

Let's gather together
Every girl and boy

"Mary Bonner." He aimed at her head. "Do. Not. Move."

CHAPTER FORTY-TWO

BONNER TURNED FAST, almost as though she'd been expecting him. In the same motion, she stretched out her arms to hold Joshua over the pot of boiling water. "If you shoot me, he will drop." Her voice was sharp, yet also somehow a whisper, like the scrape of a tree branch against a window in the dead of night.

Bonner angled her body so she was partially blocked by Joshua's torso as his feet dangled just above the top of the pot, a six-inch drop into the water. He wore a little Santa onesie, complete with red and white booties. He kicked his legs and let out a terrifying shriek.

"You do not have to do this," Austin said. "There are ways out of this, I promise you. How about you put Joshua in the other room, I put down the gun, and we talk this out?"

"You took my sister."

"I did my job." Austin had a shot. From this distance, he'd kill Bonner a hundred times out of a hundred. But there was no way he could take it. Joshua would either fall in the boiling water or onto the floor, which could break his neck. "Please, Mary. Set Joshua on the floor. I promise I will not shoot." The baby's cries were growing louder, more panicked, bouncing around the small kitchen, off the windows and the linoleum floor. He didn't think the steam was enough to burn him given the booties he wore, but the cries sounded like he was experiencing great pain nonetheless.

Her look was one of puzzlement, as though she was weighing her options. "Put down your gun first."

When he didn't move, she began to sing, her words strange and ominous against Joshua's shrieks.

Christmas is
A time for joy
Let's gather together
Every girl and boy

On the word "boy" she gave Joshua a little jiggle. "Stop being so fussy."

"Okay," Austin said. He crouched slowly, extending the gun in front of him. "I will put it down. Please do not hurt the boy. He has parents. They love him like you love your sister."

"Love of parents is nothing compared to what Lorraine and I had. She would do anything for me. *Anything.*"

The way she said the last word unnerved him, as though it carried layers and layers of meaning he couldn't grasp. What else had they done? How many more had they killed, he wondered?

He set down the gun.

"Kick it over here," she hissed.

He gave it a gentle tap with his foot and it slid across the kitchen. "Now put Joshua down and we can talk about this."

Slowly, she moved the baby away from the pot. His cries had reached a hysterical pitch. His breaths fast and ragged like he was hyperventilating.

"What did you do to him?" Austin demanded.

"You've never had children. Sometimes they are fussy no matter how much you love them."

Bonner leaned over slowly, not taking her eyes off Austin, and placed Joshua next to the gun, holding him up by his shoulders. Austin recoiled. Joshua wasn't strong enough to pick up a gun, let alone to pull a trigger, but still, the sight of a baby next to a loaded gun made him sick.

She'd set him down on his butt, but he was too top-heavy, too young to sit up on his own. When she stood, he began to slump to the left. Austin lunged forward instinctively, trying to protect his head from the fall. He made it, grabbing Joshua's shoulder just before his head hit the floor.

He saw her move out of the corner of his eye. She let out a horrific shriek as she brought the knife down into his arm.

Austin rocked back, letting go of the baby and falling backwards, striking his head on the kitchen table.

Then everything went black for a few seconds and all he heard were the hinges of his screen door screaming into the night.

CHAPTER FORTY-THREE

AUSTIN LEAPT up and tried to race toward the door, but staggered into the stove and careened off the steaming pot. It fell, splashing scalding hot water onto his clothes and soaking through his shoes, burning his feet. He slipped, smashing into the counter and crushing the carafe of his coffee pot with his shoulder. As he fell, glass and water were everywhere.

Then he realized the knife was still in his arm.

The first rule of a knife wound was not to remove the knife. But that was assuming you were going to seek medical attention. If he chased after Bonner with the knife in his arm, it could cause even more damage than removing it. Grabbing a wooden spoon from a drawer, he bit down hard, then braced himself for the pain and yanked the knife out. He spat out the spoon and dropped the knife in the sink, then tore a dishrag lengthwise and used a strip to tie a tourniquet just above the puncture. He flicked off the burners and ran for the door.

A nearly full moon cast silvery light over the yard and glimmered off the metal gate, which Bonner had left open when she fled. He ran to it, checking for footprints. Crouching, he pulled out his phone and trained the flashlight on the ground. It was still moist from the rain and there were clear tracks leading away from his yard toward the beach.

He saw her the moment he hit the sand. Lights from the beachfront properties cast sharp, angular patches of light onto the beach, leaving other stretches shadowed. Carrying Joshua Green in her arms, Mary Bonner ran along the stretch he'd just walked, back toward Point No Point. In and out of the patches of light, in and out of shadow, she ran faster than he would have thought possible while carrying a baby. Or maybe he was running slower than he thought. With his bruised hip, gashed head, and punctured arm, he was limping in more ways than one.

He heard sirens in the distance. They'd be at his house within the minute. He knew this patch of beach had no signal, and he wouldn't risk slowing long enough to make a call even if there was.

He was gaining on Bonner, running at least half again her speed. The shoulder wound wasn't terrible, but he was also losing blood. The more he ran, the worse it felt.

Mary Bonner entered the stretch of beach next to the lighthouse and, for a moment, she disappeared up the path toward the parking lot. The same path he'd walked with Sarah and Benny.

Austin hit the path, accelerating up the gentle slope. He stopped. She was gone. The parking lot appeared empty.

He tried to quiet his breath, listening in the semi-darkness. He heard nothing, not a twig creaking, not a car door opening or closing. Nothing.

He tried the lighthouse door. Locked. Inside was dark and silent.

He was about to try to kick in the door when he saw movement.

Past the lighthouse, a path led through a small section of marshlands, then up a long wooden staircase to the bluff above the beach, the same spot Sarah and Benny had been when Trisha dropped the bag of bones. He sprinted down the path, reaching the bottom of the wooden staircase when Bonner was halfway up.

"Stop," he called.

Austin took the stairs three at a time, right on her heels now. When she reached the top of the path, she veered suddenly toward the water, dodging a bench and disappearing in a gap in the brush where the blackberry brambles had been cut down.

For a second he thought she was going to dive off the bluff at full speed, but she stopped a yard away from the edge and turned, gripping Joshua tight in her arms. "Do not... come closer." She was panting, her hair and eyes wild. Joshua had stopped crying.

Austin could not see if he was breathing. Oh, God, let him be breathing.

Austin stopped on the other side of the bench, maybe ten yards from Bonner. His breath was ragged. "Is... he...al- alive?"

"He's resting."

"It's over, Mary."

She backed up a pace. "I will throw him over the ledge."

Austin couldn't see the shore, but he'd been up on this bluff before. Thirty feet below, driftwood and jagged rocks populated the beach. A strong adult would have a tough time surviving a fall. Joshua would have no chance. "You don't want to do that." He stretched both arms out in front of him, palms up, trying to make himself as unthreatening as possible. "Just stay steady. Set Joshua down and walk away. I swear to you, I will not pursue you. I only want the baby. You can be safely in Seattle in a couple hours. Please. Just leave Joshua."

Her face was pure pain, a dark scowl of loss and anger. "You have no idea what you did to me, did to *us*."

"Tell me, then. Let's talk it through. Just set the baby on the ground." He inched closer. "Tell me about Lorraine."

She looked at the ground as though considering his offer, then gripped Joshua tighter.

"If you don't want to tell me about Lorraine, tell me about Trisha."

Bonner looked confused.

"The woman you asked to bring the bag to the beach. Did you hire her because she looks a little like you? A little like Lorraine?"

"I thought if someone saw her..." She shook her head violently, like she was trying to force something loose. "If someone saw her they might arrest her and then think she did all the... all the..."

"Killings?"

Bonner nodded. She only barely thought of what she and D'Antonia had done as killings, and couldn't say the word.

"All of this was so they'd let Lorraine go, right?"

Bonner nodded. "They split us apart when we were babies. Our mother did not want us but she wanted us to stay together. *They promised her they would keep us together! It's all in the papers.*" Her voice had become the pained shriek of a dying animal. "They *split us apart.*" She stopped to take a few angry breaths, then continued. "Lorraine was put with a rich family. Italian. A *good* family. Owned a chain of restaurants. She got chicken Parmesan, fresh-baked bread and a fluffy bed. I was raised by the Bonners." She almost spat the name. "I got milk toast and a dog cage."

Austin inched closer, hands still outstretched. "I'm sorry." She was right about Lorraine D'Antonia's background. She'd been raised in relative wealth, with parents who owned five or six Italian restaurants in Seattle. Fiona had told him once that D'Antonia's murders were proof that nature mattered more than nurture. After all, D'Antonia had been given every advantage and had turned into one of the most sadistic killers in history.

He took another step forward. "I really *am* sorry. And you didn't deserve what happened to you. No one deserves that. When did you and Lorraine meet?"

She smiled, her face illuminated by moonlight filtering

through the trees above them. "We found each other more than thirty years ago."

"*Before* the news about the orphanage?" He was even more surprised than he let on. He took another tiny step forward. "I assumed you'd met when the news broke of the twins study."

She grimaced at the mention of the study. She was only a few feet from the cliff and she leaned toward the water, as though she might just let herself fall backwards, taking Joshua with her. "Don't come any closer."

He stopped. "Okay, just tell me more. Let's keep talking and see what we can work out here."

"We met because of nursing school. She had gone to UW. Her *parents* paid. I went to community college. I washed dishes to pay my way. A nurse I was shadowing told me she'd had a nursing student a few years earlier who looked *exactly* like me. I ignored it at first, but she showed me a photo, and I knew it was her. I'd always felt like a piece of me was missing, and I finally knew what it was. Lorraine and I met a little later."

Austin heard a twig snap to his left, from the bushes halfway up the staircase. He didn't allow his head to move but he shifted his eyes just long enough to see Anna Downey, crouched and creeping, clinging close to the bushes that framed the staircase. "So let me see if I can understand, because I *want* to understand, Mary, I really do." He shifted to the right slightly, drawing Mary Bonner's eyes with him, away from Anna. "You think I might be only out to stop you. But I genuinely want to understand what happened. I want to understand *you*."

She nodded.

"So tell me if I have this right. You meet Lorraine while you're in nursing school, and you form a relationship. Immediately you start discovering all the ways you're similar, despite having such different upbringings." From the corner of his eye, he saw Anna reach the top of the stairs. On her hands and knees, she moved in the shadows toward the cliff. "But at some point Lorraine begins acting strange, becoming erratic, maybe even cruel. She starts talking more and more about her childhood, complaining that she hadn't had her real mother, that nothing was as it should have been. And part of that, you could agree with. You'd had it rougher than her, after all." Anna was only about twenty feet away, hiding behind the trunk of a large evergreen that hugged the cliff. "And I'm guessing that she told you about her plans even before she carried them out. Her plans to begin taking babies. But you're not like her, Mary. She's your sister and you love her, so you didn't stop her, but I bet you knew that what she was doing was wrong. That's why you didn't help her. She was given everything and went on to do very bad things. You had it much more difficult, and the only reason you started doing these things was out of love. You wanted her to be released from prison. You thought that if babies started turning up dead in the same way, they'd have to let her go. Do I have that right?"

Mary Bonner was silent for a long moment, then let out the most disturbing laugh he'd ever heard. It wasn't the high-pitched cackle of a movie villain. It was a low, hoarse grumble, a mocking laughter that carried a darkness blacker than midnight. When she spoke, her voice was as dark as the laugh. "No, Thomas Austin. You have it completely backwards."

Anna bolted suddenly for Bonner, shoulder lowered. She was about to connect with her side, but when she was a yard away she tripped, colliding with Bonner's legs just as the woman turned. Joshua fell from her arms, letting out a sharp cry as he fell onto Anna's back and rolled onto the soggy ground.

Austin leapt forward, but it was too late.

Kicking violently, Bonner connected with Anna's side, then lunged for Joshua. Anna rolled and reached Joshua first, snatching the baby as she slid toward the ledge. She gripped him tight in her arms and, for half a second, Austin thought she'd saved him.

Then Mary Bonner dropped to her knees and used the momentum of Anna's slide to push them off the bluff.

CHAPTER FORTY-FOUR

BONNER IMMEDIATELY DISAPPEARED FURTHER up the bluff as Austin sprinted to the ledge and looked down. He couldn't see Anna or Joshua but he heard a single word. "Help."

Sitting on his backside, he grabbed a root that cascaded down the bluff. Sliding carefully, he lowered himself down, thankful to see that the cliff had a slight angle. It wasn't a sheer drop to the beach below.

As he descended five feet, then ten, then fifteen, he bumped over rocks and roots, causing a minor avalanche of dirt. His feet struck something, an outcropping of rock.

"Thomas?" It was Anna's voice.

To his left, barely visible, she was tangled in vines and covered in dirt, clinging to both Joshua and the root system of a fallen tree protruding from the bank.

Austin squinted at Joshua's face in the moonlight. "Is he..."

As if in answer, Joshua let out a scream.

Anna said, "He's okay. I don't think he hit his head. Drop down the rest of the way, then I will hand him down."

Austin used the vines to descend the last ten feet to the beach, then Anna slowly lowered Joshua into his arms.

She followed him down, then took Joshua from him. She pointed back up the bluff. "Follow her."

Austin gave her a long look, an appreciative nod, then used the roots and vines to pull himself back up the cliff.

When he'd reached the top, he listened, breathing hard. He glanced back toward the parking lot and saw flashing lights. Backup was here.

He took off up the bluff, walking fast but stopping every few paces to listen. He followed the cliff's edge as he thought Bonner had done. He knew this path. To his right, it continued up through the woods, eventually coming out on the road not far from Bonner's little house on Heron Avenue. Her other option was to find a spot to slide down to the beach. From there it was eight or ten miles to Kingston, where she could catch a ferry, find a car, or, perhaps find a place to lay low.

He reached a point where the path jutted off sharply to the right, and the beach curved to the left. He couldn't stay halfway between them anymore. He paused. Would Bonner cut off in the direction of the road and the house, drop down to the beach, or would she stick to the forest and the cliff?

"Austin." Her voice came clear and strong from the edge of the cliff.

He turned.

"Do you want to know what I meant? How you got everything wrong?"

He stepped toward her. She held a rock about the size of a baseball above her head, the moonlight illuminating its jagged edges. He wasn't sure what she was thinking. There was no way she could hit him with it from that distance. When he'd bolted from his kitchen, he'd been too out of it to grab his gun, but if he wanted to take her down, it wouldn't be hard. One way or another, he had her.

"Mary, I—"

"I will do the talking, Austin."

"You're not going to throw that rock at me. Face it, it's over."

She stepped back toward the cliff. "You will look better if you take me alive." She turned, glanced down, the rock still over her head.

She had no intention of throwing it at *him*. She was going to hit *herself* with it.

"Do not do this, Mary. Do not jump. It may seem like the best thing, but it isn't. If you live, you will be able to see Lorraine again."

The truth was, he wanted her alive for a lot of reasons. He'd worked dozens of murders. Between those and his own experience, he knew that nothing could ever fully heal the wounds the families of victims suffered. But he'd also learned that the process of seeing the killer brought to justice usually offered *some* solace. Murderers who took their own lives when captured left an even bigger wound in the families they'd destroyed.

"Talk to me, Mary. It's just you and me. I know people in the news. I can help you get your story out there. About the Bonners. The orphanage. It won't undo what you've done, but it will make people understand. What did you mean when you said I had it wrong?"

Again she laughed, and this one was even more disturbing than the last. It was as though darkness itself had taken up residence inside her and was trying to escape. "When I said my sister was innocent, I wasn't lying. You've had the wrong person locked up this entire time."

CHAPTER FORTY-FIVE

A SICKENED, broken feeling took over Austin's whole body. He tasted moldy oatmeal flecked with the burnt-toast bitterness of dread. He did not know what she meant, but somehow he knew she was telling the truth. He could only manage two words. "Tell me."

"*Lorraine* was the good one. When we met she was already a successful nurse. I was in school. We thought it was funny that we both decided to be nurses even though we'd never met. Must be in the blood. We were so similar, and yet so different."

"How?" Austin asked.

"She had grown up rich. Private schools, nice parents. Of course she'd wondered why our mother didn't want us, but she had had a good life. She was prettier than me, too."

"What did I get wrong?"

"I'm the one who killed the babies. Not her. It was *me* the whole time."

"That's not possible. Sonya Lopez in New York. We had video evidence. DNA. A confession."

"Oh, she killed Sonya Lopez. Because I *asked* her to. But little Sonya was the only one she killed. You're not as good a detective as you think you are."

Austin's mind raced. When she'd been sent back from New York to Seattle, Lorraine D'Antonia had confessed to all the murders in Seattle. She'd been off on some of the details, but she knew enough that the confessions seemed legitimate. "The details of the Seattle killings..."

"She couldn't remember everything I told her."

Austin doubled over, his stomach turning as his mind flashed back on the thousand moments he'd spent interrogating D'Antonia. He didn't want to know but he had to know. "Jonathan Gruber. Seattle. 2015."

"He was chubby, just like little Joshua. *I* took him. *I* killed him. She confessed."

"And the others?"

"All me."

"So why—"

"In 2018, I read in the paper that Seattle detectives were closing in on a suspect in the killings. Lorraine had moved away by then, was already living in New York. I begged her to do it. Told her exactly what to do. Made her do it when I was at work so they'd know I was innocent. That's why she only did the one in New York."

"You had her kill Sonya Lopez so detectives would think they'd been on the wrong suspect in Seattle?"

She nodded. "We didn't think she would get caught."

"And when I caught her, she confessed to all the killings to protect you?"

She nodded. "So they'd never come looking for me again."

They stood in silence, staring at each other. Her face ran through an odd series of contortions, like she was feeling a dozen emotions at once.

Finally she said, "Do you have a soulmate, Detective Austin?"

"I do. I mean, I did. I still do."

"Your wife?"

He nodded.

"I had one, too, until they took her away. Until *you* took her away."

"But how could she kill? How could you convince her to?"

"Would *you* have killed for your wife?"

"Not like this. Not an innocent baby. Not even for her."

"Our bond runs deeper even than love."

It was all coming together in Austin's mind now. Lorraine D'Antonia was evil, there was no doubt, but she'd had to be pushed to act on it. Mary Bonner got there all by herself. "You can *see* Lorraine again." Austin pointed down the bluff toward the parking lot, where swirling red and blue lights lit up the lighthouse and the beach. "Come back with me. I promise I'll help you see Lorraine again."

"When you wake up tomorrow, when you're drinking coffee and playing with your dog... when you're at your wife's grave and out on a date and reading your books... when you're fishing on a boat or taking a shower or eating lunch... now and for the rest of your life, you'll always have a single thing in the back of your mind. You have the wrong person in prison for four murders. And you will *never* have the right person."

Mary Bonner looked up at the rock, smiled faintly, then brought it down with a violent crash into her forehead, knocking herself backwards over the cliff.

The next thing Austin heard was the wet thud of her body smashing into the rocks below.

CHAPTER FORTY-SIX

AN HOUR LATER, Joshua Green's parents leapt out of their car and ran across the parking lot. His mother Deidre took him in her arms and dropped to the ground, cradling him and inspecting him at the same time.

Paramedics had finished their initial examination of the baby and found him bruised in a few spots, clearly in some kind of shock, but nourished and hydrated. Miraculously, he seemed to have no permanent physical damage. From here, his parents would accompany him to the hospital, but it appeared as though he'd be okay. His cries had lost the hysterical pain, but there would be a lot of healing to do.

After crouching with Joshua and his wife for a few minutes, Damian Green, Joshua's father, walked over to Austin. "She's really dead?"

Austin nodded grimly. Mary Bonner had been found on the beach, head caved in by a large rock, a spear of driftwood through her chest. "I'm sorry. I tried to bring her in alive. People who haven't been through it don't know why it matters. I know."

Austin had thought about it a hundred times. Of course there was part of him that wanted the men who'd killed Fiona to suffer the same fate. But not by their own hands. He'd rather see them face the humiliation of arrest, a public trial, and spend the rest of their miserable lives in prison.

Damian nodded. "I have to thank you."

Austin held up both hands. "It's alright. Go be with your family."

"No, really. I looked you up. Your wife." He grimaced and looked at the ground. "I felt so powerless the last few days. I just read everything I could about you, about the other detectives, about Lorraine D'Antonia. Just obsessed and obsessed. Couldn't keep myself off the internet." He shook his head. "You know what it's like losing someone. I knew what it was like for three days. Now..." he gestured to his wife and to Joshua, who were getting into the back of the ambulance. "Now I don't have to anymore."

"You should be thanking *her*." He pointed to Anna's white SUV, which the tow truck hauled to the parking lot next to the lighthouse. He doubted the thing would run anymore, but Anna sat on the hood, typing up a story on her phone.

"I will," he said. "And I'll apologize to the other detectives. I was..."

"Out of your mind?"

Damian nodded. "I was pissed I'd been caught. I was stupid and angry."

Austin shoved his hands in his pockets. "I'm no relationship expert. But I'm pretty decent at reading people. Just a skill I developed." Austin paused.

"And?"

"Sometimes tragedies destroy relationships, sometimes they bring people back together." He nodded toward Deirdre, who held Joshua tight in the flashing lights of the ambulance. "Maybe your wife gives you a second chance now. If she does, don't blow it."

"I won't, I—"

"No, listen." Austin waited until Damian Green looked into his eyes. "I used to have it as good as you have it right now. Not a child. We were going to try. But a wife. A wife who..." He dropped his eyes to the ground, tears forming in his eyes. "I thought I appreciated what I had, but I didn't. Use this horror to take stock of your life. If she gives you another chance, do anything you can, move heaven and earth to make it work."

～

It was past midnight by the time Austin sat down next to Detectives O'Rourke and Ridley on the beach, balancing three paper cups carefully. He handed each of them a coffee. "On the house," he said. "Andy is making sandwiches and coffee for everyone who's working."

Joshua's parents had left for the hospital, Anna had filed her story from her phone, completed the first round of statements about the case, and gotten a ride home. She'd deal with her car later.

Lucy toasted him. "Merry Christmas Eve."

Ridley glanced at his watch. "Technically, it's Christmas morning already."

"When do you want my official statement?" Austin asked.

Ridley sighed. "It can wait until tomorrow."

Austin was glad to hear that. He hadn't felt this tired in years.

"How are you holding up?" Lucy asked, pointing at his arm. The paramedics had bandaged him up, but he'd refused to leave the scene until everything was settled.

"I'm heading to the hospital after this. Probably a few stitches, but it didn't go too deep." He took a long, slow sip of the coffee and stared at the blackness of the Puget Sound. "What's this going to mean? Lorraine? Mary?"

Ridley let out a long, tired sigh. "It's not good. D'Antonia's lawyers will use what happened to try to get her out of prison, whether or not they hear about what Bonner told you. We've got forensics in your apartment, dusting for fingerprints and looking for other evidence. We're in the cabin, in her apartment. My guess is we're going to find evidence that what she told you is true. That she killed the babies in Seattle and let her sister take the rap."

"But if D'Antonia did the New York murder?"

"It's complicated. Maybe her confession gets thrown out and she's released, but she's still set to stand trial in New York, so—"

Austin considered this. "I know people in New York. Prosecutors. I can help smooth the path if she's got to stand trial there."

"That would be good," Ridley said.

They all stared out at the water for a long time, then Austin said, "Fiona and I used to argue about nature versus nurture. You know, what made a criminal a criminal. Whether people were born evil and all that."

Lucy turned toward him. "Must be messing with your brain that Mary Bonner committed most of the murders."

Austin shook his head slowly and rubbed his hands together, trying to get warm. He'd thought that Lorraine D'Antonia was an example of nature being more important than nurture when he knew her as the child adopted into stability. But the fact that the vilest evil had been in Mary Bonner, who'd had one of the worst upbringings imaginable, had him rethinking everything. "I don't know. Reminds me of something Fiona's brother told me once. He was an alcoholic. Recovered now, but he was trying to explain why he drank. In his mind, it wasn't exactly a disease he was born with, but it wasn't *not* that, either. He shared a quote with me from this physician who studied addiction. The point was, in the real world, the nature versus nurture argument is nonsense. Our lives are complex in a hundred ways we can see and a thousand we can't. Millions of moment-by-moment interactions between genetic and environmental factors. These interactions work together to create our minds, bodies, and our actions. To create the world. He was talking specifically about addiction, about whether people become alcoholics because of their genes or because of the circumstances of their lives. Maybe the same holds true for evil. Maybe we're not born evil, and maybe we don't become evil because of what happens to us. Maybe evil is something in between that we'll never fully understand."

"That sounds about right," Ridley said quietly.

"We may never be able to fully understand it," Lucy added. "But sometimes we can stop it."

That sounded about right, too.

CHAPTER FORTY-SEVEN

A LITTLE AFTER noon on Christmas Day, Austin walked into Jimmy's hospital room carrying a brown paper sack.

Jimmy pushed himself up by his elbows and offered a faint smile.

"Brought you lunch," Austin said. He pulled out a foil-wrapped burger. "Recipe I've been working on in the café. Already sold eight of them."

Jimmy raised an eyebrow. "Eight doesn't sound like a lot."

Austin chuckled. "What'd you expect, 'billions and billions served'? It's got bacon and roasted green chiles. Tomato jam adds a kind of sweet and sour thing."

Jimmy slowly opened up the foil. He moved deliberately, like a man in pain who would have to re-learn some of the basic motions of being a person. "Tomato jam?"

"Think of it as fancy ketchup."

"Missed the gym the last couple days," Jimmy said, inspecting the bun. "Not sure about the carbs."

Austin laughed. "That bun might bring you all the way up to six percent body fat." He pulled out a paper soda cup. "It's Bud. On draft." He handed it to Jimmy. "Usually it would go against my principles to serve a man a beer with a straw in it, but it was the only way to get it past the nurses. Drink it, and eat the damn bun."

Jimmy took a sip and smiled. "Nothing has ever tasted so good."

"Brought it over in an insulated bag to keep it cold."

"Thanks." He set the burger back in the foil on his lap. "I'll get to this later. Pain meds are killing my appetite."

Austin sat on a chair beside the bed. "You heard?"

Jimmy nodded. "Ridley and Lucy were here with Sheriff Daniels. Ridley got a call and I think they all went to get coffee or something."

"They told you about Mary Bonner?"

He nodded.

"And Joshua?"

Jimmy dropped his head. "I was within ten feet of him. Can't believe I let her get the jump on me."

"Not your fault. Could have happened to anyone." He nodded down to his arm. "They tell you she got the drop on me, too?"

Jimmy nodded. "Lady wasn't bad with a knife."

"I got lucky. I'd been stabbed like you, she'd have gotten away. And if you hadn't made that call, we might not have gotten her."

Jimmy sucked the beer through the straw. "I..."

"What?"

"How'd you come back from it?" Jimmy asked. "From the shooting in New York?"

"I didn't. I tried, but I never really made it back. Why do you think I moved three thousand miles away and started making burgers and selling bait?"

"If you'd stayed with it, think you would have made it all the way back?"

Austin had thought about this almost every day since leaving the NYPD, and he honestly didn't know the answer. "If it had just been me getting shot, yeah. I would have. I can take a punch. Most punches. But it was Fiona. And we never caught the guys who did it."

"What's the status of the case?"

"Colder than that Budweiser. Black Escalade left the scene. No plates. Witness saw three shooters. That's it."

"You saw nothing?"

Austin shook his head. "I got hit first, bullet spun me around. Dove in front of her with my back to the shooters. Next bullet got me in the shoulder blade. I fell. They think someone jumped out of the Escalade and shot her in the head. One bullet. An execution. Shot me in the back and leg on his way back to the car."

Jimmy was silent a long time, then sipped his beer. "You think you'd feel better if it was solved?"

"Would I feel good? Or healed? No, that'll never happen. But better? A *little* better? Yeah. I know I would."

Jimmy drained the rest of the beer in a long pull on the straw. "You got any Guinness? I'm more of a dark beer guy."

Austin laughed. "One beer maximum here." He stood and walked to the window, looking at the city and the mountains in the distance. "You want some free advice?"

"I feel like I need it."

"You're alive. No one you loved died. You get to work with a woman who's crazy about you."

"Lucy?"

Austin nodded.

"She told you that?"

"Not in so many words, but, well. Let me put it this way: you two are as good at hiding your feelings as I am at ballroom dancing."

"Wait, so..."

"Very bad."

Jimmy laughed. "She hasn't come to visit me alone yet."

"She's trying to be a pro. Give it time."

The door creaked open behind him. "If it isn't our New York cowboy."

Austin turned. "Sheriff Daniels, I—"

Daniels extended a hand. "No shit. Thanks, Austin."

They shook hands as Lucy and Ridley walked in.

Daniels said, "Austin. Look. As much as this pains me to say, you did a good job. Ridley filled me in."

"And you kept the FBI out of the way long enough for us to get this done," Austin said, accepting the olive branch and offering his own. "Thanks for that. Six pack and a bucket of bait on me next time you're fishing in Hansville."

Daniels smiled. "I'll let Ridley fill you in on everything else. I've got an interview."

"TV!" Lucy said. "It's not often Seattle TV comes over here."

Jimmy said, "Was wondering why you were dressed so well, Sheriff."

Austin had barely noticed, but Daniels wore a nice blue suit and looked more put together than Austin had ever seen him.

Daniels brushed imaginary dust off his lapel. "When I win re-election, maybe I can get our budget increased enough to bring this guy in for good." He gestured at Austin.

"What?" Austin asked.

Daniels glanced at his watch. "Like I said, Ridley will fill you in." He gave Jimmy a thumbs up and strolled out of the room.

"What was that about?" Austin asked.

Lucy offered him a strange smile.

Ridley said, "Tell you in a sec, but first, good news: just got off the phone with the Seattle DA. They're gonna want everything that ties into the D'Antonia prosecution. For now, her confession stands and she'll stay in prison. I got her word: The Holiday Baby Bu—" He glanced at Austin. "Lorraine D'Antonia will never see the light of day. If her confession is eventually thrown out, she'll be given a one way ticket to Rikers Island five minutes later."

That was good news. Austin hadn't been back to New York

since the move, but he'd happily fly back to testify against her if the Sonya Lopez murder ever came to trial. "So what was Daniels talking about?"

"That's what we were talking about down in the coffee shop," Lucy said. She looked at Ridley. "Can I tell him?"

Ridley nodded.

"Daniels okay'ed three-grand a month stipend. To bring you on part time."

"Bring me on to what?" Austin asked.

"The force," Ridley said. "As a consultant on retainer. As-needed basis. The county is growing fast. Tax base is growing fast. More people means more crime. But it also means bigger budgets. Daniels said I could bring you on board."

"Like Batman," Jimmy said. "We get a tough case and we throw up the bat signal and you roll out from the little kitchen in Hansville."

Austin laughed, shaking his head. "No way. That was more than enough action for me. Plus, my truck isn't nearly as fast as the Batmobile."

"Will you think about it?" Ridley asked. "No regular hours. You could still run the café—"

"And restaurant and bait shop," Lucy added. "You'd need to get a PI license, and something about insurance. But Daniels said he could get it into the budget."

Austin walked a slow lap around the hospital room. He could feel the eyes of the three others on him. "What made Daniels turn around on me?"

"Couple things," Ridley said. "First, you helped solve this thing. Believe it or not, he actually does give a shit. And not just about his reelection, which he's going to win in a landslide."

"And you got him on TV," Lucy added. "He cares more about that than anything."

"Good news is," Jimmy added. "If he gets famous enough, maybe he'll run for governor and leave the department to Ridley."

"Then we'd *all* owe you a debt of gratitude," Lucy said.

They all shared a long laugh and the room fell into an awkward silence.

"So, how 'bout it?" Ridley asked. "You want to join the squad?"

Austin walked to the doorway. "I need to get back to Run and take her for a walk on the beach. It's the closest thing I have to an annual Christmas Day tradition. This'll be the second Christmas I've done it. On the offer, I don't know. Gimme a week to think about it."

He gave Jimmy and the others one last look and strolled out of the hospital for what he hoped was the last time for a long, long time.

CHAPTER FORTY-EIGHT

TWO WEEKS LATER, Austin was in his yard with Run when Anna's white SUV pulled up. It was a rare sunny day in January, the air cold and crisp. He'd spent the morning with Andy, training a new cook and testing out some pancake recipes on the regulars. Mr. and Mrs. McGuilicutty had agreed with everyone else: the bananas foster pancakes were the clear winner and should be added to the menu.

Anna made eye contact from across the parking lot, and she appeared to be holding a package.

He hadn't seen her since the night everything came to a head with Mary Bonner. They'd texted a few times, but Anna had been busy. Her first-hand report on the night Joshua Green was saved had gone viral across the country. She'd been interviewed on morning shows, true crime shows, and a dozen different podcasts and blogs.

Austin was pleasantly surprised to see her and offered a warm smile as she approached. He couldn't remember another time he'd been happy to see a reporter strolling toward him. "You got your car back."

"Who knew you could sink a car in the Sound and it would

be back up and running in two weeks?" She leaned on the railing. "Mechanic here in town is a miracle worker." She handed him a small box wrapped in brown paper and tied with white ribbon. "I never had a chance to give you your Christmas present. Well, to be honest, I had it made last week. I didn't actually plan to give you a Christmas present."

"I hope it's a coffee pot."

"What?"

"Mine was broken but usable. Now it's ruined." He'd been drinking coffee from the café for the last two weeks because he hadn't yet gotten around to buying a new one.

Run dropped the ball on Austin's foot, gave a soft pleading growl, then picked it up and dropped it again. It was her way of getting his attention when he stopped playing for more than a few seconds.

"Do you want to walk?" Austin asked, picking up the ball. "She needs a bigger space to roam."

Anna nodded and they walked down to the beach, where the water was still, the sun glittering off the calm water like a million sapphires.

He tossed the ball as far as he could, watching Run take off at a sprint.

"Are you gonna open it?" Anna asked.

Austin stopped and opened the box. Inside was a wooden plaque, the same shape as Fiona's. The bright sun reflected off the silver plate stamped into it. Etched into the plate were five words.

The World is Worth Saving.

He read the inscription twice, then looked out to the water, across the Sound. In New York, even on the clearest days, the views were nothing like here. To the northeast, the snowy peaks of the north cascades glistened against a clear blue sky.

"Thank you," he said quietly.

Anna said, "I thought you needed another one."

"How'd you know I kept Fiona's after she died?"

"A hunch. I read about her plaque in a profile about her."

"A hunch? I'm not sure I'm comfortable with how much you know about me." He paused. "I never got a chance to tell you, if you hadn't texted me, Jimmy would have died. Doctors said he'd have survived maybe another half hour. He owes you his life." He cracked a sarcastic smile. "Maybe the first good deed a reporter has ever done."

She punched him in the arm playfully, then gestured up the beach, where Run had collapsed on the sand to gnaw on a piece of driftwood twice her size. "I did what anyone would have done."

They walked in silence for a long time, Anna glancing over every now and then like she had something to say but couldn't find the right words. They reached the park at Point No Point, Run following behind them but staying at least ten feet away at all times. Austin had learned that she feared getting too close because she didn't want to be captured and leashed. Maybe he should have trained her better, but the treats in his pocket were the only way he could be sure she'd let him catch her when it was time to go home.

Anna sat cross-legged on the bench. "You're not ready, are you?"

Austin stretched out his legs and laced his hands behind his head. "Ready for what? Did Ridley tell you about the consulting gig he offered?"

"He *did* tell me about that, but that's not what I was asking."

"Then what did you mean?"

"Ready to *date*."

Austin looked at her. She wasn't asking for a story. She was asking for herself. He smiled. "I'm flattered."

"But you're not ready?"

He shook his head. "Fiona and I had a running joke. I told her once that if anything ever happened to me, I'd want her to find someone new. I knew my job came with risk. I told her I'd want her to be happy, whatever that meant for her."

Anna cocked her head. "So what was the joke?"

"She told me that if anything ever happened to *her*, she'd want me to live the rest of my life as a monk. Celibate and miserable."

Anna laughed. "Like you said, it was a joke. You know she wouldn't *actually* want that."

"I told her I wouldn't remain celibate and miserable for *her*. I'd do it because I wouldn't want to subject any other woman to being married to me. That was part of the joke. She'd signed on early—had no way out—but I couldn't with a clear conscience subject another woman I cared about to a life with me."

"Why not?"

Austin took the ball from his feet and tossed it down the beach to the edge of the water. Run sprinted after it, spraying sand behind her.

Anna pointed at a large sailboat gliding by, far out on the water. "You ever see anyone standing on the bow of one of those boats, arms raised, shouting '*I'm king of the world!*'"

He shrugged. "I'm guessing that's from a TV show I should have seen?"

She shook her head. "Did you spend the nineties under a rock? You can't tell me you didn't see *Titanic*. You just can't. I mean, Celine Dion, 'draw me like one of your French girls,' could Jack have fit on the plank at the end?"

He stared at her, blank faced.

"I simply have to find out how you've spent your time. Like, what do you watch?"

"Interviews with suspects, mostly. Sometimes sports."

She laughed. "Well, invite me over sometime, we'll watch *Titanic* together."

"Maybe. As friends."

"So, why not? Why'd you tell Fiona you wouldn't date again?"

"The danger. I have a way of doing things. Reckless." He frowned at her. "And by the way, you've got the same damn problem."

"I know."

"The way you came at Mary Bonner like a Seahawks linebacker? Not exactly by-the-book."

"I know. It's how I do my reporting, too."

"I told Fiona that if anything ever happened to her, I'd never subject anyone else to the stuff she had to worry about."

"But you're not an officer anymore. Ridley said he didn't think you were going to accept his offer. Not much danger flipping burgers and selling bait, is there?"

Austin pulled a folded piece of paper out of the back pocket of his jeans and handed it to her. It was the business license that had come in the mail that morning.

She read it, then handed it back. "Thomas Austin, Private Investigator. I like the sound of it. So you took the job with Ridley?"

Austin gestured down the beach, where Run was battling a piece of kelp that had washed ashore. "No, I didn't."

"I don't understand. I thought he said he needed you to get a PI license as a formality to make it all legal."

"He did, and I'll work with them. Maybe, from time to time. But not on contract. I'm going it alone."

She considered this. "You're going to be an actual PI? For hire?"

He tapped on the plaque she'd given him. "Comes down to it, I agree with the sentiment. The world is worth saving. And I agree with Fiona's plaque, too. But I can't sign on to another police force, even as a consultant. Not now and not ever again. Case by case, I'll work for anyone who has a just cause. But that's not limited to Ridley and his team."

"Have you taken on your first case yet?" she asked.

"Haven't even hung my shingle."

"Then buy me a beer and a burger." She pointed up the beach to his café. "I hear that joint has the best burgers in town."

He laughed. "We've got the *only* burgers in town."

"Good enough for me."

THE END

A NOTE FROM THE AUTHOR

Thomas Austin and I have three things in common. First, we both live in a small beach town not far from Seattle. Second, we both like to cook. And third, we both spend more time than we should talking to our corgis.

If you enjoyed *The Bones at Point No Point*, I encourage you to check out the whole series of Thomas Austin novels online. Each book can be read as a standalone, although relationships and situations develop from book to book, so they will be more enjoyable if read in order.

In the digital world, authors rely more than ever on mysterious algorithms to spread the word about our books. One thing I know for sure is that ratings and reviews help. So, if you'd take the time to offer a quick rating of this book, I'd be very grateful.

If you enjoy pictures of corgis, the beautiful Pacific Northwest beaches, or the famous Point No Point lighthouse, consider joining my VIP Readers Club. When you join, you'll receive no spam and you'll be the first to hear about free and discounted eBooks, author events, and new releases.

Thanks for reading!

D.D. Black

ALSO BY D.D. BLACK

The Thomas Austin Crime Thrillers

Book 1: The Bones at Point No Point

Book 2: The Shadows of Pike Place

Book 3: The Fallen of Foulweather Bluff

ABOUT D.D. BLACK

D.D. Black is the author of the Thomas Austin Crime Thrillers and other Pacific Northwest crime novels that are on their way. When he's not writing, he can be found strolling the beaches of the Pacific Northwest, cooking dinner for his wife and son, or throwing a ball for his corgi over and over and over. Find out more art ddblackauthor.com, or on the sites below.

- facebook.com/ddblackauthor
- instagram.com/ddblackauthor
- tiktok.com/@d.d.black
- amazon.com/D-D-Black/e
- bookbub.com/profile/d-d-black

Printed in the USA
CPSIA information can be obtained
at www.ICGtesting.com
LVHW041528240823
756170LV00002B/200